Hidden Eyes

A Dr. Edward Lester Mystery

By Eric Levison

Originally published in 1918

Hidden Eyes

© 2016 Resurrected Press
www.ResurrectedPress.com

Published by Resurrected Press

This classic book was handcrafted by Resurrected Press. Resurrected Press is dedicated to bringing high quality classic books back to the readers who enjoy them. These are not scanned versions of the originals, but, rather, quality checked and edited books meant to be enjoyed!

Please visit ResurrectedPress.com to view our entire catalogue!

For updates on future releases, LIKE us on Facebook:
http://www.Facebook.com/ResurrectedPress

ISBN 13: 978-1-943403-14-1

Printed in the United States of America

RESURRECTED PRESS BOOKS IN
ERIC LEVISON'S
DR. EDWARD LESTER MYSTERY SERIES

Hidden Eyes

Eyewitness

Ashes of Evidence

RESURRECTED PRESS BOOKS FROM *THE ETHEL THOMAS DETECTIVE STORY* SERIES BY CORTLAND FITZSIMMON'S

RESURRECTED PRESS CLASSIC MYSTERY CATALOGUE

Journeys into Mystery
Travel and Mystery in a More Elegant Time

The Edwardian Detectives
Literary Sleuths of the Edwardian Era

Gems of Mystery
Lost Jewels from a More Elegant Age

Anne Austin
One Drop of Blood
The Black Pigeon
Murder at Bridge
Murder Backstairs

E. C. Bentley
Trent's Last Case: The Woman in Black

Ernest Bramah
Max Carrados Resurrected:
The Detective Stories of Max Carrados

Agatha Christie
The Secret Adversary
The Mysterious Affair at Styles

Octavus Roy Cohen
Midnight

Freeman Wills Croft
The Ponson Case
The Pit Prop Syndicate

The Uttermost Farthing: A Savant's Vendetta

Arthur Griffiths
The Passenger From Calais
The Rome Express

Fergus Hume
The Mystery of a Hansom Cab
The Green Mummy
The Silent House
The Secret Passage

Edgar Jepson
The Loudwater Mystery

A. E. W. Mason
At the Villa Rose

A. A. Milne
The Red House Mystery

Baroness Emma Orczy
The Old Man in the Corner

Edgar Allan Poe
The Detective Stories of Edgar Allan Poe

Arthur J. Rees
The Hampstead Mystery
The Shrieking Pit
The Hand In The Dark
The Moon Rock
The Mystery of the Downs

Mary Roberts Rinehart
Sight Unseen and The Confession

Dorothy L. Sayers

Whose Body?

Sir William Magnay
The Hunt Ball Mystery

Mabel and Paul Thorne
The Sheridan Road Mystery

Louis Tracy
The Strange Case of Mortimer Fenley
The Albert Gate Mystery
The Bartlett Mystery
The Postmaster's Daughter
The House of Peril
The Sandling Case: What Would You Have Done?

Charles Edmonds Walk
The Paternoster Ruby

John R. Watson
The Mystery of the Downs
The Hampstead Mystery

Edgar Wallace
The Daffodil Mystery
The Crimson Circle

Carolyn Wells
Vicky Van
The Man Who Fell Through the Earth
In the Onyx Lobby
Raspberry Jam
The Clue
The Room with the Tassels
The Vanishing of Betty Varian
The Mystery Girl
The White Alley
The Curved Blades

FOREWORD

Hidden Eyes is the first of the three mysteries written by Eric Levison, featuring Dr. Edward Lester, and set in Jacksonville, Florida and published in the years immediately following the end of World War I.

This period is an interesting one in the evolution of the detective story. For the first time, the novel was overtaking the short story as the most popular format for the genre. The expanded length allowed for the greater development of characters and for the presentation of more intricate plots. In the short story, the emphasis had been on presenting a puzzle and then revealing the solution. The novel allowed for the exploration of *motive* which had tended to be glossed over in the briefer form.

The novel also allowed for a much fuller description of *place,* the locale of the crime. The mystery novel began to be read as much to allow the reader to be transported to a different place, whether it was an English village, the heart of major cities such as London or New York, or, as is the case with the mysteries of Levison, Jacksonville, which in 1920 was probably as exotic a location to most readers as the moors of Devonshire. Levison describes his Florida in great detail, using actual street names and real suburbs to give the reader a real feel for the area.

The detective genre was undergoing a transition at this time on both sides of the Atlantic. The year 1920 marks a kind of watershed between the Edwardian period and the post war era. It witnessed the birth of what has been called the "Golden Age" of British mysteries, and saw the publication of Agatha Christie's first mystery, *The Mysterious Affair at Styles*. In America the first hard-boiled detective stories were being published in magazines such as *Black Mask,* though the first hard-boiled detective novel, *The Snarl of the Beast* by Carroll John Daly would not be published for a number of years.

Levison, as with many of the other authors that first wrote in this period, was exploring the form, still trying to establish what the new mystery novel should consist of. His mysteries are not mere copies of earlier American authors such as Carolyn Wells or Anna Katherine Green, nor an imitation of their British counterparts, but instead, is a unique regional expression of the genre, very much tied to the culture and climate of northern Florida at the time they were written.

Florida was a different place in 1920. Miami, Tampa, and St. Petersburg were still backwaters, and the great land-development boom was just getting underway, made possible by the extension of the railroads and the invention of the air conditioner. In Levison's depictions, fortunes are being made and lost, but the pace and manner of business still is definitely Southern.

For his detective, he has chosen Dr. Edward Lester, a general practitioner who seems to know and be known by everyone in Jacksonville. He is intelligent, corpulent, gruff on the exterior, but kind and genial at heart. Dr. Lester is neither the first or last physician to take on the role of amateur sleuth. Doctors, after all, are often called in when murder occurs, they are familiar with the many faces of death, and they also are equipped with the scientific background and habit of deductive reasoning required to solve crimes, and Lester is no exception to all these traits. His approach is decidedly scientific, and the doctor is familiar with all of the latest scientific developments, and not just those of a medical nature. As for deduction, a plaque with the single word "THINK!" adorns his office.

In *Hidden Eyes* the doctor is presented with a string of break-ins at the banks of Jacksonville, in which it appears that the criminal knows the combination and has some way to circumvent the time locks on the vaults, all of which are of the latest design. To solve the crime, the doctor relies not only on logic, but on a knowledge of psychoanalysis and hypnotism. The modern reader should remember, at the time the book was written, Freud and Jung were still fresh faces, and their theories and methods were still novel to the public.

Levison, as have so many of his contemporaries, has sunk into obscurity, but the three Dr. Lester mysteries still are of interest, both because of their depiction of the time and place, and because they are worth reading in their own right. It is with pleasure that Resurrected Press presents this new edition of *Hidden Eyes*.

About the Author

Eric Levison was an American author who wrote three mysteries, *Hidden Eyes, Eye Witness,* and *Ashes of Evidence,* set in

Jacksonville, Florida and featuring Dr. Edward Lester as the detective. He also wrote a number of short stories, including at least one co-written with Octavus Roy Cohen. Some sources indicate that he was born in Prussia in 1894. No other biographical information about the author was available.

Greg Fowlkes
Editor-In-Chief
Resurrected Press
www.ResurrectedPress.com

TABLE OF CONTENTS

I. THE ROBBERY

THE heavy-faced chief of detectives reached irritably for the jangling telephone on his desk, and, without removing his cigar, grumbled into the transmitter:

"Headquarters!"

Then a look of amazement supplanted the irritable gleam in his eyes. He leaned forward and jerked the cigar from his mouth.

"What?" He bellowed the question and slid forward eagerly to the edge of his chair. "Disappeared? Sa-a-ay, what 'r' you givin' me?" His face stiffened suddenly. "Oh, er—all right, Mr. Hayes." Profound respect replaced the incredulity in his voice. "Yes, sir, I'll wait."

He replaced the receiver on the hook and his eyes roved about the office.

"Great sufferin' mackerel!" he whispered in awe, straightening slowly in his chair.

He jabbed hurriedly at a button on his desk, and addressed the uniformed officer who entered: "Who's here?"

"Riley and Franklin, sir."

"Franklin? Good. Send him in." The chief picked up the cigar he had laid aside as a plain-clothes man entered, and took the chair to which the chief waved an imperious hand.

"You watched 'em put that vault in the Second National, didn't you?"

Franklin nodded.

"Stayed with it all the time."

The chief bit down on his cigar.

"Burglar-proof vault, ain't it?"

Franklin grinned.

"Lightning-proof, Chief!"

The chief eyed the man before him.

"Umph!" he grunted skeptically. "How'd you like to tackle the job of breaking into it?"

Franklin's grin expanded and ended in a laugh. Evidently it pleased the chief to be facetious.

"I don't know that I'd mind trying it, Chief—with a ton of dynamite!" he chuckled.

"Who else was watching it?"

"Who else?" The plain-clothes man's chuckle ended abruptly. "You mean when they placed it? Nobody; that is, I didn't—"

"Well, somebody did, and we've got to get a line on him, and get it quick."

Franklin leaned forward interestedly.

"Yeh? What's up?"

"Twenty-five thousand dollars in currency disappeared out of that vault last night," advised the chief grimly.

"Twenty-five thou—" gasped the astonished detective. "Not a yegg's job."

"Evidently not," nodded the chief. "It was discovered when the vault was opened this morning. I just got the notice from the Second's president. He's coming down and—"

The uniformed officer reentered.

"Mr. Hayes of the Second National," he announced.

The bank official followed close on the heels of the officer. The chief rose to greet him.

"Glad to see you, Mr. Hayes; have a seat, sir. Mr. Hayes, this is Ben Franklin; he was detailed when they installed that vault of yours."

The banker nodded shortly to Franklin and turned again to the chief.

"Well?" The chief's monosyllable was expressive.

"As I told you over the phone, Chief," the banker began, "we had a package of twenty-five thousand dollars, small denomination currency, in the vault. Put it there last night; in the outside vault; it came in late. We were to send it down the state this morning to pay off the turpentine hands near Manatee. This morning it was gone."

"Who opened the vault?" The chief's question was purely a formal one.

"Kingsley, the vice-president, and Harkiss, the cashier—you know them. This new Defy vault works with a double combination. I have them both, but Harkiss and Kingsley have only one each. Both of them must be there to open the thing. The time lock was set for eight-thirty, as usual."

"And there was no sign of anything having been—"

"None; absolutely none!" The banker anticipated the chief's question.

"H-m. You're sure the package went into the vault."

"I put it there," answered the bank president simply. "Harkiss was with me. Went out to the house with me, in fact, to talk over the new government loan; and stayed there all night. We came down together this morning."

"Of course, I'd no thought of Mr. Kingsley or Mr. Harkiss," the chief smiled apologetically. "This town has known both of 'em long enough to be certain what they are."

The banker nodded.

"But somebody—somebody last night opened that vault."

"Opened it?" Franklin interjected. "Opened it and closed it?" The detective made small effort to hide his growing disbelief. "Say, that ain't possible. Why, I—"

The chief ended the expostulation with a wave of his hand.

"You've got old Jensen for a watchman, haven't you?"

"Had him ever since he retired from the force, and his time-clock by the vault shows that he was there every half-hour. Nor was he ever out of the building; he's watching the entire building, you know."

The chief nodded.

"Of course, you don't want any publicity about this—" he began.

The banker waved an expressive hand.

"It doesn't matter," he said shortly. Then: "Of course, the loss of the money hurts, but the Second National can replace it easily enough." A note of pride sounded in the man's voice. "What I want to know," he finished, "is how we can be certain that this same man can not go into our vault at will— any time—opening it as easily as though it were a tin box, and not the latest word in vault construction?"

"Say," cut in the detective again querulously, "how could anybody—"

"That is just what I wish to discover, Mr. Franklin," the banker broke in coldly.

"Have you seen any of the safe people?"

questioned the chief.

The bank official shook his head.

"Not yet; you advise it?"

The chief frowned.

"I don't know—a factory man, perhaps. How was that vault set, Franklin?"

"In eight feet of solid concrete, three sides, top and bottom," answered the detective shortly. "And three feet of eight-ply steel," he added. "I'd like to see the man who can get into that!"

"I'd like to go up with you." The chief turned again to the banker. "That is, if you think we can look around without having the whole town buzzing at our ears."

"All right." The banker glanced at the clock. "You'll just be looking over the new vault."

The chief rose to his feet.

"You come along, Franklin," he ordered, and the detective, with a shrug, turned to the door.

"It ain't possible," he grumbled. "Why, nothing short of an earthquake could jar that box. As for opening it—" The detective's shrug of incredulity was eloquently expressive.

The president smiled ruefully.

"That was exactly my opinion, Mr. Franklin. That vault is burglar-proof, or the words are a joke; yet that currency went into the vault—I'll take oath to that fact."

The three men left the office together and climbed into the banker's car.

"Who knows of this?" The chief was chewing thoughtfully on his cigar.

"We three; Harkiss and Kingsley."

"Maybe we'd better keep it to ourselves a while,"

suggested the chief.

"Whatever you say." The banker nodded agreement.

The car moved rapidly up an avenue, turned into a crowded, building-lined street, and came to rest before a ten-story building, the home of the Second National Bank of Jacksonville.

Not without some cause did the Second National boastfully proclaim in its advertisements that its banking house was second to none south of the Mason-Dixon Line, and the first in Florida. Other banks in Jacksonville might lay claim to a larger capitalization; might boast of a larger figure to represent the amount of loans outstanding, but none could point to the structure which housed it, and show a more businesslike and modern banking floor than the Second National.

A month previous, the officers of the bank received the congratulations of the city and the newspapers on the installation of the latest model burglar-proof, fire-proof, "everything-proof," as one would-be wit of a reporter termed it, Defy steel vault.

The papers, quick to laud what they praised as "up-to-dateness," held up the Second National Bank as a model institution, boasting that nowhere else in the South, not even in New Orleans, Birmingham or Atlanta, could there be found a more magnificent and pleasing banking floor, nor a better equipped and better officered organization.

The vault had been a seven-day wonder when it was placed, for the curious were barred from the building, and the workmen—all brought down from the Defy factory—worked behind a board wall that baffled the curious eyes of passers-by. With the workmen had been detailed a plain-clothes man, less because it seemed necessary than to add a touch of "official supervision" to the work.

The Defy vault, so the papers had said, was the last word in construction. The huge, circular door, which inspired a feeling of utter safety, was opened, first by aid of a time lock, which, at a certain hour, permitted the working of the double combinations. The combinations, two in number, were independent of each other; one a number combination, and one a word.

Even the builders themselves did not know them, for the combinations were set by the president of the bank, and by his two officers; Kingsley, the vice-president, assisting with the number combination, and Harkiss, the cashier, with the word combination.

The steel of the vault defied the inventions of science to pierce it; short of literally blowing the vault to pieces.

The most expert safe men in the country had stood before a replica of this same vault, and tried, with all means at their command, to effect an entrance into it. The exhibition was staged at the Defy factory, and the experts' failures had furnished many columns of advertising for the manufacturers.

It was impervious to the oxy-acetylene blowpipe, and heat served only to throw into operation the sensitive plates, cunningly hidden in the metal, which, in turn, operated the electric alarm connected with police headquarters, the office of the chief of detectives, and the home of President Hayes.

Drills blunted against the vault's eight-ply nickeled surface, and acids flowed as harmlessly as so much water from its door. As near as could be, the vault of the Second National Bank of Jacksonville was proof against burglars, fire and the elements. But it appeared that the impossible had been accomplished, and the chief of detectives leaped eagerly to the ground as the car drew up before the bank's building on Forsythe Street.

With a nonchalance that none of the three men felt, they entered the building.

The vault itself, glistening in the sunlight that filtered through an overhead lighting space, seemed to carry a message of absolute impregnability to the two detectives; for they both shook their heads as they viewed the wide-open, tremendous door, and glimpsed the shiny row of safe-deposit boxes beyond the bronze grille.

A word from the president, and the three men entered. They were alone in the vault, and, hastily, in an undertone—although a revolver shot could not have been heard, save through the open door—the banker explained:

"Here's where I put it, put it personally."

The chief noted the steel shelf—empty.

"And I was the first man to enter this morning when Kingsley and Harkiss opened." The banker spread his hands in a wide gesture.

The two detectives glanced hurriedly over the side and steel glistening roof of the monster, but found only the reflecting, solid, impassable adamantine steel meeting their scrutiny.

Finally the chief turned to Franklin; but Ben Franklin, usually more than ready to venture an opinion—and a good one—only shook his head.

"It just naturally ain't possible, Chief."

The chief grinned sourly.

"Huh! But it was done."

They followed the banker from the vault and made their way into his private office.

"Just one thing, gentlemen," urged the financier; "don't let the papers know the amount of the loss, should they learn something and come to you. They'll hardly magnify it, knowing nothing, and I'd rather—" he eyed the chief speculatively, leaving the sentence unfinished.

The chief frowned.

"The Southern National is installing one of these, isn't it?"

The president shook his head.

"A Defy vault, yes; but a much smaller one; one of the old kind."

"I think," began the chief, "I think I'll get in touch with the factory and see—no, by George!" He broke off with the ejaculation.

"Yes?" The banker was eager.

But the chief only frowned.

"No, I think I'll wait a day or two," he added slowly. "There's no use raising the devil until we have to."

And a moment later the two detectives turned from the building, crossed Laura Street and made their way toward Hemming Park. Near the corner of Adams the chief turned to Franklin.

"There's one man," he nodded, "one man who might be able to work this thing out. I mean Halvey Thornton/'

Franklin's face lighted.

"By heavens, yes! Know him, Chief?"

"Um! No," grunted the chief, as the two men

crossed the park toward the St. James Building. "He's a steel man, though, and now and then one of the papers boosts him up."

Franklin nodded.

"I know him, and say! what he don't know about steel! And he's forgot more about vaults than we'll ever know." Franklin hurried along at the chief's side. "At least he'll be mighty interested," he agreed. "And he's a dandy fellow, Chief. Office next to Doctor Lester's. I see him once in a while."

"Was he ever around when the vault was assembled?" the chief questioned slowly.

The detective nodded.

"He'd drop in now and then to kid me along."

The chief frowned.

"A chemist, ain't he?"

Franklin nodded again.

"Yep; working on some steel problem for a Birmingham company; I've heard him talking to Doctor Lester about it."

"That's the man I want to see!" The chief clipped off his words sharply. "Maybe he knows a little too much about—metal."

Franklin eyed his superior.

"You don't really believe that anybody without the combinations got into that vault, do you?"

The chief stopped.

"Just get that idea out of your nut," he demanded. "That vault was opened all right; I'll take Hayes' word for it. And whoever opened it knows a blamed sight more about steel vault construction than is good and healthy for a crook."

At the entrance to the building the two men stopped a moment, and Franklin eyed his chief with an expression but little short of disgust.

"Say, what's the big idea?" he demanded. "Ain't it occurred to you, Chief, that the man who copped that money *knew it was there?*"

The chief passed a thoughtful hand over his chin.

"H-m. That *is* so. It was unusual, the money being there—wasn't it? That's what Hayes said."

The detective smiled superiorly.

"As for this Thornton chap—wait till you meet him. He's harmless."

The chief's eyes darted a look of interest at Franklin, who pushed through the swinging doors.

"Too certain," muttered the chief thoughtfully, as he followed, "too damned certain."

II. A Lead

DOCTOR EDWARD LESTER sat hunched comfortably in a huge chair in his private office, reading industriously. Now and then he scratched his head thoughtfully, as though puzzled, and twice he looked up, staring long and abstractedly at a framed motto above his desk which bore the one word: "Think."

The word, however, hardly impinged on his consciousness, for he was evidently deeply engrossed in the huge volume that lay outspread on his knees.

The office girl tiptoed lightly through the room and into the laboratory beyond, passing close to the huge bulk of the man in the chair, but he paid no attention, muttering thoughtfully to himself, his eyes fixed on the book before him. For an instant the girl hesitated in the doorway and gazed smilingly at the oblivious man in the chair.

Such friends as the big doctor had swore by him with all earnestness. There was something more than lovable in the heavy-faced man, whose little black eyes, peering intently from their puffy, fat lids, seemed always to see something just a little removed from the actual.

His clothes he wore patently to hide his nakedness; certainly for no vain purposes of adornment, for they hung from his massive frame with a ludicrous air of having been flung on haphazard. His coat-pockets bulged chronically with half-empty packages of his favorite Virginia cigarettes, and more often than not, cigarette ashes decorated the front of his weirdly colored shirts.

The doctor looked up from his reading, stared a moment at the girl, then shook his head heavily.

"Did I forget something, Mae?"

The girl laughed.

"Not that I can think of," she replied. "I just wanted to cut off the heat from the sterilizer."

The big doctor nodded, and almost immediately immersed himself in the book before him.

Returning through the office, the girl hesitated a moment, and, as the doctor continued his reading, pushed sharply against a chair.

A heavy forefinger descended on the doctor's book to mark the place and he raised his eyes.

"Now what's up your sleeve?" he grumbled.

The girl extended her bare arms laughingly in evidence.

"No sleeves even," she mocked.

The doctor hoisted himself groaningly to his feet.

"Well, what's it all about, Mae? You might as well tell me what's worrying you, and have done with it."

The girl grew serious.

"I'm—I'm going to get married."

"In the name of all the gods at once!" The doctor's little eyes grew large. "What for?"

"What does anybody get married for?" the girl countered, and the doctor's vast bulk shook with a soundless laugh.

"Don't ask me," he rumbled, "I'm not married, am I?"

"Just the same, I wanted to tell you I'm going to leave—next month."

The doctor cocked his head grotesquely to one side and eyed the girl before him.

"Say, what's going to become of this office, you reckon?"

The girl shook her head.

"It isn't that bad, Doctor Lester, and you know; it. Besides, it will be more than a month probably before I—"

The doctor lowered himself into his chair.

"Thank the Lord for small blessings," he grumbled. "I might die of apoplexy in the meantime; that's one consolation." He picked up the book again. "Now let me finish this chapter, and don't let anybody pester me—hear?"

The girl turned to the door which led into the reception-room. Even before it was closed the doctor's heavy head was sunk once more on his chest, and the words before him occupied his entire thoughts.

For a half-hour he read industriously, stopping only to light and relight cigarettes.

He sighed hugely as he came to the end of the chapter, then raised his head as the door opened and there appeared on the threshold a young man over whose coatless shirt, and to his knees, extended a leather apron, stained and burned. In the man's hand were a pair of huge goggles which he jerked nervously by a cord.

"Oh, hello, Hal; come in."

Halvey Thornton entered.

"Lord, Lester, you dig yourself in as though you had a thousand-dollar fee in view. I've been waiting outside for fifteen minutes, and that girl of yours"— here the girl passed through the office. "Here, Mae!" Thornton's voice was laughingly complaining. "Why didn't you tell me there wasn't any one in here with the bear?"

The girl turned and laughed.

"You said you didn't want to be bothered, didn't you, Doctor?"

And Doctor Lester, putting aside his book, chuckled as he nodded.

"What can I do for you, Hal?" grumbled the doctor good-naturedly, as the girl passed into the laboratory.

"You can lend me a couple of test-tubes; my fingers are all thumbs this morning, and I've broken a half-dozen tubes, more or less."

"Help yourself." The doctor replaced the book in its case and as Thornton turned into the laboratory, he stretched his huge bulk yawningly and followed:

"Still working on the steel, Hal?"

Thornton, running an appraising eye over a rack of test-tubes, nodded slowly.

"Yes, but I'm not making progress."

The doctor lighted a cigarette.

"Rome wasn't built in a day," he grunted. "That mercurial solution—any 'count at all?"

Thornton shook his head.

"Absolutely no good." And he frowned thoughtfully. "Dog-gone it, Lester, I'm more tempted than ever to chuck the whole business. I feel like a rotter taking the company's salary and turning out nothing. A fine job to give a man, isn't it?"

The doctor chuckled and nodded.

"You should worry about the company," he rumbled. "If they're a lot of asses, what do you care?"

"Just the same," the younger man went on, "it's a silly proposition. For a while I thought I was on the track of it, but Moses himself can't treat iron and make steel of it. Why, man, it's the very bulk of that Bessemer steel that makes it worth while. Oh," and he waved an all-embracing arm, "it's asinine! How the devil can a man cut the thickness of a metal in half and still have the same resistancy and strength?"

The doctor grunted.

"That's your problem, isn't it? Why the Gloomy Gus attitude all of a sudden?"

"Money, Lester. I'm just hard up, that's all. Now, none of that—" as the doctor made a movement toward his coat-pocket. "Keep your checkbook out of sight."

The doctor shrugged and turned to his table as Thornton continued:

"It isn't temporary relief I'm needing, Lester," and he smiled at the expression. "But I'm getting nowhere, and a man my age ought to be accumulating a little, you know."

Thornton hoisted himself to the edge of the operating-table and played thoughtfully with his glasses while the doctor turned to a microscope and lifted the protecting bell-jar.

"Anything new with you, Lester?"

Doctor Lester selected a glass slide, held it to the light to see that the smear thereon was even, then passed the glass rapidly through the flame of a Bunsen-burner to "fix" it.

"Is there ever anything new, Hal?" he questioned in turn, as he carefully dropped methylene-blue stain from a tiny dropper on to the glass slide. "If there is, it doesn't happen in the St. James Building, nor anywhere else in this beautiful city of Jacksonville-on-the-St.-Johns."

The doctor washed the stained glass carefully, allowed it to dry between the blotting-pads, then, gently placing a drop of cedar-oil in the exact center of the tiny blue smear, he fitted the slide into the holder, turned the lenses until the oil-immersion lens rested over the slide, and, hunching over the microscope, twisted the adjusting-screw.

In a moment he raised his head.

"If everything worked out as easily as that, Hal," he indicated the microscope, "we'd have a cinch, and you'd make a million."

Thornton smiled.

"And there are still a good many men, Lester, who say the germ theory is all bosh!" Thornton's brown eyes twinkled; he knew how to arouse the huge, hulking medico, who seemed impossibly blase and calloused.

Doctor Lester snorted.

"Umph! And the fools deny ocular proof. Any man whose eyes aren't satisfied—" The doctor broke off disgustedly.

The office girl passed the doorway, and the huge doctor nodded after her heavily.

"There's another good girl gone flooey!"

Thornton's raised eyebrows expressed surprise.

"Mae? What's she up to? Wants to go in training, I suppose?"

The doctor shook his head.

"Naw. Married. That's worse. Seems there's a gum-shoe man down at headquarters—Ben Franklin—"

Thornton laughed.

"Gee, I *am* thick. That's what he's been hanging around this floor so much for. And I thought he was interested in steel vault construction!"

"Speaking of marriage," began the doctor tentatively, replacing the bell-jar over the microscope, "it seems to me, Hal—speaking as a friend of all concerned—that it's about time you and Isabel—"

A laughing voice in the doorway interrupted.

"Who's taking my name in vain?"

And into the room came a smiling, blue-eyed girl, apparently in her early twenties, accompanied by a well-built, impressive-looking man whose sharp black eyes drifted quickly to Thornton, in his stained leather apron, and to the doctor.

Doctor Lester nodded cordially.

"Come in—come in, Isabel, you're welcome. You, too, Ralby." He extended a fat hand to the man who accompanied the girl.

"Are we breaking into a conference?" the girl mocked, eying Thornton mischievously.

"Sufferin' mackerel, no! I was just trying to cheer up our Gloomy Gus friend. He's as pessimistic as a German philosopher this morning."

The girl came around the table toward Thornton.

"That's not like you, Hal."

Thornton turned to the window and stood gazing out on the city beneath them.

"By the way, Ralby," the doctor turned to the man who had accompanied the girl. "Got a little time? I've got something here I think would interest you."

The man addressed as Ralby glanced toward Thornton and the girl, then nodded.

"Trot it out, Lester; I'm not exactly rushed to death," he laughed. "They're struggling along in the office all right without me." And he followed the doctor into the adjoining office.

The girl turned to Thornton.

"What was he saying about me?" she demanded smilingly.

Thornton grew suddenly embarrassed. "I—really, I don't remember, Isabel—that is—"

"Never mind," the girl laughed. "I'm not afraid of any remarks Doctor Edward Lester might make. Did you ever know a more wonderful man?"

Thornton smiled his appreciation.

"No, nor a grumpier one, and sloppy—ugh!" He turned to the doctor's table and cleared away the remains of the blue stain, the water and the blotting pads.

"That's what makes him such a dear," she said finally. "He never seems to do anything right, but he is a dandy, isn't he?"

Thornton nodded.

"Indeed, yes, and you've no idea how patiently he helps struggling young chemists."

"Meaning you?" The girl smiled at the thought of Thornton's needing help.

He nodded and picked two test-tubes from the rack before him.

"These are what I came to borrow," he explained.

"Oh, but you aren't going to get away!" The girl raised an admonishing finger. "You're going with me, and with Morton, to see his new launch. We're to go as far as Ortega in her."

Thornton shook his head, and a tiny frown appeared on his face.

"Mighty nice of you to ask, Isabel, but you run along with Ralby; he seems to be a gentleman of leisure; I'm rather busy."

The girl pouted.

"I will not," she said; "besides, Morton is head over heels in some case by now with the doctor; let's sneak. I'd rather—rather—" the girl blushed, "I'd rather talk to you anyway, and you never come to see me any more."

Thornton took an impulsive step toward her, but drew up sharply.

"Shucks, Isabel; you know I want to come—"

"Well, why don't you?"

Through the open door behind them came the doctor's heavy voice, rich in its southern brogue:

"A plain case of obsession—persecution-mania—eh?"

And Ralby's close-clipped words in answer: "Evidently. Have you tried psycho-analysis? How about hypnosis?"

This was followed by the doctor's: "By jove, Ralby! You're wasting your time monkeying with real estate! Hypnosis; that's the thing—maybe I can do something for the poor kid—"

Thornton and the girl drew nearer the window, away from the open door.

"Why don't I?" Thornton repeated the question inanely. "Oh—well, you see, Isabel—I—oh, I've been busy; I guess that's it."

The girl smiled quietly.

"That won't do, Halvey." She shook her head. "Morton's busy, too, yet he comes. And you even cut my last dance."

Thornton played with the test-tubes in his hand in an embarrassed fashion.

"Oh, Morton! I'm afraid Ralby's not the busiest man in Jacksonville, lady. He's almost never in his office; goes around making calls with Lester, and then—"

The office girl appeared in the doorway, and Thornton turned, seemingly glad of the interruption.

"Want me, Mae?"

The girl nodded.

"I'm sorry—there's some one to see you. I heard the knocking and looked—it's my—it's a man from the police department and some one with him."

Thornton nodded. "Thanks, Mae."

He turned to the girl beside him. "You see, Isabel, I am busy. And—thanks, lady, for missing me."

The girl smiled and shook her head. "No thanks necessary, Mr. Chemist-who-is-always-busy—I'm counting on you to-night? You're coming, aren't you?" She extended a slim hand which Thornton took in his own a moment.

"Well—thanks, Isabel—I—" he stuttered hopelessly, and the girl looked at him earnestly. This was unlike him. Finally: "Yes, thanks, Isabel—I'll be there," he blurted, and hurried from the office.

In the hall he confronted Franklin.

"Howdy," he greeted, and chuckled. "I've just learned, young man, why you frequent this neighborhood so much."

A flush overspread the officer's face, but he turned to his superior.

"Chief, this is Mr. Thornton. Mr. Thornton, the chief."

Thornton bowed and shook hands.

From the doctor's doorway Mae waved a furtive greeting to the detective in the hall, who smiled and waved his hat in answer, while the chief eyed him heavily.

Thornton turned toward the girl in the doorway. "Tell the doctor I'll drop in later," he requested, then turned smilingly to the man beside him. "You wanted to see me, Chief?"

The chief nodded.

"If you please, Mr. Thornton; and privately."

Thornton opened his door.

"Step in, Chief," he invited, and the chief of detectives entered the office; nor did he fail to notice the half-puzzled expression in Thornton's eyes.

III. CHECK

THORNTON dropped into a chair before a flat-topped desk, and waved his visitor into a leather chair at the desk's side. He passed a humidor of cigars, helped himself, extended a match to the chief, and settled back in his chair.

The detective turned in the doorway.

"I'm going down the hall, Chief," he mumbled; "be right next door when you want me," and he left the room, his face a brick-red under the caustic eyes of his superior.

"Well, Chief?"

The chief scrutinized the man in the chair before him, and nodded slowly as though satisfied, in some fashion, with Thornton's appearance, although that young man did not take the examination coolly, and fidgeted nervously under the chief's gaze.

"You're by way of being a vault expert, ain't you?"

The chief's eyes followed Thornton's gestures closely, but saw only a mild interest in the face of the young man before him.

"Well, not exactly an expert, Chief—but I know a little about them." Thornton smiled politely. "Any information I can give you—"

The chief pondered a moment.

"You were connected with the Defy people once, weren't you?"

Thornton shook his head.

"Connected? Hardly. They're using a patent of mine on their newest vault; a synchronizing device that makes the time-lock and double combinations possible."

"Pretty rotten crowd to deal with; those Defy people, weren't they?" The chief stabbed blindly. "I imagine they held you down pretty tight when it came to talking terms."

Thornton nodded.

"They did that, and no mistake. Still—" he shrugged. "What I get, I get; otherwise, the thing would have been a dead loss. But, they aren't exactly pleasant to deal with."

"Had some trouble with 'em about your patent, didn't you?" The chief seemed weighing each word carefully.

Thornton nodded again.

"Didn't know any one knew about it," he remarked quietly.

The chief chuckled.

"Oh, we know all sorts of things, young fellow. Believe me," and the chief grinned expansively, "there ain't much going on in Jacksonville that I'm not wise to. Did the vault people come across?"

"Come across?" Thornton wondered what the chief was talking about, and that individual, scenting an evident blunder, hurriedly added:

"I mean, you settled your differences all right, didn't you?"

"Oh, as to that—yes. It wasn't of great consequence." Thornton shrugged. "They went to work installing my device when I repeatedly told them I wasn't ready. I dropped the whole business, that's all. Of course," he added hastily, noting the chief's manifest interest, "there's nothing really that they can't do as well as I could, but—" he gestured with his cigar.

"Yes? But—what?" The chief leaned forward.

Thornton's eyes narrowed.

"Mind telling me why you're so suddenly interested in this, Chief?" he asked mildly. "I settled with the Defy people over a year ago, and it isn't perhaps—"

The chief leaned closer to Thornton.

"That vault in the Second National," he asked carelessly, "know anything special about it?"

"Meaning—?" Thornton knocked the ashes from his cigar, thoughtfully wondering to what all this was leading.

"Oh, nothing special." The chief leaned back in his chair. "It's a pretty good type of vault, ain't it?"

"The best on the market," the other man agreed enthusiastically. "I don't know of a better or a more satisfactory type."

"Equipped with one of your devices?" A nuance of eagerness crept into the chief's disinterested tones.

Thornton nodded. "Oh, yes; I watched the men install that vault, by the way."

"Well, young man"—the chief pointed his cigar at Thornton and leaned forward—"that device of yours don't work! There's a hole in it as big as the St. Johns River."

He watched Thornton sharply, but the younger man's shrug seemed innocence itself.

"I know it," he commented briefly. "But how do you?" Thornton sat straight in his chair.

"What's the idea, Chief? You didn't come here to talk generalities, nor to discuss the merits of the Second National's vault."

For a minute the chief sat silent. Then he

removed his cigar, and his voice dropped as he said very quietly:

"Happens that twenty-five thousand dollars disappeared out of that Second National vault some time last night, Mr. Thornton."

"What!" Thornton's eyes grew large with surprise. The chief nodded slowly.

"I said it; twenty-five thousand, in currency."

"And who—who—what—" Thornton stuttered in his astonishment. "Blown up?" he questioned incredulously.

The chief's reply was a look of disgust.

"Naw—opened."

Thornton laughed shortly.

"What's the joke, Chief?" he questioned mildly.

The chief snorted.

"Joke? A hell of a joke. It happened. And what's more, I—"

Thornton raised his hand.

"You mean to tell me that the vault in the Second National Bank was *opened* and money stolen?" A smile played over the young man's face. "Somebody's been kidding you, Chief."

"Then it's the president of the bank," grunted the chief, "and if you'd had a look at him you wouldn't think he was kidding. Hayes ain't the kind to report a twenty-five-thousand-dollar loss just for the fun of it."

"But who—" Thornton began, and the chief's shrug interrupted.

"That's what I want to find out, Mr. Thornton. I've come to you because I've been told you know these vaults, and I want to know whether—well, if you think it could be done?"

Thornton laid his cigar aside.

"Just a second, Chief; you're asking me seriously if I think any one could open that Defy vault, working at night, and in one night? Lord, man, no!"

The chief nodded.

"Not workin' all night either; the watchman came 'round every half hour."

Thornton picked up his cigar again.

"Then, all I can say, Chief, is that you'd better look inside the vault for what's missing. My word for it—it'll be there."

The chief shook his head slowly.

"But it isn't," he insisted.

Thornton's gesture of impatience was manifestly sincere.

"Let me tell you something, Chief." He spoke slowly, as a teacher would address a very stupid pupil. "The best vault men in the country have tried to get into a vault of this kind. They tried in the open daylight, with everything from dynamite and the oxy-acetylene blowpipe on down. And they had half a day to work on it. I happened to be there myself to watch the experiment. You read of it probably, up at the Defy factory. And they didn't get in! You can understand how I feel, Chief, when you sit there and tell me a wild yarn like that."

"And I'll tell you this much," the chief wagged a minatory ringer before Thornton's face. "The Second National's vault was opened, and to hell with your experts!" The chief's face purpled slowly.

A touch of color appeared in Thornton's face.

"Very well, Chief. You came to me for information, and I give it. Now I'll tell you further that whoever entered the vault of the Second

National Bank last night—as you say—entered by
opening the vault door in only one fashion; that is,
by means of the combinations!"

The chief puffed silently on his cigar, then shook
his head slowly.

"I beg your pardon, Mr. Thornton," he grumbled.
"You see how I feel about this," he added
apologetically; "that vault was got into; that's my
only information, and the three men who know the
combinations, well, they're Hayes, Harkiss and
Kingsley, and Harkiss was at Mr. Hayes' house all
night."

Thornton, mollified by the chief's tone, shrugged
slightly.

"About this—this imperfection?" the chief
continued. "I mean in this device of yours; just what
is it?"

"Not such as to make burglary even remotely
possible," Thornton answered quickly. "It isn't really
an imperfection, but it is something that should be
improved. It hasn't a thing to do with the vault itself;
it is in the time lock—in the clock, that is."

"In the clock?"

Thornton nodded again.

"The clock depends on electricity for its winding
power; that's the trouble. It winds automatically and
only for one hour at a time, by my new tension
arrangement, without the usual springs. Shut off the
electricity and the clock stops—stops and   drops
automatically into the time set for the vault to be
opened."

"Just a minute." The chief puzzled with the idea,
thoughtfully eying his cigar. "If you cut the juice
from the Second National's vault clock, the

mechanism immediately throws the clock to eight-thirty?"

"If that is the time set—yes." Thornton smiled at the chief's expression of bewilderment.

"Then it ain't got a thing to do with the opening of the vault itself, this invention of yours?" He seemed, somehow, disappointed.

"Just as I told you, Chief; it doesn't affect the vault one way or another. The cutting off of the power merely permits the working of the combinations—not another thing."

With a murmured request for permission, the chief reached for the telephone and growled a number into the transmitter.

"Hello!" The chief frowned thoughtfully. "Get me the superintendent. That you, Karks? Yes—yes. Tell me, was your power shut off, even for a second, any time last night? What's that? I mean the up-town power, no, not the lights—hell, I don't know. I mean the juice at—well, say, the Second National Bank. All right, I'll hold the wire."

Holding the receiver, the chief turned to Thornton.

"I've got the power-house out in Springfield. They'd know. Say, if the juice was cut off and sent back on later, what'd happen?"

"If the power were turned on again, it would not affect the clock," Thornton explained. "The clock stops, and the only way to start it is to open the vault, close it, and reset the clock."

The chief nodded and opened his mouth to speak again—but turned instead to the telephone.

"Hello. Yes. All right, Karks. It was not, eh? You're sure? All right, Karks, thanks. Naw, it's not important, just wanted to know; s'long."

He turned again to Thornton.

"That eliminates the clock."

Thornton's eyes had narrowed puzzlingly, and he was frowning thoughtfully before him.

"There was power all night?"

The chief nodded.

"Then," Thornton stated positively, "that makes it doubly impossible. There's not a man in the country who could get into that vault. I know it couldn't be done with the power off, but with the clock running—well—it just simply can't be done, that's all."

The chief grinned slightly.

"Sounds fine, Mr. Thornton, but you're over-looking the fact that it *was* done."

Thornton turned to a cabinet beside his desk, and drew from a flat drawer a series of blue-prints. These he spread out on the desk before him.

"Take a look at these, Chief; here are your measurements, and here," he sought a moment among the prints, "here's a cross-section of the door; this one—" and he indicated a drawing. "Now, honestly, Chief, does it look possible to you?"

The chief looked thoughtfully at the prints, although the drawings meant little to him. After a moment he shot a side glance at Thornton, and pursed his lips thoughtfully.

"Mind telling me, Mr. Thornton, how you happen by these prints?" The chief's voice was mildly inquiring, but the look in his eyes betrayed his keen interest.

Thornton   flushed   slightly,   but   answered promptly:

"Of course not. Got them from the Defy people after the work was installed. They had no need for them, and I wanted a set—just to have in my files, you know."

The chief relighted his cigar.

"And there's no man—mind you, nobody you ever heard of—who you think could open this Second National box?"

Thornton studied the blue-prints before him, then raised his eyes to the chief's.

"Well, it might sound silly, after what I've already said; but I'd like to tackle the job of getting in there myself. Oh, not in a few minutes," he laughed at the chief's startled expression, "but I'd like to have a week to try out the combinations, that's all."

The chief pondered this.

"But you don't really think you could do it?"

Thornton laughed outright. "Well, frankly, I do, Chief, although I've been laughed at about it before. The Defy people offered to let me try .when they carried on the experiments up north. I did try, as a matter of fact, but they'd bunged that door up so it wasn't really a fair trial. Still, I think if I had a week to work over that vault, undisturbed, I *might* be able to get into it."

"You mean by working out the combinations?"

Thornton nodded, then waved his cigar in a dismissing gesture.

"But what's the use talking about it?"

The chief grunted.

"Oh, I don't know. I come in here and you tell me that nobody in the world can work into the place, and a minute later you turn around and say you think you could do it yourself."

Thornton reddened. "That's what I get for boasting," he smiled ruefully.

"You don't know the safe-men, Chief. Ask any one of them the questions you asked me and you'd get the same answers. And talk to any of them about vaults—except their own make, of course— and you'll find them blowing that they can get into anything from a two-by-four strong-box to the vaults of the Bank of England.

"It's just our way, I suppose, even though I'm not the most expert safe-man in the country---not by a blamed sight."

The chief got slowly to his feet.

"Well, some one got in there, Mr. Thornton, and, what's more, I'm going to find him."

Thornton rose.

"You can count on any assistance I can give you, Chief. I'd be mighty interested if you'll let me help. But don't be too sure about it. I'm afraid you'll find that Mr. Hayes is just mistaken, that's all."

The chief smiled grimly.

"Well, we'll see. I'm pretty sure, though, that Hayes knows what he's talking about. By the way, Mr. Thornton, the two combinations: what are they?"

"The first a five-letter word, and the second a five-figure number; that's the extent of my knowledge, Chief. I don't know which comes first, or whether they alternate, or anything else."

The chief turned to the door.

"If you'll drop around this afternoon, Mr. Thornton," he said slowly, "maybe I'll take you up on that offer to help."

"Do. I'll be glad to." Thornton shook hands with

the detective, and turned to gather up his blueprints, which he replaced in their cabinet. "But," and Thornton turned again to the chief, "I'm mighty afraid you'll find that somebody's made a bad bull somewhere." He closed the print file with a snap, and shook his head slowly. "That vault's simply impregnable, Chief; that's all there's to it."

And when the door closed behind him the chief stood for a moment in the hallway, gazing abstractedly at the ground-glass panel of the door marked "Halvey Thornton—Chemist."

He stuck his cigar thoughtfully in one corner of his mouth, and smiled slightly to himself: "Too certain," he grunted, "too damned certain."

IV. THE LAUNCH

THE Brannon home, set far off on the Ortega Road, some five miles from the city, shone brilliantly, and the spacious grounds were crowded with a moving throng of men and women.

Isabel Brannon's dances were important affairs in the social life of Jacksonville; informal almost in their frequency, but affairs to be looked forward to.

Here could be met, in the cool of the early evening, many whose names were written large in the social and business register of the city, and the broad veranda, which encircled the house, and which faced, for a portion of its length, the swiftly moving St. Johns River, had witnessed the beginning of more than one important civic movement—and matrimonial.

To be counted among Isabel Brannon's regular guests was in itself a badge of social distinction, and to be an intimate of the circle was proof positive of the possession of an intellect above the ordinary.

Near a large sycamore on the lawn before the house Max Railey, the youngest and most brilliant prosecuting attorney that the city of Jacksonville and the county of Duval had yet produced, held forth oratorically in the center of an intensely interested crowd.

It was generally conceded that Railey's next step was the mayor's chair; then Congress, and later perhaps he would be Jacksonville's contribution to a gubernatorial campaign, and after that—

At any rate, the powers that be in Florida politics hoped great things from the young prosecuting attorney.

"And the sort of reform we need, we're going to get; we'll get it, I tell you, if I have to go to Tallahassee and bulldoze the Legislature in person!"

The bright moonlight drifted down on the speaker, clearly outlining his deceivingly youthful face and the shock of black hair thrown carelessly back from his forehead.

"*Bravo! Muchissimo bravo!*" chuckled the professor of Spanish from the university, flipping a cigarette across the grass.

Ralby laughed aloud.

"Come out of it, Max!" he cried. "The next dance begins in a minute, and I guess the city won't go to the demnition bow-wows entirely."

"The devil it does!" Apparently the young attorney placed more importance on the immediate present than on the possibility of future reform.

"Where the deuce is that girl?" he laughed, looking about him. "Seen Bernice around, Ralby?"

Ralby nodded.

"Disappeared when you began to hold forth concerning the relative merits and demerits of John Barleycorn's reign.

"Here, Isabel!" Ralby hurried across the path to where Isabel Brannon stood smiling at her guests. "My dance, Isabel," he claimed, his dark face lighting.

The girl nodded, then called: "Oh, Max—"

Max Railey hurried to her side.

"Fair lady, behold Pierrot disconsolate! Columbine has vanished!"

Isabel Brannon nodded.

"And I don't blame her—there! And the very next time, Mr. Pierrot, that you bring your nasty politics into this—"

"Pardon, Heaven-born, pardon! I would kneel—I would make obeisance—but—the grass is damp, alas! Where, oh, where is my lady?"

Isabel laughed, taking Ralby's arm.

"I think I saw Bernice hiding in the library," she said lightly. "And I've missed all of this dance I intend to."

"Pierrot thanks you, Heaven-born."

The young attorney hurried to the large porch and made his way to the side of the house, while Ralby and the girl entered through the large open windows from which came the lilting, infectious strains of a fox-trot.

Out of hearing of the music from the house, near the bank of the river, thoughtfully and judiciously throwing stones into the water, was Doctor Edward Lester, and beside him stood Halvey Thornton.

The doctor, in his evening clothes, looked, if anything, more grotesque and awkward than he did in his laboratory, while Thornton's appearance left little to be desired from the standpoint of masculine effectiveness.

The contrast between the two men was sharp and distinct. The doctor's six feet of pulpy flesh, his double-creased chin and puffy cheeks, set off to good advantage the clean, lithe appearance of the younger man who was speaking earnestly:

"I tell you, Lester, the thing bothers me. It's uncanny. How could any one have got into it?"

The doctor spun a flat stone into the water,

watched it ricochet and disappear.

"Why worry over it, Hal? None of your business. Let the detectives and the bank worry."

"But, man alive!" expostulated Thornton. "I feel as though it were a personal affront to me—as though it were my vault they'd broken into—if they have."

"If they have?" The doctor turned his little eyes on the younger man.

Thornton fidgeted under the direct gaze.

"Oh, I thought Hayes might have put the money somewhere and forgotten about it. Such things do happen, you know. But both Harkiss and Kingsley were with him when he put the package away, and when the vault was opened. I talked to Hayes this afternoon; dammit, Lester, show some interest!"

The huge doctor chuckled.

"Go on, I'm listening—you're too infernally nervous these days, Hal."

Thornton shrugged.

"By George, it's enough to make any one nervous. Hayes reminded me that it was my recommendation that finally induced him to get that Defy vault instead of the others, and—well, don't you see, Lester, the position I'm in?"

The doctor shook his massive head.

"Can't see that I do, Hal. What if you did boost the Defy product; you had an ax to grind, didn't you? There was the royalty from the patent—"

The doctor lighted a cigarette. "Quite a distinction for this burg of ours, eh? A cracksman who can calmly get into the pride of the Defy people and walk off with what he likes."

"Confound it, Lester, be serious." Thornton did

not smile in answer to the doctor's rumbling chuckle. "Some one did it—I believe that now—the question is, who? I don't believe there's a man alive who could—"

The big doctor laughed again.

"Ralby would tell you, Hal, that there's a man alive who can undo anything that another man has ever done. Got a good argument, too. Jam up on criminology. Ever argue with him about it?"

Thornton turned impatiently and walked slowly away.

"Bother Ralby and his stupid ideas."

The doctor grinned at Thornton's back.

"Just the same he's a coming young man," he taunted. "Isabel's taken a notion to him, too, it seems."

Thornton stopped short.

"What's the idea, Lester?" he asked shortly.

The doctor's laugh boomed out.

"Got you, eh?" His huge frame shook heavily. "Nice chap, Ralby, mighty nice chap," he grunted. Then: "By the way, where were you last night?" he finished banteringly.

"That's not as funny as you think, Lester," Thornton flamed. "I even considered that, too, for if there's a man in this town—and I'm not boasting and you know it!—who could get into that vault, well, I'm the man. But, lord, it would take me weeks to work out the combinations. However, if I—"

The doctor waved a fat hand. "Of course I was joking."

Thornton nodded.

"I know you were; but I've puzzled over it all day; and if a man can get into that vault that easy— why, there isn't a vault or strong-room in the United States that's safe!"

"Well?" The doctor was plainly bored.

"And yet," Thornton continued speculatively, "I *might* be able to do it."

The doctor grumbled something unintelligible and uncomplimentary.

"I was with Isabel until about ten," Thornton mused aloud. "Met her down-town and didn't go home with her; had a headache. By ten-thirty I was in bed, and I awoke this morning about seven—"

"Come on, let's get back." The doctor took Thornton's arm commandingly. "You'll find there's something wrong somewhere, for if that vault can't be got into—well, that's all there's to it, I guess."

Thornton shook his head gloomily.

"I wish I thought so," he muttered.

The doctor laughed. "You offered your services to the chief, of course."

"Yes. But what can I do against this—against this—whoever he is. I don't think you realize, Lester, that a man who could do a thing like that is a genius—a man who could command—"

Doctor Lester shrugged his massive shoulders and yawned mightily.

Together the two men made their way across the grounds and were met by their hostess.

"For goodness' sake, Hal," greeted the girl, "why the portentous frown?" And Thornton smiled.

"There, that's better," she remarked, taking the arm relinquished by the doctor. "As for you," she addressed herself to Doctor Lester, "Morton has been looking for you all over the place. He found a book in the library, and seems to have proved you wrong about something—something with a funny name—I don't know what it is."

"H-m," Doctor Lester frowned jestingly. "That's a fine way to try to shake an old friend. But—all right, young lady; it means something that tastes nasty the next time I get a chance at you—just wait."

And he heaved his huge bulk across the narrow path toward the house.

The girl turned to Thornton in the semi-darkness of the lawn. The music from the house came to them but faintly.

"Well, Mr. Chemist-who-is-always-busy, what's the matter?"

Thornton shook his head slowly.

"Nothing much, Isabel, except that I'm bothered. The impossible has happened, and even Lester is laughing at me, I think."

He outlined the situation briefly, telling her of the chief of detectives' visit to his office and of his conversation.

After a moment the girl nodded quietly.

"Every one seems to know about it," she remarked. "Max was telling Morton of it a few minutes ago. The papers didn't mention it, however. I suppose you are to help?"

"Try to help," he corrected- "What does Max think of it—and Ralby?"

The girl laughed.

"You know our 'brilliant young prosecuting attorney,' " she said lightly. "He vows they'll find whoever it is in a week. Of course Morton doesn't agree with him. I left them arguing Morton's idea that there's always some one who can undo things that have been done. I think Max was getting the worst of it, too."

Thornton noted the note of enthusiasm in her voice.

"You like Ralby a lot, don't you, Isabel?"

The girl shot a quick glance at him.

"Why—why do you ask, Hal?"

Thornton shrugged.

"Oh—" he waved a hand helplessly. "I don't know; everybody seems to like him."

The girl smiled at his vagueness and shook her head a little.

"I don't know, Hal," she said frankly, "sometimes Morton is a little short of wonderful, and sometimes—"

"Yes?"

"Sometimes I just despise him without any reason." The girl laughed. "And if you ever breathe a word of it—" she threatened.

Thornton came back to the subject which occupied him.

"You know, lady, I believe there is just one man in town capable of getting into that vault."

The girl looked up quickly and bit her lip. It seemed that the sudden switch of conversation was not too pleasing to her.

"Yes?" she questioned dully.

"I could."

The girl laughed quickly.

"Nonsense. In a month, perhaps. You didn't succeed the last time, did you?"

"Oh, it was different at the factory," Thornton explained. "So many things had already been done—"

"I've heard enough about vaults and such, Mr.

Chemist," the girl broke in archly. "And I've been saving this dance for you."

When the dance ended, a half dozen clamoring men claimed her attention and Thornton drifted outside. His mind would not leave the problem, and he wandered toward the river, turning it over and over.

Near the dock lay Ralby's new launch; a mahogany-finished, glistening thing, with the lines of a yacht, and gleaming beautifully in the moonlight.

Absently Thornton wandered aboard and looked about him, first on the deck and the little wheelhouse, and then below in the two cabins the launch boasted.

Two or three times, between the dances that followed, Isabel searched for Thornton. Neither Ralby nor Doctor Lester had seen him, and she determined to seek him out later, the while she laughed at the doctor's suggestion to check over the list of feminine guests and find an absentee that would explain Thornton's disappearance.

It was past midnight when Thornton made his reappearance in the ballroom.

The doctor drew him aside, scanning closely with his little eyes the slight pallor which rested on the young man's cheeks, and the bewildered expression in his eyes.

"What's wrong, Hal?"

Thornton smiled weakly.

"I think I'll be a patient of yours pretty soon," he laughed. "That is, if I don't buck up. I went out for a stroll toward the river. Saw Ralby's launch at the dock and clambered aboard. I must have fallen asleep in the cabin. Anyway, I was there two hours."

"You come to me in the morning, young man," grumbled the doctor heavily. "I'll have no breakdowns at this stage of the game." He drew the younger man into an alcove. "That girl has been hunting for you all over the place. Tell me, Hal—I meant to ask you this morning—what's the verdict?"

"Isabel?"

The doctor nodded.

"I'm afraid, Lester, afraid to ask her. She seems to like Ralby so—"

"Faint heart—" broke in the doctor heavily, and Thornton flushed.

"I know, Lester," Thornton laughed shortly, "but suppose she turns me down? Why shouldn't she? She's a thousand times too wonderful—"

"None are so blind—" Again the doctor broke off his quotation. "Look," he nodded across the room to where the girl could be seen making her way through one of the large windows. "Whom do you suppose she's looking for?"

"Me?" Thornton queried inanely.

"No, oh, no. Maybe she's looking for me," the doctor answered sarcastically.

Thornton stepped out into the room to follow the girl. A butler caught his eye and hurried across the room.

"You're wanted on the phone, Mr. Thornton."

Thornton cast a glance after the disappearing girl and followed the servant.

The doctor's huge face creased into smiles.

"The gods," he muttered, "don't seem ready for this thing to happen." He produced the inevitable cigarette, stepped out to the veranda, and, musing thoughtfully, wandered off beneath the trees.

"It's a good match," he soliloquized, "mighty fine match. He's a boy with a future, and she's a—what the devil!"

The doctor drew up near the tiny dock in the river, and his eyes grew large as he gazed at the launch made fast to one side. The moonlight glinted on the polished bow of the little craft, a bow that was pointed down the river.

"Now, who," muttered the doctor heavily, thoughtfully eying the little launch, "who turned that craft around?"

V. THE SECOND VISITATION

THE doctor returned to the house unnoticed in the babel that attended the leave-taking of the guests. He shook hands absently with whoever presented himself, his eyes searching for Thornton. Finally he discovered him leaning gloomily against a post far down the veranda, and waddled gravely to his side.

"You look like a study in pessimism," the doctor greeted. "What's up now?"

"Nothing."

The doctor eased his huge bulk into a wicker chair, lighted a cigarette and meditatively puffed a moment.

"See the lady?" he queried, and Thornton gloomily shook his head. "That's the occasion of the funereal expression, I suppose," the doctor continued, eying Thornton.

The younger man scowled and dropped into a chair beside the doctor's.

"I came out," he explained glumly, "and Ralby was with her. He always is, dammit. And just when I—"

The doctor laughed encouragingly.

"Had your courage screwed to the sticking-point, eh?" He contemplated Thornton from out his little shrewd eyes. "Nothing important in the call?" he hazarded.

Thornton shook his head. "They'd rung off; don't know who it was."

A little frown appeared in the doctor's forehead.

"Idiots—call a man this time of night and decide they don't want him. I've been trembling in my boots that somebody'd have a young fit and drag me away from here. Must be my lucky night."

Thornton remained silent, staring intently at the floor before him.

The big doctor smiled.

"I'll probably have a string of calls waiting when I get home," he rumbled on.

Still no word from Thornton, and the doctor snapped his cigarette in a wide arc across the rail of the veranda.

"'Rah for the fireworks!" the young prosecuting attorney cried approvingly as he approached. "Gee, that was a push—eh, Bernice?"

The girl at his side nodded in turn.

"You wait for me," she demanded poutingly. "I won't be five minutes. I'm ready to go home, too."

"Lady, whenever have I failed you?" protested the young man theatrically. "Here shall I make my home until you return." He took a chair next to the doctor's.

"You keep him for me, Doctor," the girl laughed her request at Doctor Lester. "He's the onliest man I've got, you know." And she turned into the house.

Railey accepted a cigarette from the doctor's fat hand and leaned back comfortably.

"A corner on feminine loveliness; that's what I've got," he exulted cheerfully.

Doctor Lester grunted unintelligibly, and Thornton remained silent. The young attorney smoked a moment, then:

"What's the idea?" he demanded. "Come out of it,

Thornton; this isn't a sphinx party."

Thornton raised his head.

"Oh, hello, Max; didn't know you were here."

"What?" The young man drew up in his chair. "And you did not see the blinding vision of beauty that commanded me to remain here until she returned?" he mocked. "You must have been dreaming."

Thornton turned toward the speaker.

"What's your idea about this Second National business, Max?"

Railey laughed.

"The expert—the steel oracle—desires information? Well, frankly, I haven't any theory, Thornton." His voice dropped from its light tone and took on a vein of seriousness. "Just how do you explain it yourself?"

"Explain it?" Thornton frowned. "By heaven, there's no explanation to it. I think the chief is wrong somewhere, that's all."

"H-m." The young attorney hummed thoughtfully. "The chief told me he'd talked to you, Hal, and that you'd sort of thrown a bluff that you could get into that vault. He's rather struck with the idea. Why did you do that?"

"There you are." Doctor Lester seemed to rouse into wakefulness. "That's what you get for blowing, Hal. Shouldn't be surprised if the sleuth had an eye on you."

Thornton shrugged.

"I'm going to satisfy myself to-morrow," he said quietly. "I want to see if I can do it. Suppose they'll let me try, Max?"

"Why not? But I wouldn't make an ass of myself,

Thornton. I looked at that vault to-day, and, believe me, it looks about as solid as Gibraltar."

Thornton nodded.

"That's what I say; but I can't get the idea out of my head. I've been bothering with it all night. It seems so ridiculously impossible."

"Glad Ralby's not around," chuckled the doctor. "He'd read you a lecture on what isn't possible and what is, eh, Max?"

"Gosh, yes. He had me in a corner to-night," laughed Railey. "Brilliant chap, that Ralby."

The doctor agreed readily. "Keeps up with things well," he admitted. "Got the finest little library on the new psychoanalysis movement I've seen yet; from Freud on down."

Thornton listened without interest.

"Just how good is the city's detective force, Max?" he questioned.

Railey started.

"Hey? Oh,"—and he laughed slightly—"nothing to brag about. The chief's a fat-headed, bulldog sort; he gets some results, through sheer luck, it seems to me. No, Hal, don't pin your faith of working out this thing on the detective force. They're about as much up in the air as I've ever seen them."

The doctor grunted.

"I'm up in the air, too," he admitted, "what with Thornton's insistence that the blamed thing is bulletproof and all. Damme! I'm beginning to wonder about the thing myself." The doctor lighted still another cigarette and grumbled heavily as though blaming himself for his interest.

"Here's an idea," suggested Railey slowly. "Let's see. Wouldn't it have been possible, Hal, for the men who put the vault in the bank to fix it so that they could come back some time and work the combinations?"

Thornton shook his head.

"If they did, they're marvels, that's all. I saw considerable of that work, Max, and it looked all right to me. Of course," he continued thoughtfully, "I wasn't looking for anything wrong, but—" he shrugged slightly. "It's too far-fetched, I think. That vault is so delicate that it would not close if a sheet of moderately thick paper were placed on the side of the door. No, that's not a good guess, Max."

The prosecuting attorney laughed.

"Oh, well, I can guess again, then; it just occurred to me, that's all."

"Seems to me," rumbled the doctor heavily, "seems to me that I read somewhere once—some detective story, probably—of a bunch of crooks who got into a vault like this by coming up from underneath, after working months to open the way. Sounds silly, doesn't it?"

"No-o," Railey began speculatively; "think I read the same thing, a long time ago." He tapped a foot consideringly on the floor. "As good a guess as any, I suppose, and worth looking into. What do you think of that one, Hal?"

Thornton shook his head.

"Won't do," he declared. "The base of the vault — its setting, that is—is on a solid concrete base from the ground; about eight solid feet of concrete, and some three feet of steel. Getting through that would be more of an impossible feat than opening the door itself."

The doctor yawned.

"I guess I'm not a Nick Carter," he grinned. "Besides, it's morning, and time to get in. Coming with me, Thornton? I'll drop you at—"

"Mr. Thornton"—the butler approached again—"the telephone, please."

Thornton turned to the doctor.

"I don't know who it can be this time of night—or morning—" he smiled; "but wait a minute and I'll go with you." He followed the servant.

Railey rose to his feet.

"That fair lady of mine is taking too much time," he commented. "Think I'll chase in and see— Hello, Ralby— not gone yet?"

Ralby drew near the two men.

"No," he said shortly. "I've been talking to Isabel. Everybody seems to have left, though, except the younger bunch. Where's Thornton—seen him?"

The doctor raised his eyes.

"Just went inside to the telephone. Wait a minute; we'll all go together. I've got my three-cylinder buzz-wagon outside."

The doctor invariably spoke of his roadster as a three-cylinder, claiming that the fourth cylinder had chronic something or other, which prevented it functioning, and no small part of the doctor's profanity was perfected while swearing over this same cylinder.

"You're still in the Riverside Apartments, aren't you, Ralby?"

Ralby nodded.

"Yep—third floor. Thornton's down on the first. Thinking of coming in with us?"

The young prosecuting attorney laughed.

"Yes, whenever I can bring Bernice to terms," he

chuckled. "In the meantime my diggings will hold me."

"Glad to have you," said Ralby easily. "We'll make you feel at home there. And if we can get you too, Lester—" He turned to the huge doctor.

"Huh." The doctor humphed his displeasure. "I spend half my time there now, doctoring that Haines kid."

"Oh, yes, our little mania patient," Ralby commented. "Think you'll try that suggestion business when— Oh, good night, Max, see you to-morrow—I mean later in the day." Ralby nodded and, shook hands with the young attorney, who moved off,

"Thanks for taking care of him, Doctor," the girl in the doorway cried laughingly. "And it's time you people were abed."

"Thornton's an infernally long time at that phone," grumbled the doctor.

Ralby nodded.

"Yes, and we're keeping Isabel, I think. Want to go dig him out?"

The doctor shook his head. It just occurred to him that Thornton was with the girl.

"No, I'm not especially tired," he grunted. "Had an easy day of it."

Meanwhile Thornton passed through the empty library and to the telephone on the table.

"Hello. Yes. Thornton speaking." He frowned into the transmitter trying to recall the voice. "Oh, hello, Chief—what's the idea? Did you call me a minute ago? Well, about twenty minutes. You did? All right. What is it?"

A look of astonishment crossed his face.

"The devil!" he gasped. "When? Yes. Yes. All right. I'll come down now. Yes. All right. Be with you in a few minutes."

He hurried to the porch.

Doctor Lester looked up.

"What's the rush?" he grumbled, and Ralby looked expectantly at Thornton.

"I just heard—" Thornton began, as the girl appeared in the doorway.

"Shoo! All of you!" she demanded laughingly. "I'm going in and it's past one o'clock."

She smiled impartially on the three men as they made their adieus.

Thornton was manifestly excited.

"Now, what is it?" demanded the doctor, stopping still.

"The St. John's National has been robbed!"

VI. Dr. Lester Makes a Bet

THORNTON'S voice was melodramatically quiet.
"The devil you say!" Ralby brought up short.
"When? How?"

The doctor whistled softly through his pursed lips.

"In the same way," continued Thornton, moving on. "I was just talking with the chief. Another vault entered—the loss is ten thousand."

They stopped before the doctor's car.

"Want to come to town with me?" Thornton turned. "I'm going down to the chief's office and see what I can learn of the affair."

"By George, I will!" The doctor clambered into his car. "Come along, Ralby; this'll interest you. A nice study in criminal psychology—a damned nice study."

Ralby shrugged and laughed.

"At least he's an engaging sort of thief, this. And he's got the nerve."

They crowded into the doctor's small car and sped toward the city. As they were crossing the Riverside Viaduct toward Bay Street Ralby broke the silence.

"Well, Doctor, doesn't this demonstrate again that there's always some individual who can—"

The doctor, driving, made the turn into Bay Street on two wheels.

"H-m," he grunted. "It begins to be interesting, certainly."

"Interesting?" Thornton's voice was tense. "By heaven—it's more than that. You don't understand.

It's almost unbelievable. The man who is doing this is a marvel!"

The doctor grunted again.

"Just the same," he threw the words at Ralby, "they'll get him—just as they get 'em all."

"Never in the world," laughed Ralby. "I think our gentleman will be too shrewd to be caught napping."

Thornton concurred. "Any man who can do things like that," he agreed, the words jolting from his mouth as the doctor swung the car around a corner, "isn't likely to be caught."

The doctor pressed his heavy foot on the accelerator.

"What'll you bet?" he questioned.

Thornton gestured with one hand.

"Not me," he frowned. "The whole business is too queer."

"Bet what, Doctor?" Ralby was interested.

"I'll bet five hundred they'll catch him in two weeks," grumbled the big man.

"Five hundred? Done with you," Ralby laughed aloud. "That's a sporting proposition."

The car swerved abruptly and brought up before the detective's offices with a screech of brakes. The three men descended and the doctor chuckled aloud:

"Good bet," he agreed, "and I'll split fifty-fifty with you, Hal, if you can work it out. You're on the case, you know."

*   *   *   *   *

"All that I can say," finished Thornton, leaning back in his chair, "is that whoever is responsible for these robberies is a safeman, par excellence."

The chief nodded heavily, and turned to Franklin at his side. The room in which the men sat adjoined the chief's office; the air was heavy and redolent with tobacco smoke.

Doctor Lester, who had spoken but little, scanned the faces of the men about the table. There were Thornton, the chief of detectives, Franklin, two other plain-clothes men, Morton Ralby, and the doctor himself.

It was Ralby who broke the momentary silence that followed Thornton's remark.

"Isn't it a bit peculiar, Chief, that the man should just grab one package of currency? Surely there were bonds in the vault?" He tapped a cigarette over an ash-tray.

"Hell!" exploded the chief. "Whoever it was probably realized that it was a cinch to get more when he wanted it. Why should he bother with bonds, and take chances on being located by the serial numbers?"

"Then you expect still another attempt might be made?"

"Why not?" the chief demanded. "The man seems to be able to get through anything; even into what Mr. Thornton says"—here the chief's voice grew heavily sarcastic—"is burglar-proof."

Ralby smiled, and Thornton blurted out:

"I tell you again, Chief, as I've told you a half-dozen times already: there isn't a man in this part of the country who knows as much about these things as I do, and I doubt that I could get into—"

The chief waved a pudgy hand.

"All right, Mr. Thornton, I'm not disputing you; but—" he grinned weakly, "you'd better look to your laurels then."

"That's all very well, Chief," Thornton returned quickly, "but my idea is that these—this—whoever it is—isn't just one man, but a gang of them. They must have planned this thing for months."

"What makes you think so?"

Thornton flushed at the chief's tone.

"I don't know," he said slowly. "But—oh, it isn't reasonable to suppose that suddenly a man appears—a man of whom the police have no record, no history—who is able to get into an absolutely burglar-proof vault." Thornton scowled thoughtfully at the detective. "You know yourself, Chief, that any single man of this extraordinary ability would be known somewhere, and you admit you've no record —nor any history of a—a—"

He broke off, and the chief scratched his head musingly, while the detective, Franklin, nodded.

"It does sound reasonable," he admitted.

"Of course it does," Thornton flashed. "It would be queer if a man of this power suddenly decided to turn thief and chose Jacksonville as his field. It's ridiculous. He would pick a place where his robberies would net him ten times the amount they do here. That's simply common sense."

"Was there any sign of damage in the St. John's vault?" Doctor Lester's heavy voice broke in, more to turn the conversation from Thornton and the chief than for any other reason.

Franklin answered the doctor.

"Not a sign. The guy just knew the combinations—or worked 'em. It's an old single-door box, and he walked in, helped himself, shut the door, and—flooey!" The detective's gesture was all embracing.

The heavy doctor chuckled.

"Quite an easy way of making a living, eh?" ha grunted.

Franklin nodded, grinning.

"But you watch, Doctor," he commented, "that guy's going to get too blamed biggety, and we'll get him. He'll think it's too easy."

The chief dropped his cigar into a cuspidor.

"I'll tell you this much, Doctor," he offered. "If Mr. Thornton and you and Mr. Ralby here are interesting yourself in this—er—affair—"

Ralby hastened to nod.

"With your permission, Chief, though there isn't much I can do, I know. I'm interested, well, less in the robberies, frankly, than in the personality of the robber. Psychology, you know—a harmless hobby, and—"

Doctor Lester heaved himself heavily to his feet.

"Anything I can do, Chief, just say the word." The big doctor chuckled. "But there doesn't seem to be much use for me."

The chief smiled grimly.

"Never can tell, Doctor," he snapped. "We may have use for you at that—you, too, Mr. Ralby."

"Well," the doctor yawned, "don't give that lunatic too much to do." He nodded heavily toward Thornton. "He's nervous as a jumping-jack already."

"What do you propose to do first?" Thornton ignored the doctor's remark.

The chief shrugged. "At least I can prevent a recurrence of it. I've got men stationed at each bank in the city"—the chief looked straight at Thornton—"and it's unlikely that we'll have another chance—"

"Surely you don't think this is going to continue?" Ralby's voice was incredulous.

"Huh!" the chief grunted. "Doesn't it look like it?"

"Why not?" Thornton asked bitterly. "It seems to me that one of the things we can expect is a repetition of the robberies."

The chief nodded his agreement, and Doctor Lester eyed Thornton thoughtfully.

"It may be down the state," Thornton went on, "but I doubt it. If it is one man, and I don't believe it, he'll have the whole country in an uproar in six months."

"Not if I know it," growled the chief, viciously biting off the end of a fresh cigar.

"I'd like to go down with you in the morning, Chief," Thornton continued as he rose to his feet, "later on, that is, just to see whether it is possible for a man to work the combinations of the vault in the Second National."

The chief eyed Thornton again.

"All right, young man. You can have a fling at it, and also at this St. John's—"

Thornton laughed.

"I've no doubt about the St. John's, Chief. I know what can be done with that, and I'll bet I can get into it inside of thirty minutes. It's that Defy vault that's worrying me."

Doctor Lester, moving toward the door, took it up:

"You folks," he commented, "seem to be overlooking the fact that watchmen are supposed to be in these banks."

Franklin turned to the doctor.

"No, we ain't, either. But this guy works like streaked lightning. Why, he didn't have fifteen minutes between the watchman's rounds at the St. John's."

"What time was it when this last robbery took place?" Doctor Lester was beginning to manifest an interest in the proceedings.

"As near as we can make out, a little after midnight," answered the chief promptly.

"That was when you first called me, wasn't it, Chief?" Thornton questioned.

"Er—yes." The chief nodded embarrassedly, and hurriedly held a lighted match to his cigar.

"Why did you ring off?" Thornton queried curiously.

The chief turned visibly red.

"Er—I—that is—I was at my house," he stuttered, "and you were so long coming to the phone" —he fidgeted about in his chair—"I was in a hurry to get to the office, of course," he explained. "Called you again right after I got here."

Doctor Lester's heavy face creased into a grin and he winked broadly at Ralby, who wondered what the reason was.

It was patently evident to the big doctor that Thornton's questions embarrassed the chief of detectives, nor did the shrewd physician for a moment doubt that the chief's call was made for any other reason than to fix definitely the fact that Thornton was at the Brannon home, five miles from the city.

The doctor eyed Thornton speculatively, but the young man seemed entirely unaware of the chief's nervousness or of the doctor's gaze fixed on his face. The chief's answer evidently satisfied him, for he was frowning at nothing, staring straight ahead, evidently endeavoring to solve the problem by sheer thought.

Doctor Lester shook his head heavily, and a puzzled light came into his little eyes as he met those of Morton Ralby fixed on him. He shrugged hugely and turned aside. Ralby was undoubtedly puzzled, and showed it. He had been listening intently:

"Tell me," he began again, "who discovered the St. John's robbery at this time of the morning?"

The chief's guttural laugh answered him.

"I thought you'd get away without asking that," he admitted. "Our gentleman left a light burning before the vault. The watchman reported it to Hollwood, the cashier. He went down and investigated; then called me."

Ralby shook his head slowly.

"A man such as this one appears to be," he speculated, "would hardly leave a light—"

"Oh, there's none of 'em perfect," the chief assured him positively, glad to get away from the subject of his telephone call for Thornton. "That's why I'm morally certain we'll land him. But—thirty-five thousand dollars in two days."

"Will the papers have it?" queried Ralby.

"That's the hell of it," agreed the chief. "They will, by to-morrow—by this afternoon, that is—and they'll be on me like a pack of hungry wolves."

"Did you look for finger-prints?"

The chief smiled tolerantly at Ralby's questionings.

"About fifty hands a day touch that vault," he grumbled. "Besides, Hollwood had opened the vault before I got there."

"There isn't any inner vault there?"

The chief shook his head.

"Nope. Only one. A small inner safe, one of the circular kind, which they use for securities."

Ralby frowned, and Thornton broke in:

"There wasn't any effort made to open the inner safe?" he questioned. "That sounds queer. To a man who can go through the outer vault-door, the inner safe would be like a cigar-box."

The detective, Franklin, had been listening carefully, especially when Thornton was speaking. It was easy to see that he considered Thornton but little short of an infallible oracle.

"I guess he didn't have time," he volunteered. "He must 'a' had a line on the watchman's rounds all right."

Ralby, carefully studying the tip of his cigarette, asked Thornton:

"How long, Thornton, do you think it would take a man, knowing the combinations, to open, enter, and close the St. John's vault?"

Thornton pondered the question, and the big doctor again eyed him closely. The chief leaned forward interestedly.

"Ten minutes," Thornton answered finally. "That is, if he had the combination down pat, and got it the first time without a slip."

Ralby whistled.

"He's some fast worker then. And if he had to work out the combination, what then?"

Thornton frowned.

"That's just what I've been trying to get out," he explained, "if a man had to work those combinations out—any man short of the most expert vault constructor in the world—it would take him at the very least an hour."

Doctor Lester glanced at his watch.

"Well, I'm off," he announced, satisfied that there was but one way to end the apparently interminable discussion. "Coming along, Thornton?"

Thornton nodded and turned to the door, accompanied by Ralby.

"See you later, Chief; don't forget I'm to have a hand at that Second National vault."

The chief nodded and the men withdrew.

Left alone with his men, the chief turned to Franklin.

"Well?" he demanded.

Franklin shook his head.

"It seems to me, Chief, that that guy Ralby's mighty interested."

The chief shrugged his shoulders.

"One of these scientific guys," he commented caustically, his voice plainly indicating his opinion of the scientific fraternity. "Supposed to be in real estate, ain't he?"

Franklin nodded.

"Yep. Offices on the first floor of the St. James Building, but he's never in 'em. Always seems to have money. Always did have—but where he makes it beats me."

The chief shook his head.

"Nix," he commented briefly. "He's harmless."

"All the same," continued Franklin tenaciously, "he sat up a little when you mentioned that light."

Another of the men laughed.

"Come off, Fran," he grinned. "So did you. Said it wasn't so at first, didn't you?"

"I don't know," commented the chief thoughtfully. "It's a good point, that light." He turned to the man who had spoken to Franklin. "You pick this Ralby up and stick with him," he ordered.

The detective nodded.

"A pipe," he declared.

"And you," the chief continued, turning to Franklin, "you hang with this Thornton chap who's so damned certain that he's the only man in town with brains enough to pull a thing like this."

The assignment pleased Franklin, for it meant, as he knew, the spending of considerable time on the third floor of the St. James Building—next to the offices of Doctor Lester.

"But I wouldn't advise you," the chief finished heavily to Franklin, "to worry more about that girl in Doctor Lester's than your job."

"When's it coming off, Fran?" laughed one of the men jeeringly.

Franklin turned red.

"Seems to me," he growled, "that if you guys paid as much attention to your blamed business—"

A guffaw of laughter interrupted him.

"Enough of that," grunted the chief. "I'm not talking just to make noise," he went on, "but I'm tellin' you boys there'll be some mighty loud howling going on in this town in a day or two, and we've simply got to get on the job—and get there right." The chief's fist pounded the table before him.

"I want you," the chief turned to one of the men beside him, "to start up Bay Street to-day with this list." The chief grinned as he drew a list from his pocket. "Serial numbers of some of the big bills in the St. John's package," he explained. "I ain't spilling all

I know, you see. You make copies of this list, and spread it pretty well over town—on the q. t, mind."

The detective nodded and pocketed the slip.

"And you, Franklin," the chief turned again on Franklin. "You pick up Thornton at his apartment, and just forget that girl of yours a little bit."

Franklin turned red.

"I'll do my end of it, Chief," he began, but the chief waved his hand to end the discussion.

"That's what you're here for."

"How about the doctor?" commented Franklin ironically, digging back at the chief. "Hadn't somebody better—"

The chief flushed slowly.

"Aw, get to hell out o' here," he grumbled good-naturedly. "Give me a rest. We'll all be needing to work together to land this steel-vault Johnnie of ours."

"Then why waste my time watchin' Thornton?" Franklin demanded. "I could do twice the good hanging around Bridge Street, gettin' a line on some of the new faces, or down to Pablo."

"Nix." The chief slapped the desk heavily. "The guy who's pulling this stuff isn't your Bridge Street kind, and you won't find him hanging 'round down the beaches, either. I've got a hunch this is one o' those gentlemen crooks you're always ravin' about, Franklin, and—well, we've got him to get, that's all."

Franklin shrugged, picked up his hat, and made for the door.

"Just the same," he insisted, "they'd laugh you out of the place if they knew you were wasting time on Thornton and his crowd."

The chief wagged a finger at the retreating

detective.

"I ain't saying a thing, Fran, but when a man shoots off his mouth so much and frequent that he's the only guy who could pull a thing like this, well, I reckon I'd keep an eye on him—even if he was my own grandfather. And that's your job; get me?"

VII. AN UNPROFESSIONAL VISIT

DOCTOR LESTER'S car coughed its complaining way along the deserted streets, the doctor hunched far down in his seat behind the steering-wheel.

Thornton was moody and silent, and Ralby, after twice trying to light a cigarette, gave it up as a bad job, and watched the huge doctor as he twisted the car about, picking the best spots in the going, and grumbling over the cylinder, which missed chronically.

As they swung into Riverside Avenue Thornton broke the silence.

"Remember coming across any case analogous to this in your reading, Ralby?"

"What?" Ralby sat up with a start. "Beg pardon, Thornton; I was dreaming. What was it?"

Thornton repeated the question, and Ralby mused silently a moment.

"No," he finally answered, "can't say that I have. There was that Tennessee case of the man they called Midnighty Somebody-or-other; I forget what. He was a pretty wise one, but hardly up to a game like this. Besides he's still doing time in Tennessee, if I remember aright."

"You mean that fellow Josephs," Thornton remarked. "I remember reading of that. No; it would take a better man than he was at his best. Josephs depended on the sense of touch to tell him when the tumblers began to fall in the doors, and I don't believe he could get very far on these new vaults."

The doctor at the wheel grunted skeptically.

"Is there anything in this Jimmy Valentine business?" he questioned. "I mean this opening of vaults by the sense of touch." He half turned to Thornton, who nodded immediately.

"You're mighty right there is. There's a man up at the Defy plant who is a wizard at it." Thornton chuckled reminiscently. "I can do it myself sometimes."

Ralby shrugged.

"A matter of practise, I presume. Same old argument, Lester: there's always a man to do *anything*, provided he works hard enough."

The doctor grunted unintelligibly. Then he chortled:

"By the same reasoning, there's a man who can catch this cracksman of ours then."

"Of course," Ralby admitted immediately. "But I doubt if our worthy chief or his colleagues have the necessary imagination." He was silent for a minute, then: "If I were running this bunch of sleuths, I think I'd work on Thornton's idea of a gang of them; a well-laid, plotted scheme; not just one man."

"But one man must do the actual work," argued Thornton. "It's almost impossible to believe there is a man capable of it. If there are more it simply makes it so much the more improbable."

Ralby shrugged. "Well, we've beefed about it enough. For my part I'm willing to forget it and go to bed. Something is bound to turn up—it always does."

"I hope it turns up quick," grumbled the doctor. "Five hundred dollars' worth. You're not forgetting our bet, Ralby?"

"Don't worry, Lester; you've got the losing end.

Thornton's experiments later on will demonstrate that. Personally, Thornton, I doubt that you'll be able to manage, although, of course, I don't know a blessed thing about the darn vaults."

"I'm almost sure myself," Thornton admitted. "Still I want to determine to my own satisfaction that it can't be done. There's always the possibility of a flaw in the mechanism, you know. That's what I'm hoping to find. You'll be there, won't you?"

"If they'll let me," laughed Ralby. "Gosh, but the chief's face would be a study in emotions if, by any chance, you should succeed."

The doctor's laugh boomed aloud.

"It'll be worth seeing," he admitted. "Think I'll drop around myself. Ought to see Hayes anyway. Haven't dropped in on him for a coon's age."

Thornton spoke enviously. "Wish I hadn't;" and Ralby's eyes shot a side glance at him.

"Why?"

Thornton laughed.

"Oh, nothing, except he's carrying a little paper of mine. Not enough to amount to anything—but bothersome, just the same. Oh, yes, I see our friend Mr. Hayes every now and then."

Ralby made as if to speak, hesitated, and finally dropped a hand in a friendly fashion on Thornton's arm.

"Be glad to help you out on that—er—paper, Thornton. Just say the word."

"Thanks, old man." Thornton was genuinely pleased. "It's good to know that I've got a couple of you fellows to fall back on if I need you. Lester here," he nudged the doctor beside him, "tries to swat me with a check every once in a while, but I'm pulling through all right. If those infernal Defy people would do the right thing, and come across as they should for that synchronizing device, I'd be on Easy Street."

"Take 'em into the courts," grumbled the doctor. "You've got 'em tied now, since they started using the thing definitely."

Thornton laughed.

"What's the use? I'll take what I can get—what they'll come across with, but, believe me, the next time I offer a patent to a corporation I'll have it tied up so tight they can't monkey with it."

The car slid to a halt before the ornate front of the Riverside Apartments, and Thornton and Ralby alighted. They stood for a moment talking with the doctor.

"You'll remember to drop in at the office, Thornton," the doctor remarked. "These sleeping fits need looking into."

Thornton smiled. "I am a bit all in," he admitted. "Too much work, probably."

"Too much dancing, I'd say," laughed Ralby. "We'd begun to think you were going to cut all of the lady's dances this year," he bantered, and Thornton flushed.

The doctor humphed. "If you'd been wasting your nights more profitably," he growled, "I'd say all right. Now there's Isabel—"

Ralby's voice cut in.

"Well—it's time to turn in, and then some. If Thornton wants to burn the midnight oil tinkering with that steel mess, it's his business. I can dig up some mighty good authorities, though, Thornton, to prove that a too constant application to work tends to degenerate the capacity for it. Great strides we're making in the modern psychology."

The doctor grumbled his displeasure.

"I'm not saying a word about the psychologists, Ralby," he said, "but a whole raft of them could very profitably go back to James and learn fundamentals. The whole trouble is Freud became popularized too blamed sudden, and every whippersnapper on earth thinks he's a psychologist, because he's read that Brill translation on psychoanalysis. Why, demme! Any man without a groundwork of anatomy and medicine trying to grasp the modern psychology is simply butting his head into a brick wall, and—"

Thornton interrupted:

"So-long, pill-roller!" he laughed, knowing there was but one method of stopping the avalanche of words when the doctor started on his pet subject. "I'll drop in on you and let you thump me over a bit. Good night!"

"Good night!" The doctor's heavy voice rumbled as he slid in the gears and the car trembled at the curb. "And, say—" But Thornton and Ralby were out of hearing.

Carefully the doctor picked his way down the dimly-lighted streets, flashing and dimming his lights alternately.

By the time he arrived at his home all thoughts of the events of the evening had been methodically put from his mind, and he was once more the phlegmatic, unimaginative doctor. As he deftly steered his car into its garage, however, he muttered absently:

"Blamed strange, just the same, and thirty-five thousand dollars. Whew!"

He entered the house and paused mechanically

before the telephone, picking up the note-pad by its side. On the pad he read:

"Call Mrs. Haines—Riverside Apartments."

He noted that the call was recent and picked up the receiver. In a few minutes he was frowning intently into the transmitter.

"Didn't make her sleep? You gave it to her? All of it? Um! Seems afraid; eh? Yes, I'd better come out, I reckon."

He hung up the receiver, glanced at his watch and yawned hugely; then turned once more into the night.

Puzzling over the case, he rolled his car from the garage and started off, muttering beneath his breath as he lamented his lot, and stopping only to yawn prodigiously.

In a few minutes the doctor's car brought up again before the apartment-house it had quitted but a short time before.

The heavy doctor frowned at the dark empty elevator, sighed resignedly and turned to ascend the steps. His destination was the fifth floor, and he was puffing mightily before he had gone half the distance, grumbling and muttering in his own grouchy fashion:

"You'd think—oof—they'd have more lights in a first-class apartment-house—whew—doctors not supposed to sleep, I reckon—run 'em all the time—a hell of a profession—and get no thanks for it—oof—noble profession, yeh—heal the sick—dammit!"

This last ejaculation as his shin caught sharply against a protruding part of an ornate bit of iron on the third floor.

The doctor stopped to rub the injured leg, panting

heavily.

From beyond a door, opening on the corridor, came a soft, well-modulated voice:

"You *must*, I tell you—you *must!*"

The doctor looked up, noting the apartment number.

"Humph!" He frowned disgustedly. "Ralby; eh? That's why he was so blamed anxious to get in." The big doctor shook his heavy head, a silent commentary on the morals of the age, and once more began his ascent.

Arrived at the fifth floor he knocked softly on a door, and an eager-faced woman answered.

Gone was the doctor's grouchy manner and grumbling. With his hat he seemed to shed the pessimism that cloaked him, and he became the kindly, eager and extraordinarily proficient physician that the name Doctor Edward Lester stood for in the city of Jacksonville.

His big voice grumbled soothingly as he stooped over the bed of his patient, a young girl, apparently about eight years of age, whose troubled, burning eyes carried their own message of the fever of sleeplessness.

The doctor's clumsy hands were very tender as he took the wrist of the little girl, and nodded his head heavily as he checked the pulse against the watch he drew from his pocket.

Ten minutes later he was again in the hallway.

"Oh, yes, she'll sleep now," he rumbled. "You'd better go to bed, too," he admonished heavily, and the woman smiled slightly. "You needn't worry. She'll sleep, I tell you. Call me again, if you want me—but there'll be no need. Not at all—not at all.

No trouble—no trouble—demme—that's my business, isn't it?"

And he began his slow descent, puffing laboriously and growling:

"Fine profession—damned fine profession—the hell it is!"

He carefully skirted the obstruction that he had bumped into on the third floor, glanced at the dark transom above Ralby's door, shook his head heavily and eased his huge bulk down the remaining two flights of stairs and out into the night.

The door to the street slammed shut behind him, and a man in the front (right) apartment jerked violently erect at a little table at which he sat.

"Sleep again—dog-gone it!" Thornton muttered, rising to his feet and snapping on the electric light. "Couldn't even wait to get into bed." He stretched luxuriously and yawned.

A knock on the door interrupted, and, wonderingly, he opened it. The doctor's huge figure filled the opening.

"For th' love of Mike, Hal, why ain't you in bed?"

Thornton laughed.

"Come in, now that you're here. Pretty late, isn't it? What brings you back?"

The doctor lowered himself into a chair.

"Mountain climbing," he grumbled. "That Haines kid has got 'em bad again. She'll do now, though — but what's been keeping you up?"

Thornton turned to a cellaret and brought out a decanter and glasses.

"Frankly, Lester"—he poured out a drink into the doctor's glass—"I don't know." He leaned over the table with a seltzer bottle. "I came in— let's see—of course I did. I must have. And say —say when!"

"'S'nough—thanks. Then what?" The doctor stirred his drink meditatively as he eyed Thornton.

"I must have fallen asleep at the table here. Something woke me up just now—"

The doctor choked and put down the glass he had raised. "Let's see." He extended a great fat hand and grasped Thornton's wrist, squinting the while at his watch. He shook his big head slowly.

"What's it doing?" Thornton queried lightly, though the tiny wrinkles about his eyes showed his worry.

The doctor replaced his watch and swallowed the drink.

"How do you feel?"

"All right," the younger man answered easily. "Nothing wrong, anyway—except a little dizzy, as though I'd suddenly stopped spinning around."

"Light points before the eyes?"

Thornton shook his head.

"The devil! I'm not bilious," he laughed.

"It's no laughing matter. Come here!" The doctor turned a table light until it shone clearly in Thornton's face. "Bend down here, dammit, I ain't a giraffe!" He gazed earnestly into Thornton's eyes, squinting with his own until they were mere pinpoints behind their fat, puffy lids.

Thornton grinned at his seriousness.

"You look like Gargantua!" he taunted.

The doctor snorted, "You'd be better off not reading that rotten Rabelais!" he commented. "French smut!"

"Aw, come on, Lester! You chuckle over it yourself!" Thornton smiled under the doctor's steady scrutiny. "What's the idea?"

The big doctor carefully lifted the lid of one of the young man's eyes and frowned in a puzzled fashion. Then he arose.

"Yellow jaundice?" Thornton mocked.

The doctor didn't answer, but groaningly dragged out his hypodermic case.

"Get in bed," he grumbled; "I can't stay here until this afternoon." And Thornton, joking lightly, obeyed, while the doctor turned into the bathroom from which came the sound of running water.

He returned in a few moments, commenting under his breath about the heat of the water, while Thornton, pajama-clad, sat swinging his legs from the edge of the bed. The doctor drew out a battered stethoscope and began listening intently, with the disk pressed here and there on Thornton's chest.

Thornton was beginning to be genuinely worried.

"What seems to be the trouble—" he began, but the doctor, the ear-pieces of the stethoscope firmly in place, only rumbled a heavy "Shut up, will you?" and continued his examination.

He worked very carefully, stopping now and then to thump experimentally.

"Say 'Ah,'" he grunted, and Thornton obeyed, although he seemed to consider the whole business a lark.

Finally the doctor replaced the stethoscope, carefully doubled up, into his hip-pocket. "You've got a heart like an elephant," he grumbled, "and lungs made of leather—or I'm a liar!" He seemed disappointed, and Thornton laughed at the lugubrious expression on his face.

The doctor turned again into the bathroom, and

returned in a moment, waddling ludicrously. In one fat hand he held a hypodermic.

Thornton objected weakly.

"Aw, I don't need anything like that, Lester— say—what—"

The doctor cocked his heavy head on one side.

"Who's the doctor here?" he demanded. He passed Thornton a piece of alcohol-saturated cotton. "Swab off that arm," he ordered, holding the hypodermic to the light and pressing easily on the plunger until a drop of fluid appeared at the needle's end.

"Bet a dollar it's not a thing but a touch of indigestion," Thornton bantered from the bed. "And you come along dragging a funereal face as though I was all but buried."

"Yeh?" The doctor was elaborately sarcastic. "Maybe I'm hanging around here at three in the morning for my health; eh? For two cents I'd stick you in a hospital where you could be watched. A fine place to get sick in—I don't think!" The doctor eyed the disarray of the apartment.

Thornton laughed aloud.

"All right, if you're going to fill me full of habit-forming dope, here's your chance!" He extended a bare forearm.

"Habit-forming—tommyrot!" The doctor jabbed in the needle sharply. "Maybe you'll get enough nerve this way to talk business to—don't sit there, dammit! Get in bed. Cover up. I ain't going to hang around here a week."

Obediently Thornton slipped beneath the covers, while the doctor continued his grumbling:

"Now you sleep," he ordered, "and come in when you get down-town." He picked up his hat and turned once more to the door, while Thornton, already dozing, muttered a sleepy "Good night!"

The doctor darkened the room and slouched into the corridor, closing the door quietly behind him. He waddled into his automobile, noted that it was nearly four o'clock, and groaned mightily, grumblingly complaining and lamenting his choice of a profession, shoved down the starter and glided down the street—streaked with the gray of the approaching dawn.

Fifteen minutes later, his Brobdingnagian figure clad in brightly-striped pajamas, the doctor smoked a final cigarette. On his fat knees lay an open volume, but his eyes had drifted from the book until they surveyed the placid St. Johns River, which flowed peacefully a quarter of a mile to the south.

Finally he let himself gently into his creaking bed.

"Just the same," he muttered drowsily, "there's no reason for that spasmodic reflex of the eyeball unless—" But the doctor's speculations drifted into nothingness, and his heavy breathing bespoke sleep.

VIII. The Third Visitation

FRANKLIN, the detective, shuffled uneasily in his seat in Doctor Lester's reception-room, while from the open door, leading into the doctor's office and the laboratory beyond, came the sound of airy humming, accompanied by much needless noise.

Franklin smoked a cigarette, drummed impatiently on the arm of his chair, looked at his watch, and finally lounged into the doctor's laboratory.

The office girl, busy with her cleaning, made as though she did not notice him for a moment. He cleared his throat clumsily and began to speak two or three times before he finally blurted:

"How long before the doctor will be in, you reckon?"

The girl turned as though but that moment aware of his presence. "Ben Franklin, how many times must I tell you that I don't know? And if you don't quit bothering me—"

"Honest, Mae," the man pleaded, "I want to see him—I ain't kiddin'."

The girl tossed her head.

"Well, wait then," she advised curtly, but relented at the sight of his woebegone expression.

"And if you want to make yourself useful you might turn that switch there for the sterilizer—no, stupid—the other one—here—" And she turned to the man to show him the proper switch-button.

Perhaps it wasn't her fault that their hands met

at the switchboard; certainly it appeared to be her
intention to press the button. As a matter of fact, the
sterilizer remained dead, cold and neglected for
many minutes.

Later the girl fixed her hair.

"I think you're just staying because—" She left
the sentence unfinished, but a side glance spoke
volumes.

Franklin laughed, but shook his head.

"No, honest, girly—not that I wouldn't want to
stay, anyway, but—well—er—that is—I got some
business up here."

"Go on!" The girl busied herself at a table.
"There's nobody up here for you to gumshoe around!"

Franklin shook his head.

"Don't you be too sure of that," he smiled; "maybe
I'm watching you!"

The girl puckered her mouth and whistled
tauntingly, but broke off abruptly in the middle of a
bar:

"If you don't go into that outside office and let me
work—" she gasped, pushing the man away, "I'll—
I'll—"

Franklin turned obediently to the door, and, for
perhaps five minutes, the sounds of renewed activity
proceeded from Doctor Lester's laboratory.

Then the girl tiptoed quietly to the door of the
reception-room. Franklin, however, was not there.
She pouted and made her way across the room, but
ducked back hastily as she saw him pacing the
corridor.

For a moment she sat quietly near the door; then,
as Franklin did not seem to have immediate
intentions of returning, she called to him:

"All right, then—you might as well wait in here —if you just must."

Franklin reentered the room.

"Say, Mae," he seemed embarrassed, "what time does Mr. Thornton come down? Seen him yet?"

"You've been here as long as I have," the girl replied. "You were here with me, weren't you? Have you seen him yet?" she mimicked.

"Pretty nice sort, ain't he?" Franklin's questioning was extremely clumsy.

The girl nodded.

"Uhuh. And a mighty good friend of the doctor's, too; the doctor thinks he's going to—" A step in the corridor interrupted, and Franklin jerked about sharply to see who was passing.

When he turned again the girl was regarding him scornfully.

"Ben Franklin—do you mean to sit there and tell me that Mr. Thornton is the man you're watching?"

Franklin turned red. "Aw, come off, Mae. I ain't told you a thing. You know I ain't. What d'you think I'd be watchin' him for?"

She eyed the red Franklin a moment and picked up a magazine.

"I don't know," she commented caustically, "but it would be silly enough for you to be doing it."

"When does he come in—usually?"

"Haven't I told you that I don't know?" The girl paged through the magazine indifferently.

"I don't mean the doctor," Franklin explained hurriedly, "I mean—er—Mr. Thornton."

The girl slammed the magazine back on the table.

"Ben Franklin, tell me right out now—are you watching for Mr. Thornton?"

"Aw, say, Mae," the man began once more to expostulate, then, noting the scornful expression in her eyes: "Well, you needn't yell it out loud," he grumbled.

The girl's eyes flashed.

"Of all the idiotic things!" she gasped. "Just wait till I tell Doctor Lester. What on earth do you think you can learn from watching Mr. Thornton?"

The detective fidgeted in his chair.

"It ain't my fault, honest it ain't, Mae, but the chief's such a nut." He got slowly to his feet and crossed the office, sitting next to the girl. "Gee whiz, Mae; don't jump on me about it." Tentatively he reached out for the girl's hand, but she withdrew sharply.

"Are you sure you didn't ask to watch him?" The hint of a smile began in the corner of her eyes.

Franklin, perceiving her reasoning, chuckled aloud, but made no other reply, although he possessed himself of the girl's now unresisting hands.

"Say," Franklin prefaced most of his remarks that way, "as soon as they clean up this job, Mae, I'm going to get that vacation."

"Yes?" The girl drew closer.

"And then—"

Doctor Lester waddled heavily into the room, breaking into Franklin's speech to the girl. The two slid hurriedly apart, but the huge doctor only nodded smilingly.

"Good morning. Why the detective force so early? Didn't get much sleep, did you?" The doctor chuckled. "Better watch out, Mae," he warned.

Franklin came to his feet.

"Good morning, Doctor," he grinned, "maybe it's Mae here that brings me. I'd like—," He turned awkwardly to the girl, who blushed rosily.

"Don't pay any attention to him, Doctor," she remarked, "he's just a stupid fly-cop." She flung out the expression and ducked hastily behind a table as Franklin made a grab for her.

Laughing his huge rumbling laugh, the doctor continued into his office. From there he called in a moment:

"Seen anything of Mr. Thornton this morning, Mae?"

The girl's eyes leaped to the man's beside her.

"No—no, sir, not yet," she called back.

"All right." The doctor was evidently already thinking of something else, for, in a moment, the sound of running water came from the laboratory.

The detective turned to the girl again.

"He ain't coming up right away, I don't think. He was going down to the bank with the chief this morning."

"Is *that* what you're watching him for?" Suddenly the girl laughed aloud. "Oh, that's too funny! Of all the men in town, you stupid—"

Doctor Lester appeared again in the doorway.

"I'm going down to the Second National, Mae," he explained. "Be back in about an hour. You can get me there." He turned to Franklin. "You're going down, too, aren't you?" he invited.

Franklin nodded and picked up his hat from the table, while the girl smiled, then made a face at him as the doctor turned his back.

Together the two men left the office and made their way to the Second National Bank, a few blocks away.

An interested group stood about the closed door of the big vault in the Second National Bank building. The skeptical chief of detectives, with his cigar clamped tight in the corner of his mouth; Hayes, the bank president, and the two junior officers, Kingsley and Harkiss; likewise old Jensen, the ex-policeman and now watchman of the bank property, and, last, Thornton, a puzzled frown on his face, and a queer look in his eyes.

"Well, how about it?" grumbled the chief, and Thornton threw aside his coat and rolled up his shirt-sleeves as he stood, legs apart, gazing frowningly at the closed circular door, with its double combination dials and the large wheel that controlled the levers.

The bank president nodded.

"I admit, Mr. Thornton, that we are somewhat skeptical—" he began, and stopped as the detective approached, the huge doctor waddling gravely behind him.

Thornton apparently did not hear, and it was only when the big man slapped him on the shoulder that he looked up, startled.

"Oh, hello, Lester," he smiled, seeming again his natural self. "Well, I'm going to take a shot at it, but it looks strong, doesn't it?"

Doctor Lester eyed the glistening surface of the vault-door.

"Huh!" he grunted, "the devil himself can't break into that thing. Go to it, Mr. Jimmy Valentine, Jr."

"Yeh," sneered the chief heavily, "go to it."

Thornton turned again to the vault, fixing his eyes on the clock at the top, the face of which was sunk flush with the vault's surface. The clock had been set, arbitrarily, at five minutes past eight.

The bank officials smiled smugly as they watched the young man. It was patent that, to them, the idea of entering the vault was ridiculous.

Thornton nodded slowly, muttering his thoughts aloud.

"First the clock, of course." He seemed puzzled a moment, and turned to an electric light switch to one side of the vault. "What does this control?"

Hayes, the president, smiled as he answered:

"Merely the lights inside the vault, Mr. Thornton."

Thornton pondered this.

"Is your current independent of the building, or are you all on one circuit?"

The president shrugged.

"I haven't an idea, Mr. Thornton—all the same, I suppose."

The watchman stepped nearer to Thornton.

"Beggin' your pardon, sir, there's a string of fuse-plugs in that box there."

He indicated a boxlike affair on the wall to one side, which Thornton approached. He opened the front and stared a moment at the row of shiny plugs. Then he smiled and his hand went out with a certain gesture to one side and began to unscrew one of the isinglass-topped fuse-plugs.

Suddenly the chief of detectives gave a startled grunt as the hands of the clock dropped suddenly to eight-thirty.

The doctor's eyes grew a bit larger, and he fixed them intently on Thornton, while wondering expressions appeared suddenly on the faces of the bank officials.

Thornton returned to the vault-door smiling.

"Well, Chief, that's how the current went," he boasted. "Silly, too, to connect it that way."

He bent over the vault-door and began toying with the numbered dial of a combination, and Harkiss, the cashier, turned to the chief and grinned behind his palm.

"He's got the wrong one," he whispered, and the chief only frowned in return, shaking his head for silence.

Thornton worked hurriedly a few moments, then passed to the dial on the face of which letters took the place of the numbers. In perhaps five minutes, during which time only the heavy breathing of the spectators broke the silence, he straightened slowly from his task, relaxing his muscles, and shook his head.

"Can't make it, eh?" The bank president smiled.

"'S matter?" grunted the chief sarcastically.

Thornton turned. "There's absolutely not the slightest quiver," he said shortly. "One thing sure, no one learned those combinations by their sense of touch. There's no *feel* there, that's all."

"Well," the chief began heavily, but Thornton did not heed the interruption, and turned to the doctor, saying:

"There's one other way to try. Lend me your stethoscope, Lester; got it?"

Doctor Lester twisted grotesquely and brought the instrument from his hip-pocket. He handed it over with a grin and the chortled warning:

"Careful of it, Hal, I ain't got another one."

The chief of detectives snorted his disgust, and

the officers of the bank smiled leisurely and superiorly as Thornton took the stethoscope, adjusted it carefully into his ears, and once more approached the vault.

This time, with the flat disk of the stethoscope pressed against the steel door, he twisted the combination of the letter dial slowly, so slowly that it seemed to the watching men that the shiny circle of steel scarcely turned.

After a moment Thornton straightened slowly, and, still holding the stethoscope against the vault-door, he turned the large center wheel carefully. Again he turned his full attention to the smaller combination dial. Suddenly he turned, removing the stethoscope.

"H!" he jerked out triumphantly—"six to the right to H!" And he laughed 'aloud as he caught the look of surprise on the face of Harkiss.

The chief remained silent, staring wide-eyed at Thornton, and the big doctor chuckled as Thornton explained:

"Of course, knowing the beginning, I can work it—in time—using 'H' for the key letter, and beginning with this letter each time, go through the alphabet."

"And the numbers?" It was Harkiss, the cashier, who put the question.

Thornton looked toward the man.

"That could be worked out, I think," he said quietly. "You see, I know you don't alternate numbers and letters." He smiled at the expression of astonishment that showed again on the cashier's face.

"How do you know that?" grumbled the chief.

Thornton's smile broadened.

"You're not remembering, Chief, that I know these vaults," he reminded. "I can tell by the way the combinations are placed. The alternating combination knobs in this particular type of vault are placed one under the other."

The chief was silenced for a moment, then:

"How long do you figure it would take you to get in there?"

"Working continually," Thornton answered, "and without interruptions"—he thought a moment—"I'd say twenty-four hours."

Doctor Lester interrupted heavily. "Then what in the name of common sense did you expect to learn?"

"Just what I did," Thornton answered quietly. "The man who opened this vault *knew the combinations!*"

Both Harkiss and Kingsley turned a dull-red, and the former opened his mouth to expostulate. The president's hand fell on his arm.

"Easy there," he counseled, and turned to the others. "If you don't mind"—he apologized—"they'll be needing this open in earnest."

He led the way up-stairs and into his private office.

On the steps the fat doctor drew alongside Thornton. "Feel pretty good?" he questioned.

Thornton nodded.

"Yes—all right now, thanks. I don't think there was anything really wrong."

The doctor grumbled beneath his breath, and the chief of detectives turned to whisper to Franklin as they entered the office:

"You don't want to lose this guy a minute,

understand?"

The detective nodded and detached himself from the group, wandering into the banking floor proper, which presented the usual busy Saturday morning scene.

The bank president passed around a box of cigars. The chief lighted one immediately, while Doctor Lester produced a crumpled package of cigarettes from a capacious pocket. Thornton merely shook his head, declining the invitation to smoke, and dropped into a chair.

"Ralby didn't come with you?" he questioned the doctor, and seemed nervous.

The doctor grinned.

"Stealing a march on you, maybe, eh?" he grunted. "He's got a new launch, you know—"

The bank president turned to the chief.

"You saw the papers this morning?"

The chief nodded.

"And that's just a beginning to what they're going to have to say about it," he remarked. "But how the devil can I help it? I'm doing what I can, ain't I?" He turned in his perplexity to the doctor, who had remained standing.

The doctor frowned and turned from a contemplation of Thornton's averted face.

"Don't ask me, Chief," he grumbled. "I'm not Nick Carter."

The chief nodded.

"That's just it," he complained; "from the way the *Times-Union* waded into me this morning you'd think I was Nick Carter or Craig Kennedy, or maybe Sherlock Holmes. But this—" He waved his hand helplessly. "We're just as much in the air as ever."

Thornton objected. "There's one thing you might do, Chief. Take it up with the Defy people. And isn't there some way of getting a line on the people who *might* have known the combinations?" He turned to the president: "By the way, Mr. Hayes, have you changed them?"

The banker shook his head, and dropped his voice to a low tone as he answered:

"Not yet; the board seemed to think it best to leave them in the hope that we'll receive a return visit from Mr. Burglar."

The chief groaned, and the doctor chuckled heavily. "It isn't likely, is it, Chief?"

"Huh? How'd I know? But, believe me, he'll get a warm reception if he does show up again."

"Still," Thornton continued, "you're taking useless chances. If I—"

A knock on the door interrupted, and, frowning, the president called "All right." The cashier entered, followed by a burly police officer who panted heavily.

The chief dropped his cigar and came swiftly to his feet as his eyes fell on the uni formed man.

"Beg pardon, Chief—I left my beat to tell you—-" The officer's words tumbled over one another in his excitement: "They don't know how much he got— they just found out—it's the Bay Street Bank this time—"

IX. Suggestion

HARKISS, the cashier, turned to the president of the Second National Bank, who, in turn, eyed Doctor Lester and Thornton. The chief of detective's departure had been sudden and abrupt.

"Well," jerked out the cashier finally, "that's about all of us."

Doctor Lester's small eyes fixed themselves intently on Thornton again. Thornton stood thoughtfully, still gazing at the door through which the chief had so summarily departed. It was evident that Doctor Lester was less interested in the bank robberies than in the physical condition of his friend.

He took Thornton's arm, grumbled good-by, and started with him to the door. Thornton walked silently by the doctor's side through the bank and out into the street.

"By George!" ejaculated the doctor suddenly. "I'd almost forgot a patient. Let's get a move on." And the two men hurried up the street together.

"What do you think of it now?" questioned the doctor, puffing laboriously as they neared the St. James Building.

Thornton shook his head.

"It's got me beat," he admitted slowly, "plumb beat." And he relapsed into a moody study.

Thornton preceded the doctor into the building, and a speculative gleam shone in the doctor's little eyes as he watched his friend.

The two men entered the doctor's office, and Franklin, who had followed them from the bank, grumbled as he took up a position at the end of the corridor, mentally determining to follow them into the office within a few minutes.

In the reception-room Mae was playing with the little girl on whom the doctor had called the night before.

"Ah," greeted the doctor, with heavy joviality, "how's the little lady to-day?"

The furtive look of fear that seemed to linger in the girl's eyes disappeared for an instant as she smiled: "Good morning, Doctor Lester." She extended a small hand, over which the huge man bowed with all gravity.

"I'll be ready for the lady in a minute," he chuckled, beckoning Thornton to follow him into his office. "Just play a minute more." Then:

"Anything else turn up, Mae?"

The office girl shook her head.

"Nothing else, no, sir."

Doctor Lester turned to Thornton in his private office.

"There's a poor devil of a kid with too much imagination," he grumbled. "You'll wind up with a new-fashioned mania of some kind, too, if you don't quit this infernally close application to work."

Thornton grinned.

"Work? What have I done these past few days?"

"You've done worse than work," grumbled the big man. "You're bothered too much about these robberies. What're they to you? Let 'em all be robbed—you should worry. What you need is a rest and a change. Go fishing for a week. By George, I'm half a mind to go with—" The door opened and the doctor turned. "Ah, Ralby, come in; I was wondering whether you'd show up."

Ralby, immaculately dressed, entered jauntily. He stared a moment as his eyes rested on Thornton, then nodded pleasantly:

"Good morning, Thornton—well, how did the vault opening go?" There seemed a lack of interest in his voice, which the doctor did not fail to notice. It was evident that Morton Ralby had but small faith in Thornton's vault-opening abilities.

"It didn't go," Thornton answered. "That is, I got the first letter, but it would take at least twenty-four hours to work anything from that."

Ralby nodded understandingly.

"Of course. You didn't really expect—" He left the sentence unfinished, but Thornton answered:

"Oh, I don't know. I feel sometimes as though I know I can get into the thing; then again I'm just as sure I can't—that no one can."

Ralby smiled and turned unconcernedly to the doctor.

"There's a problem in psychology for you, Lester."

The doctor didn't smile in return.

"I wonder if you heard about the Bay Street Bank?" he asked.

"Why, no." Ralby's face expressed mild inquiry. "What's gone wrong there? I've got a few dollars there myself."

"Well, our gentleman cracksman friend walked into their vault last night."

"Last night?"

"Well, I don't know just when," the doctor grumbled, "but it seems as though he made two trips —one to the St. John's and one to the Bay Street."

Thornton nodded to confirm the doctor's

statements.

"We haven't got the details—but it's a fact. That man is a genius—a pure genius—"

Ralby laughed pleasantly and easily.

"Genius? I'd call him something besides that, Thornton."

Thornton shrugged, but his eyes glistened.

"By heaven, I hope they get him!" he cried, and Ralby applauded:

"Admirable hope, Thornton; so does the doctor here—he stands to win five hundred. But two at a time *is* rubbing it in a bit. I'd give a whole lot to know that cracksman's thoughts."

The doctor, who had busied himself at his desk, heaved his huge shoulders.

"Don't be too sure about that bet, Ralby," he grumbled. "I wouldn't crow yet if I were you. Fact is, your cracksman is getting too impertinent for comfort. He'll lose out one of these times."

Ralby smiled at the doctor.

"I'm not crowing, Lester; you've still got plenty of time to win, of course, but I think—" He broke off and Thornton queried:

"What?"

"Oh, nothing," Ralby spread his well-manicured fingers in a wide gesture, "except if our friend has finished with the Bay Street bank, there's nothing left for him to do, is there? He'll probably have to move farther north."

Thornton slumped in his chair.

"That's true," he admitted dolefully, "but he might make a second trip to one of them."

"Don't you believe it." Ralby nodded positively. "The man who has been pulling these robberies isn't your typical criminal, I'll gamble on that. He hasn't the criminal mind, Thornton—and I don't believe he's the kind to run any silly chances."

The doctor looked up.

"Well, there's the Farmer's National left."

"That's right," Thornton ejaculated. "I'd forgotten about that."

Ralby laughed again.

"I wouldn't be surprised to hear of him trying it. He seems out for a clean sweep. By the way, Isabel has an account there. She mentioned it this morning."

Thornton looked a question and Ralby continued:

"We were down at the jetties this morning," he explained, "that's why I didn't show up for the experiment on the vault. Bernice and Max and Isabel and I. They're going to make a fine couple, Bernice and Max!"

"They are, indeed," Thornton agreed heartily.

"They act like a couple of school children; yet he has the responsibilities of a—"

"That's just it," nodded the doctor sagely. "The more responsibility you pile on Max the better he carries it. Now if you were the prosecuting attorney," the doctor turned to Thornton, "you'd have some right to worry yourself into a nervous breakdown, and you probably would. Did you do any fishing, Ralby?"

Ralby shook his head.

"Nope, just trying out the launch. We went pretty early—about seven o'clock—which means that nobody got a great deal of sleep last night. Just got back a few minutes ago; I came all the way in with the launch and up here direct; that's probably why I hadn't heard about the Bay Street affair."

Thornton made as if to reply, but the doctor interrupted with a gesture.

"Let's forget it," he suggested. "I want you to see this anyway, Ralby—"

He passed a history sheet over to Ralby, who took the paper and studied it carefully.

"Oh, yes, that's our little persecution-mania patient, eh? Going to try suggestion?"

The doctor nodded ponderously, and placed before him a small black box which he drew from a drawer of his desk.

"Wanted you to see it, Ralby," he rumbled. "You, too, Thornton; take your mind off this infernal bank business."

The doctor rose and heaved himself to the door.

"All right, Mae," he called, "let's have the little lady in."

He returned to the office and indicated a chair for Thornton to one side of his desk.

"You sit there," he ordered, "and you stand over here, Ralby, out of the way. I'll sit here—so." He pulled a desk chair over toward the small lounge to one side.

The girl entered the office timidly, tightly holding to the office girl's hand. She gazed anxiously about, then, as though reassured by the smiling faces which met her gaze, she smiled weakly. Doctor Lester lifted her on to the couch, and nodded shortly to the office girl, who left the room, closing the door behind her.

"So," Doctor Lester muttered, patting the girl's arm gently. "Sit there, honey. Now what's wrong, eh? Sleep all right after I left you?"

"Yes, sir." The girl smiled into the doctor's face.

"I—I did then."

"Now, isn't that fine?" The doctor's huge voice bubbled joyously. "That's just great. And nobody came running after you?"

A frightened look leaped into the girl's eyes; then she smiled wistfully.

"No—no, sir, not after you left—but—" she trembled violently—"I'm so afraid, Doctor—I—"

The doctor clucked commiseratingly with his tongue.

"Now that isn't right," he grumbled. "You know there's nothing really going to bother you. Let me tell you something;" he leaned forward confidentially. "I'm going to tell you a story about a little girl—just about your size, too—who wouldn't go to sleep at night."

He hitched his chair closer to the couch and put away his cigarette.

The girl smiled at the huge awkward man, and he winked broadly in answer.

"Now, you listen," he demanded, and began:

"Once upon a time there were two bad little boys and two bad little girls. Yes'm. The boys would run around stealing apples and—and—well, whatever little boys steal, and the little girls would hide from their mothers, and wouldn't go to sleep on time, nor wouldn't eat their suppers, nor—" The doctor's voice was low and monotonous and the little girl on the couch, her eyes fixed intently on the doctor's face, listened eagerly.

He spun out a weirdly crude fairy tale, his voice becoming slower and more monotonous as he spoke, and his hands played idly with the little black box he had removed from his desk.

This he opened slyly, and slowly began to twist in his short fingers a glistening crystal.

The girl's eyes drifted to the crystal and held there, and the doctor's low monotone continued his story, as he saw the girl's eyes hold hard in the very center of the shimmering sphere—then slowly grow dull and staring.

The doctor leaned forward and lowered her gently, until she rested easily on the lounge. Then he straightened, mopping his forehead.

"I guess I haven't got Grimm nor Andersen backed off the boards," he grumbled.

He turned to Ralby, who was intently watching the still figure on the couch. "Well, Ralby?"

Ralby nodded slowly. "Very good," he muttered, "very good. Rather easy, wasn't she?"

The doctor shrugged.

"I've got a mighty fine crystal, for one thing."

He leaned over the couch and began to speak to the unconscious girl; as he spoke a nuance of authority and earnestness crept into the heavy timbre of his voice, and Thornton glanced with surprise at this hulking bull of a man.

Once again his chronic grouchiness and roughness seemed to fall from him, and Thornton forgot the grotesque figure as he listened to the low commanding voice, making suggestions and speaking slowly and carefully.

The doctor straightened and turned to Thornton, staring at him through his little eyes, while one hand fumbled mechanically at his coat for a cigarette.

Thornton marveled at the metamorphosis. Here was again the Doctor Edward Lester he knew:

easygoing, grumbling, smoking innumerable cigarettes, and as phlegmatic and blase as the Sphinx itself.

"That's about all I can do, eh, Ralby?" The doctor puffed his cigarette, and Ralby nodded.

"I wouldn't look for too definite results immediately, Lester," he warned. "She seems— well—" he shrugged lightly. "And I'd wait about a week between treatments."

Ralby turned away from the couch, and the big doctor spun the crystal lightly in his fingers as he bent over the sleeping girl.

He spoke quickly and commandingly, then laughed gutturally:

"My, but we're a sleepy-head."

He shook a thick finger under the girl's eyes as she opened them and laughed.

"I was so awfully tired," she apologized.

"Aw," the doctor rumbled, "don't you know it isn't polite to go to sleep when you've got company?" He stooped and helped the girl into a sitting posture.

"Is mama coming for you?" The doctor's voice was jokingly inquiring.

The girl shook her head.

"No, sir; I'm going home—all the way—by myself," she boasted.

"You don't say!" The doctor lifted her from the couch. "And I'll bet you get plumb lost on the way," he chuckled.

"I'll bet you I won't, either," the girl laughed challengingly, and the doctor opened the door.

In a few moments he leaned back heavily in his chair, deep lines appearing about his eyes. He yawned hugely.

"Gosh, but I'm about played out. This business of getting home in the wee sma' hours is beginning to tell on my frail physique." He eyed his huge figure spraddled in the chair.

Ralby lit a cigarette, extending the case to Thornton, who shook his head.

It was Thornton who broke the short silence that followed:

"And you think she'll obey commands, Doctor?"

The doctor shrugged his shoulders.

"*Quien sabe?*" he muttered. "There's a good chance that she will, anyway. What do you think, Ralby?"

Ralby started.

"Eh? Oh, yes! Yes, there's a chance," he admitted.

Thornton smiled wearily.

"I wish somebody would convince me I didn't feel rotten."

Doctor Lester looked up sharply as Thornton swayed in his chair. Both Ralby and the doctor leaped to their feet. Thornton, however, recovered himself, and sat upright.

The doctor turned immediately to his laboratory and returned in an instant with a partly filled glass.

"Drink this," he snapped, and Thornton obeyed, smiling.

The doctor reached for his hat. "You're coming with me," he grumbled. "You're going home and to bed, and there you'll stay until morning if I have to sit on you."

Ralby nodded.

"Quit bothering about this infernal bank business, Thornton," he urged. "It won't do to have you go on the sick list. Stay with you this afternoon, if you like."

Thornton shook his head.

"No, thanks, Ralby, I'm just tired, that's all."

The doctor frowned.

"Don't mention it to Isabel, Ralby," he grunted, "if you see her this afternoon. I'll stay with Thornton myself; I need a rest." He turned to Thornton. "Lean on me," he directed, but Thornton laughed.

"Go on, I'm not an invalid." He passed a hand across his forehead, but walked steadily into the corridor. The doctor stopped only to leave instructions with the office girl, and the three men made their way to the street.

Thornton and the doctor climbed into the latter's car, and Ralby stood thoughtfully watching them out of sight. A puzzled frown drew his forehead.

"That's strange," he muttered thoughtfully, "damned strange."

X. Thornton has a Touch of Malaria

RALBY turned and reentered the St. James Building, stopping before a suite of offices on the ground floor, the doors of which were marked: "Morton Ralby & Company," and down in one corner the legend: "Real Estate."

It was past noon, the usual Saturday hour for closing, and but few clerks remained in the office. These seemed surprised at Ralby's appearance. It was unusual of him to come to his offices on Saturday.

Ralby spoke a word to a man behind a desk and turned into a private office. He shook his head slightly as he removed his hat and dropped into a chair before his desk. A few moments later he picked up the telephone and gave a number. When the connection was made, he tapped a pencil impatiently on his desk as he asked:

"How did Steel close? Mr. Ralby speaking." His face lighted as he listened. "Up a bit, isn't she? Hold on a while, and we'll get out from under, all right."

He hung up the receiver as the man to whom he had spoken in the outer office entered.

"Well?" Ralby rose to his feet, preparing to leave.

"Beg pardon, Mr. Ralby; thought you'd like to see the contractors' estimate for that Moncrief drainage." He extended a file of papers which Ralby took and paged through.

"That doesn't look so bad, does it?" Ralby played thoughtfully with the papers in his hands. "Properly done—you'd attend to the contract, of course— there ought to be considerable money in the sub-division."

The office man nodded.

"It looks good, Mr. Ralby," he agreed. "I'd advise handling it."

Ralby smiled.

"Well, the work will be yours, anyway; I'm willing to tackle it. Have the papers drawn up and I'll sign them Monday. How much of a guarantee are we to deposit?"

"Five thousand dollars, I believe."

"Can't beat that down any at all?" Ralby frowned over the figure.

"Afraid not, sir. But the Second National—if we let them in on it—would be glad to advance—"

Ralby waved his hand impatiently.

"Nothing doing," he said definitely. "We'll keep this for ourselves. I'll see about the guarantee, all right. It will be ready when the contract's signed."

"Good." The office man seemed pleased with the prospect. "In five years there ought to be—"

Ralby made his way to the door.

"Don't you go figuring profits on me," he laughed. "I don't want any air-castles." He stood aside as the man left the office and waited for a moment. "That's all," he added briefly, and closed the door. For a time he stood irresolute, then, with a half laugh turned to the telephone again.

"Main, four, four, two, three." Ralby was smiling into the transmitter when the answer came. "Miss Isabel, please—" He waited a moment, then: "Recovered from the trip, Isabel? Yes, this is Morton. I'm glad you enjoyed it. Listen, I've two perfectly good tickets for the show to-night. What?" He frowned slightly. "Yes—y-e-s—I saw Hal here in the building. No—no wonder you couldn't get him; he left some time ago with the doctor. How should I know?" The little frown grew deeper. Then: "Lester said something about taking him along down to St. Augustine; he'll hardly be back this afternoon." Ralby smiled again. "You will go! That's fine. I'll come for you at eight. All right, Isabel. Until to-night, then."

He replaced the receiver and leaned back, smiling, in his chair. "That's one march stolen on Hal," he chuckled as he glanced at his watch.

Then he pressed the telephone once more into service, calling the office of the prosecuting attorney.

"Hello. Hello, Max. Going to work all the afternoon?" Ralby laughed at the answer that came to him. "Yeh," he mocked. "Of all the loafers in town, you're about the biggest. What are you doing this afternoon? Oh, excuse me! I might have known the lady wouldn't let you off. Have lunch with me, anyhow. All right, at the Mason, in fifteen minutes."

Ralby passed through his deserted offices and into the street. Within a few minutes he was smiling across a small table at Max Railey, and laughing easily at that young gentleman's description of a recently acquired set of books.

"I suppose," Ralby began later, "that you heard something about the Bay Street Bank robbery," and, as the young attorney nodded his head, Ralby questioned: "He didn't take two at a time, did he?"

The young attorney ran his fingers through his hair in a gesture habitual with him.

"Demme, Ralby—as Lester says—the thing's beginning to get on my nerves, too. I only heard about the Bay Street business a few minutes ago. It wasn't discovered until late in the morning, and there's no way of telling just when it did happen. The loss was slight—of no consequence, this time; but just the idea that our bank vaults are about as safe as an old stocking is something of a jar."

Ralby lighted a cigarette and dropped the match into a tray on the table before he answered.

"Why not try to get some detectives from up North on it?" he questioned. "It seems rather silly to leave it to our crowd; they're evidently making no progress, and it wouldn't surprise me if the robber got clean away, now that he's about through here."

The man across the table dipped his fingers thoughtfully into a bowl, and dried his hands slowly.

"One thing, at least, Ralby," he said, "I'm glad I'm not in the chief's shoes. The papers are beginning to hammer him hard, and I hate to think what they'll do to him in the Sunday editions tomorrow. By the way, what came of Thornton's attempt to enter that vault this morning?"

Ralby laughed.

"Got back too late from our little trip," he answered, "but I saw Thornton and Lester. It wasn't exactly a success, and Thornton's more positive than ever—and said so—that when that vault was opened it was by some one who knew the combinations—both of them."

"Rather rough on the crowd at the bank, isn't it?" The young attorney grinned. "It's like Thornton, though. He's nothing if not positive. He doesn't look well these days, either, Ralby—physically, I mean; seems run down. Noticed it?"

Ralby nodded.

"Yes. He had a bad attack this morning; that is, he's just about worked out—collapsed. And this infernal business is worrying him a good deal. Went home, finally, with Lester, who was threatening to stay with him all the afternoon."

Ralby turned quickly to the younger man.

"Don't mention it to Bernice, Max. She'd tell Isabel, and there'd be the devil to pay. Nothing would suit Isabel better than to imagine Thornton needed nursing. And she'd be fool enough to undertake it, too."

The younger man looked slyly at Ralby and smiled at his earnestness. Ralby flushed; then laughed as he arose.

"Just the same," he boasted, "Isabel's going with me to-night."

"Theater?"

Ralby nodded smilingly. "Sure, and probably a spin on the river in the launch afterward."

"I'll see you then," the young man replied, "My own heaven-born has just announced her desire to see the play."

The two men shook hands and parted, and Ralby looked after the retreating figure of the young attorney.

"I wish I were as certain," he muttered enviously, "as Max is of Bernice."

Doctor Edward Lester was a picture of contentment. Slumped far down in a huge chair in Thornton's bedroom, an ash-tray at his side, a half-empty glass on the table beside him, and a book in his pudgy hands, he seemed more than ever to personify sloth and laziness.

Now and then he glanced toward the bed in which Thornton lay, slightly pale, but sleeping quietly, and once he laid aside his book and studied Thornton's face intently, muttering his thoughts aloud:

"Just plumb played out, that's all," he grumbled. "Needs a fishing trip—or a wife." He chuckled at his own wit, and began to muse upon the idea of Thornton married.

The book in his hands dropped unheeded into his lap, and he tapped a cigarette against the arm of his chair unconsciously. "Naw—" he grumbled aloud suddenly, "it isn't possible—of course it isn't—"

"What isn't, Lester?"

The doctor jerked erect, and his eyes fell on Thornton sitting upright in bed.

"None of your business," he growled, heaving himself heavily to his feet and lurching across the room. "You get back down into that bed where you belong."

Thornton smiled and obeyed.

"I'm afraid I'm about slept out, though. What time is it?"

The doctor looked at his watch.

"Nearly six," he answered as he switched on the electric light. "And not a single call for me," he chuckled. "Some peaceful day, eh?"

Thornton stared at the ceiling silently, and the doctor turned again to his chair, which he drew closer to the bed.

"Might as well chew the rag with you a while," he grunted. "Tired of reading anyway." He extended a cigarette to Thornton. "Here, you can smoke one," he offered, and Thornton grinned his thanks.

"From the treatment I get," he laughed, "one would think I was really sick. Is this the way you get patients, Lester? Joshing them along that they're really in a bad way?"

The doctor yawned mightily.

"Go on, rub it in," he growled. "Just the same, you were close to being a mighty sick man this morning. And if I hadn't filled you full of—"

"Go on," Thornton laughed, "I feel fit as can be. Just a touch of malaria, that's all."

"Yeh, malaria?" sneered the big man heavily. "You'd better write a book on it. When did the malaria ever act like sunstroke?" he demanded. "And when I got you into that bed you were about out— that's a fact."

Thornton turned his head until his eyes met the doctor's.

"Of course, Lester," he began quietly, "I'm not a fool, and I'm more than obliged—"

"Then shut up," grumbled the doctor hurriedly. "Let me do the talking."

For several minutes he smoked in silence, then:

"Tell me, Thornton, what happened to you at Isabel's last night? I mean, just how did you feel when you woke up?"

Thornton frowned a moment.

"I don't know, Lester. Much as I do now. Felt pretty good, in fact. Think it's the same thing?"

"Naw," grumbled the doctor, "how can I think anything? Maybe," he was heavily sarcastic, "maybe it's malaria," and he exploded in a laugh of contempt.

"Surely you're not going to keep me flat on my back here all night?" Thornton queried.

"I am just that," grumbled the doctor. "You might as well be satisfied. When I leave here you'll be with the little birdies again." He grinned at Thornton.

"And dreaming about burglar-proof vaults that aren't burglar-proof," grumbled Thornton.

"Forget it," snapped the doctor. "Just get it off your mind. You've got other things to worry about."

The telephone on the table cut in on the conversation and the doctor lumbered across the room to answer.

"Huh? Yes. Yes, he's here. Doctor Lester talking. Sorry, Chief, I've got Thornton laid up, and he'll stay laid up until to-morrow morning. No, nothing serious. Just nervous, I reckon. Nothing special you wanted, was there? All right then; I'll tell him. He'll be down-town to-morrow, but tonight he stays here in bed; you can bet on that."

He turned to the bedside.

"Your friend, the chief," he commented caustically. "Probably wanted to bother you about some of his theories. Nothing doing."

Thornton looked at the doctor.

"All right," he complained, "but don't I get anything to eat?"

"Eat? Eat?" The big doctor's face purpled. "Is that all you think about? Eat? I guess nix. If I can stand it," the doctor surveyed his corpulent self, "you can. And when you come to in the morning, don't make a dash for a restaurant. Get that?"

Thornton grumbled, and the big doctor continued earnestly:

"I'm not joshing you, Hal. You've got a fine chance to be damned sick, and that's a fact. Tomorrow I want you to eat one egg, one piece of toast, and drink one glass of milk." The doctor checked the items off on his fingers. "Understand?"

Thornton nodded.

"And come up to the office in the morning. We'll have lunch together. Now you're going by-by—" The doctor laughed hugely, and turned to the bathroom. He returned, replacing a pocket-case, and carrying a glass.

Thornton obediently gulped the contents and sank back in the pillows.

The doctor picked up his book: Alexander Dumas's *Memoirs of a Physician* and turned to the table, Thornton's eyes following him.

"There's no reason to bother with me all night, Lester," he said. "I'll stay put."

The doctor chuckled as though at a joke, glancing at the empty glass he put on the table.

"For twelve hours, you bet you will!" he grunted.

"I'll be off soon." He addressed himself to the book in his hand.

A few minutes later he looked up.

"Apropos of nothing in particular, Hal," he began, "what do you know about gas engines?"

There was no reply to the question, and the doctor lumbered over to the bed and gazed down at the sleeping figure of Thornton.

Very gently he carefully pulled the covers about Thornton's neck, yawned, picked up his battered hat and turned to the door. He stood a moment in the doorway, his heavy face immobile, and his little eyes speculatingly eying the sleeping man. Then his hand went out and the room was darkened.

Quietly the door closed behind him and he turned into the street to his automobile.

As he switched on the headlights he eyed the shiny speedometer abstractedly.

"Just the same," he mumbled aloud, "I'd like to know what turned that boat around?"

XI. The Fourth Visitation

THE chief of detectives was in anything but a happy frame of mind as he boarded the streetcar Sunday morning before his house, and his good morning to the conductor was growled surlily. It seemed to the irate chief that every passenger on the car smiled knowingly as he entered and dropped into a seat, unfolding a newspaper.

At his break fast-table he had read the *Times-Union's* heavily leaded and sarcastically adjectived account of the robberies of Saturday, and had called down all manner of vengeance on the scribes who were taunting the city's detective force with inefficiency and laxity, and who demanded instant summary apprehension of the criminal.

The *Metropolis*, Jacksonville's other paper, had handled the chief more kindly, but had rehashed all details of the three bank robberies, and hinted broadly to the administration of the advisability of calling in aid from the detective departments of at least two other towns, naming Atlanta and Birmingham especially.

The chief's breakfast coffee had been left untasted, and the telephone call that he had received from the office—an urgent request to come immediately—capped the climax.

He had snapped his answers to the unoffending official at the other end of the wire, but was able to learn only that a gentleman desired to see him immediately in person, nor would the gentleman, whom the chief's informant characterized over the phone as "a little runt," state his business further than to say that it was urgently important, and had to do with the matter of a local bank.

The chief's wrath grew with each block that the car traveled, and when his eyes fell on an editorial comment headed:

THE DEBACLE OF A MUNICIPAL DEPARTMENT

he swore heavily under his breath.

Nevertheless he read the account, which commented ironically on the inability of the detective department to apprehend a criminal who, so the editorial ran:

seems to care little whether he works in the broad
daylight or in the darkness of night, and to whom
steel, burglar-proof vaults—and detectives—are but
little more than a joke.

The chief crumpled the newspaper in his hand, and eyed a man in the seat across from him belligerently.

When the car drew up before the municipal building the chief slammed his way into his office. The man at the door nodded sourly in greeting, and jerked his head to indicate the presence of a caller in the waiting-room.

"All right, send him in." The chief chewed angrily at his cigar, and greeted his visitor, a small, stooping, gray-headed man, with little courtesy.

"Well?"

The little man, however, seemed in no hurry.

"The chief of the detective department, isn't it?" he queried mildly, and the chief purpled as he stuttered an answer.

"I'm Mr. Carney—Mr. Carney of the Farmer's National Bank"—the visitor produced a card.

"Have a seat," the chief nodded gruffly, thumbing the piece of pasteboard, on the engraved surface of which was the information that Mr. Kenneth Carney was connected with the Farmer's National Bank of Jacksonville, Florida, and that his position was that of cashier.

The little man nodded his appreciation of the chief's suggestion, seated himself slowly, and, placing the tips of his fingers carefully together, turned his mild eyes on the chief.

"I have to inform you, sir, that our vault was— er—entered to-day!"

"Damn!" the chief exploded at the mild man's announcement. "When? How?" he barked.

"And further to inform you, sir," Mr. Carney of the Farmer's National went on mildly, paying no heed to the chief's explosive questioning, "that the bank looks to your department, sir, to rid the city and the state, sir—once and for all of this—er — marauder."

"And might I inquire," grunted the chief with elaborate politeness, "just how the Farmer's Bank expects me to go about it?" The chief was heavily sarcastic, but the little man only nodded, giving but the smallest attention to the chief's words.

"There remains, sir, I am told," he answered deliberately, "no one in the city, who has—er—not yet been visited by this—er—cracksman."

The chief flung his cigar aside, growling. This individual, with his drawling advice, began to irritate him.

"I would suggest, therefore"—Mr. Carney tapped a finger on the arm of his chair thoughtfully—"that you—er—station a trustworthy officer at each banking institution in the city, sir, in order that—"

The chief grinned sardonically. "It might interest you to know, Mr. Carney, that a man was stationed at *your* bank all night."

The little man nodded, as though judiciously weighing the chief's words.

"That is what I have come to speak to you of," he admitted after a thoughtful silence. "Your—er — officer departed this morning at nine o'clock, and — er—it was between nine and ten that our vault was—er—entered, and I—"

"The hell you say!" The chief's fist clumped the desk before him.

"And I," continued the little man, unperturbed by the chief's outburst, "was about to advise you, sir, that I attribute to my own—er—sagacity the fact that it was so soon discovered." He raised his eyes to the scowling man behind the desk.

"At breakfast in my—er—home," continued Mr. Carney of the Farmer's National Bank, "it—er— occurred to me, while—er—perusing the newspaper accounts, that it might be eminently—er—advisable to see that everything remained secure in my own institution, and I immediately acted on what I considered an admirable—er—conclusion."

He looked again at the chief, as though expecting praise for his independent efforts to see that all was well with his bank, but the chief seemed not to have heard.

"And I—er—"

"What did he get?" barked the chief suddenly. "You're sure it did happen?"

"Undoubtedly." The little man's inquiring eyes fixed themselves on the chief, as though unable to account for his vehemence. "The—er—loss, fortunately, is small—less than one thousand dollars. Our—er—available cash—our surplus cash, that is —was—er—forwarded—"

The chief waved away the explanation and punched viciously at a button on his desk. The dour-faced attendant answered the buzzer, and the chief growled:

"Send me Jackson."

Jackson arrived and proved to be a bull-necked, low-browed individual whose undershot jaw boded ill for evil-doers of whatsoever degree.

"Jackson—Mr. Carney of the Farmer's National."

The chief jerked out the introduction as though he disliked doing it.

"Pleased t' meetcher—seen yuh at the bank." Jackson bobbed his bullet head industriously in the direction of the bank cashier.

"True, true." Mr. Carney nodded slowly in turn. "Your face and carriage are—er—familiar."

The detective turned a puzzled look to the chief, but the chief's thoughts seemed elsewhere engaged, and the man shuffled clumsily on his feet, scowling at nothing in particular.

"Y' wanted me, Chief?" he finally questioned, and Mr. Carney turned his head suddenly, as though startled by the fact that the bull-necked one was still visibly in evidence.

The chief nodded absently, then seemed to jerk his thoughts back, with an effort, to the present.

"You were at the bank all night?" The chief looked heavily at the man before him.

"Sure—them was the orders."

"Exactly," murmured Mr. Carney definitely.

The chief eyed the little man balefully a second, then turned again to the detective, questioning:

"Just whereabouts were you?"

"Meanin' in the bank?" asked the detective, and as the chief nodded irritably, he continued: "In the payin' teller's cage; the back of it faces the vault, and—"

"Urn!" murmured Mr. Carney thoughtfully, then shook his head definitely. "So it does, so it does."

The detective seemed rattled by the interruption and scowled at the little man in the chair. Then: "I got in there at eight last night," he continued, "and there I sat until a few minutes to nine this mornin'."

"Sure you didn't leave that cage, Jackson?"

"Sure, sir," answered the bullet-headed detective positively.

"Me an' the watchman played checkers between his rounds, and while he was gone I was dopin' out combinations on him."

"Combinations?" Mr. Carney's mildly inquiring voice broke in again. "Combinations, did you say—er—Mr. Jackson?"

"Checker combinations," grunted the detective scornfully, and Mr. Carney nodded his head relievedly. "Ah, to be sure—checker combinations," he murmured.

"Well, Jackson," the chief commented briefly, "the

Farmer's vault was entered this morning."

"Naw!" Utter amazement spread over the detective's features, and involuntarily he turned to Mr. Carney for confirmation of the chief's statement.

"Precisely," nodded Mr. Carney. "The vault was— er—entered and the—er—marauder made his—er— getaway"—Mr. Carney flushed at his own use of the police vernacular—"with—er—several hundreds of dollars."

Jackson looked blankly at the chief.

"Notice anybody about when you left?"

The detective's beetle-brow corrugated in thought. "Naw," he muttered, as though to himself. "Nobody—not anywhere near there."

The chief thought quietly a moment, chewing on a fresh unlighted cigar.

"Where'd you go when you left there? Come straight here?"

"Yep!" Jackson seemed struggling to recall his exact movements. "Lessee. I went down Bay Street and came up Hogan. Then I stopped at Demo's for a cup of coffee and talked to O'Reilly a minute. He's the man on the beat," he explained, and the chief nodded heavily, while Mr. Carney inquired:

"The regular policeman, you mean?"

Neither of the two men paid the slightest attention to the bank cashier's questioning, and, looking a little hurt, Mr. Carney relapsed into silence.

"Then I went over to the post-office," Jackson muttered on thoughtfully, and the chief tapped impatiently on the desk with his fingers. "From there —lessee—I started down Forsythe Street, and I met this Thornton guy—"

"What?" The chief leaped to his feet, and Mr. Carney jerked erect in startled surprise.

"Huh?" Jackson eyed the chief with surprise. "Whatcha mean, what?" He frowned at the chief's sudden display of interest in his movements.

"Who did you run into?" the chief questioned eagerly. "Thornton, you said."

Mr. Carney's raised eyebrows registered bewilderment.

"Yeh," Jackson nodded heavily. "That Thornton guy what was up here the other mornin'. He was coming down Laura Street, walkin' with his nose up in the air; too good to talk to a gum-shoe."

"Did you watch where he went?" The chief's hands closed on the edge of his desk and his cigar lay unheeded at his side, which in itself betokened the fact that the chief was keenly absorbed.

"Naw." Jackson spat disgustedly into a cuspidor. "What'd I want to trail him for?" he demanded. "Th' dude was prob'ly goin' home. He was headed for Bay Street. Naw, I didn't watch him—what for?"

The chief frowned and did not answer. Mr. Carney, however, deemed it time to say a few words, so he raised his eyes and looked at the chief.

"An admirable young man, Mr. Thornton," he said mildly, "quite an admirable young man."

"Huh!" the chief grunted the monosyllable, and Mr. Carney raised his eyebrows.

"What's wrong about that guy, Chief?" The bullet-headed detective scented the fact somehow that he should have followed Thornton.

The chief raised his head.

"All right, Jackson; nothing at all," he answered. "You just stick around here and I'll call you when I'm ready."

Jackson turned to the door and clumped heavily from the room, and the chief turned an attentive ear to Mr. Carney's drawled question of:

"If you care to—er—investigate the bank premises and the—er—banking structure, I shall be glad —er—"

The chief cut him off sharply.

"No need of that," he grunted. "I'll leave you now, Mr. Carney." He rose heavily and turned again to the cashier, his voice silkily mild: "And thank you for calling."

Again the sarcasm missed the little man, who rose slowly to his feet.

"Not at all." He waved his hand deprecatingly. "I—er—felt it my duty to advise you immediately, and any assistance that I—er—maybe able to render, sir—" He stopped as the chief held open the door in an invitation there was no mistaking.

"And just what advices shall I carry to my—er — superiors, sir?"

The chief turned.

"You tell 'em," he rumbled heavily, "you tell 'em I'm on the job." He turned again to the door, but hesitated as Mr. Carney inquired further:

"And when, sir, may we expect the—er—apprehension of the—er—criminal, sir?"

The chief looked scornfully at the little man.

"Just as soon," he advised slowly, "just as soon as I can get my two hands on him," and he spread out two huge hairy hands in an eloquent gesture, while Mr. Carney, evidently satisfied with the reply, minced through the open door.

As the visitor left, the chief closed the door slowly

and turned to his desk.

The officer who entered in answer to his ring stood for several minutes waiting, before the chief looked up from his staring at the desk.

"Has Hanson come in?"

"Not yet, sir," the man replied.

"He's out at the Riverside Apartments, ain't he?" The chief's question was a mere formality, and the officer nodded.

"Franklin's just left for the St. James Building," he advised, "and Hanson ought to be in any minute."

"All right—all right." The chief waved his hand in dismissal, and the officer retired, while the chief continued to gaze thoughtfully before him.

Finally he turned to the telephone.

"Get me Doctor Lester's office," he snapped, and hung up the receiver.

The switchboard operator worked swiftly, for in a moment the chief's buzzer announced that the connection had been made, and the chief turned to the telephone.

"Hello! Miss Mae in?" He grinned a little. "Is it? Well, this is—er—never mind. Is Ben Franklin around anywhere? He ain't? Know where he is? Oh, all right. Will you tell him to call headquarters, please, if you see him around? Thanks."

The chief hung up the receiver slowly and retrieved his cigar. This he clamped into the side of his mouth, and a shrewd look drifted into his eyes:

"I'm getting warm," he grunted to himself; "I'm getting mighty warm!"

XII. Ignoring His Friends

DOCTOR LESTER had been dragged complainingly from his bed at 8 A. M. by the jangle of the telephone on his little night table, and in answer to the call had splashed himself hurriedly beneath a cold shower, backed from its garage his three-cylinder automobile, and, grumbling profanely at people who fell ill on Sunday morning, had started on his call.

The "case" proved to be far from interesting. A patient had developed sudden and severe pains in the region of the stomach, these accompanied by a violent headache that prevented the man's raising his head more than an inch or so from the pillow without a feeling that a million triphammers, manipulated by as many little demons, were suddenly let loose beneath his forehead.

The doctor, his huge fingers on the man's pulse, listened to the groaning recital of symptoms, and grunted pessimistically. Also—for the doctor was wise in his generation—he sniffed the air suspiciously and promptly and correctly diagnosed the case as "the morning after," leaving his patient a moment later, and complaining aloud and bitterly to the circumambient atmosphere of having been robbed of well-earned slumber through the action of the country's prohibition laws, which necessitated the purchase of intoxicating liquors in the guise of hair tonic.

By the time he had urged his complaining

machine to the city, however, he had ceased to grumble and bemoan his unfortunate choice of a profession, and as his car drew up before the St. James Building he was puzzling, half aloud, over Thornton's condition and going over in his mind the possible reasons for it.

He entered his deserted office, threw open the windows in his laboratory, and plumped himself heavily in the chair by his desk. One hand reached for his cigarettes; the other went out for the telephone for the purpose of calling Thornton.

The doctor thought better of his impulse, however.

"Better let him sleep," he muttered heavily, yawning himself, and he turned to greet the office girl who had entered.

"Mornin', Mae. Not married yet?" The doctor seemed to grow visibly cheerful as he watched the girl put aside her hat and efficiently set about straightening the office.

"Not yet," she laughed in reply, vigorously stirring up the dust from the top of the doctor's desk.

He arose, grumbling good-naturedly.

"Can't even have peace in my own office—whew!" He coughed with every symptom of sudden choking, but the girl, entirely too well acquainted with his manners to mind the complaint, busily manipulated the duster.

The doctor reached for his hat.

"I'm going out to hunt breakfast," he growled, glancing at his watch. "Maybe you'll be through when I get back."

"If you don't hurry, yes." The girl smiled at the waddling figure as it crossed the office.

Doctor Lester stopped in the doorway.

"And don't forget to light the sterilizer!" he thundered.

For answer the girl went into the laboratory and pressed the electric switch, returning in a moment.

"That all right?" she asked laughingly, but the huge doctor had gone, and the girl heard the sound of his shuffling footsteps as he made his way down the long corridor to the elevators.

The doctor waddled across the street and made his way through the park which faces the St. James Building. A man hurrying across the green square in another direction attracted his sudden attention, and he stopped short, his heavy legs planted far apart as he squinted at the figure.

"Looks like Thornton," he muttered aloud, then took a hurried step forward as he saw the figure of Isabel Brannon step from the roadster that drew up by the curb on Laura Street and approach the walking figure.

The man who looked like Halvey Thornton continued calmly, but in seeming haste, on his way, and the doctor's face clouded as he saw the girl stop short, then gaze after the figure of the man who passed her.

"Huh!" grunted the doctor, starting across the park. "It must sure look a lot like him to fool Isabel. Isabel!" He raised his voice to a rumbling shout, but the girl had stepped again into the automobile, which darted off.

The doctor stopped in his tracks, turned slowly about, grumbled aloud, and half-heartedly continued in the direction he was going.

"Aw, the devil! I'm not hungry," he groaned, and

slowly began to retrace his steps.

The office girl seemed surprised at his return, but her laughing question went unasked as she saw the doctor's heavy face creased into a thoughtful frown.

"Was Mr. Thornton in here?" he asked.

"Why, no," the girl answered. "I haven't seen him since you left with him yesterday."

"Huh," grunted the doctor thoughtfully. "It sure looked like him." He scratched his head. "Didn't see him go into his own office, did you?"

The girl shook her head.

"He might have gone by without my seeing him," she replied. "I think I would have, though."

"Oh, all right," the doctor grumbled. "Nothing important. Get out o' here now and let me go to work."

The girl left the office, closing the door behind her, and the doctor picked up the telephone.

To the operator who answered he gave Thornton's number, and waited impatiently, nodding his big head heavily to the operator's twice repeated: "I'm ringing." Then: "They don't answer." And the doctor, scowling, replaced the receiver on the hook and turned into his laboratory.

Hurried steps came down the corridor, stopped before Doctor Lester's door, and into the room hurried Isabel Brannon, the color high in her cheeks and tears hanging threateningly in her eyes. She was dressed for the tennis courts, and the office girl smiled a "Good morning."

The girl only nodded hastily, however, and hurried into the inner office.

Doctor Lester, the sleeves of his white laboratory coat rolled high on his fat arms, turned from a row of test-tubes and faced the girl, his stolid heavy face lighting suddenly with genuine concern.

"Isabel, what's the matter?" The doctor's voice held a tense quality.

Instead of answering, the girl dropped into a chair and began to cry brokenly.

The doctor's little eyes grew large; then he turned suddenly and shut the door of the reception-room. In a moment his huge hand was patting the girl's shoulder.

"There, there, Izzy," he muttered, using the nickname that usually aroused a storm of protest. "Come on; what's the matter, girl? Out with it now— aw! sa-a-a-ay." The doctor coughed apologetically, and the crying lessened in volume. He was uncomfortably embarrassed. "'S all right, Isabel; of course it's all right; if it isn't, demme! we'll very soon make it all right. Come on now."

The girl looked up and the doctor slumped into a chair before her.

"I—I—I know I'm a little fool," the girl sobbed.

"Nothing of the kind!" The doctor straightened violently. "You hear," he rumbled, "nothing of the kind. Who says so?"

The beginning of a smile hovered about the girl's wet eyes.

"I—I—passed right by him on the street"—her voice was low—"and—and—and he wouldn't speak to me." The threatening tears rose afresh. "I haven't done anything to him, Doctor, have I?"

"Of course you haven't. How could you have?" The doctor's heavy voice was very reassuring, and although he knew, he grinned: "Who was it?"

The girl's smile broke out, as he very much hoped

it would.

"Of course, it's silly of me. He—he just didn't see me, though—though I—I walked right up to him and said 'Hello,' and—and he passed by without — without— It was Halvey," she finished hastily.

"Thornton, eh?" The doctor stroked his elephantine chin slowly. "Sure you're not mistaken, Isabel? Might've been somebody that looked like him."

The girl shook her head and her eyes met the doctor's. She blushed slightly.

"No, I wasn't mistaken."

"When was it?"

The girl turned from the doctor's gaze.

"A few minutes ago. I was just coming from the tennis court with Bernice, and stopped the car, and he—he—"

"Ho! ho! ho!" The doctor's huge laugh boomed out in the office and he grinned broadly. "And that's what's worrying you. I just remembered," he chuckled.

"What?" The girl leaned forward eagerly.

"Ah," grumbled the doctor heavily, "don't you worry; he didn't even see you. You see, he's—er— bothered; that is, he's worrying about this safe business —er—concentrating; that's it. Why, of course he didn't see you," and the big doctor's laugh boomed out again, while the girl smiled with him.

"Don't, please, think I'm a little fool," she began; but the doctor turned once more to the telephone. "I'll see if he's in," he grumbled, giving the number.

The mind behind the little beady eyes was working rapidly as he smiled at the girl. Thornton undoubtedly had passed her; had, perhaps, gone home. The doctor glanced at his desk clock to ascertain whether Thornton had had time to reach his apartments.

"Hello!" he rumbled into the receiver. "The devil it is," he chuckled, as he recognized Thornton's voice and his manner of answering the telephone. "Say, you pirate, whadaya mean by passin' your friends on the street an' not speakin' to 'em? Naw, it wasn't me; it was Isabel. You did, I tell you. Yes, you did, too; don't dispute me. Here she is; talk to her yourself." And the doctor, handing the receiver to the girl, arose and lumbered into the laboratory, where he stood attentively staring from the window as though greatly interested in the view.

Despite his apparent preoccupation, however, he nodded his head with relief when he heard the girl laugh easily: "All right, then, come to-night—at eight—and make your apologies."

But later, after the girl had smilingly gone, he slumped down in his chair at his desk, his heavy face stolid and inexpressive, and muttering aloud his mental reactions:

"It ain't right," he grumbled; "goes to sleep—keels over like a chicken with the pip—eyes reflex like a jumping jack's—cuts his best girl—demme! —it ain't right."

The doctor ran his, eyes over a row of books on top of his desk, and still muttering, picked out an especially huge tome, which bore, gilt-lettered on its back: *Theories of the Neuroses*, by Freud.

Mechanically he opened the volume and began to read, his mind occupied with the case of the little girl of the day before, the persecution-mania patient, as Ralby called her.

In a few minutes, however, he found his thoughts drifting from the learned discussion under his eyes, and he raised his head from the book, gazing blankly at the wall before him, staring with unseeing eyes at the motto on the wall, the motto containing the one word, "Think."

Slowly the word seemed to sink into his mind, and he wheeled in his chair.

"Mae!" he bellowed, and the office girl appeared in the doorway.

"When Mr. Thornton comes up, I wish you'd tell him to drop in here," he requested; and the girl nodded.

The doctor waddled again into his laboratory and resolutely picked up a test-tube.

"What's the use worrying about it?" he grumbled, holding the test-tube up to the light and squinting at the discolored fluid it contained.

He forced his mind from Thornton and the problems he presented as he poured a bit of the fluid in a small centrifuge, screwed to a stand, filled the opposite holder with water to equalize the weight, and began slowly to spin the mechanism, pursing his thick lips and whistling softly. He was soon entirely absorbed in the work before him and, in a short time, was slowly manipulating the adjusting screw of a microscope, his eye glued to the top and his mind occupied only with the small glass slide beneath his lens.

He did not hear the door behind him open, nor was he aware of Halvey Thornton's entrance as that young man stood smiling in the doorway, looking fresh and immaculate, his face glistening from the effects of the razor.

Finally the doctor raised his head.

"I've got to get some more of that violet stain," he muttered half aloud, leaning back on his white stool before the microscope and carefully removing a slide from the holder.

He heaved himself heavily to his feet, still with his back to Thornton, and began to whistle slowly and laboriously a distorted air from *Aida*, the only opera which, he often contended, was worth wasting time over.

He lumbered through a difficult passage, and Thornton behind him took up the air. For just an instant the doctor hesitated, then continued his whistling, methodically wiping the microscope slide. Finally he came to an end, and, without turning, grumbled casually:

"When'd you get in?"

Thornton laughed.

"Just a second ago. You need some practise on that air, though," he bantered.

"Yep, I know it." The doctor placed a bell-jar carefully over his microscope and turned to survey Thornton. "Well, you *look* all right," he grunted.

"Never felt better," Thornton boasted. "A little dizzy when I got up, but quite all right now." He extended a cigarette-case, and the doctor took a cigarette as he led the way into his consultation-room.

Thornton dropped on to the couch, and the doctor sat in his chair by the desk, puffing his cigarette.

"Say, Hal," he began tentatively, "what's this Isabel's been telling me about you?"

Thornton looked his surprise. Then:

"Oh, you mean about not speaking to her. Piffle!

She must have been mistaken."

"Huh." The doctor's little eyes fixed themselves on Thornton's face. "And you didn't pass her out here by Hemming Park this morning?"

Thornton blew a cloud of smoke.

"Of course not, Lester. You know I wouldn't —as to not recognizing her—bosh! I humored her over the phone; she really seemed cut up about it." He shrugged lightly and lifted his cigarette.

The doctor nodded.

"Sleep all right?"

"Like a brick," Thornton answered; then laughed: "that is, with about as much sensation as a brick. I was dead to the world."

"That's good," nodded the doctor heavily. "You look a hundred per cent, better for it."

Thornton smiled.

"Thanks—and thanks for bothering with me yesterday. I feel a hundred per cent, better, too."

"Don't doubt it." Doctor Lester lighted a fresh cigarette from his old one.

"By the way, Hal," he raised his eyes. "You didn't play tennis this morning, did you?"

"Not much I didn't," Thornton laughed. "Sorry, too, for Isabel was out with Bernice and Max."

"Didn't feel up to it?" The doctor's little eyes looked bland and blankly unexpressive.

Thornton dropped his cigarette into a tray.

"Don't know whether I did or not," he replied. "That dope you filled me with worked too well. I didn't wake up until after nine—when you telephoned, in fact."

For the fraction of an instant the doctor's eyes clouded at Thornton's answer, then he chuckled:

"Tried to get you earlier, but no answer."

"No wonder," Thornton replied, rising to his feet. "I slept like a brick, I'm telling you." He stretched luxuriously. "And I'm going to put in some work this morning, too, to make up for lost time."

The doctor nodded.

"Got up pretty late myself," he grunted, "but don't feel much better for it. You say you didn't awaken until nine o'clock—that's some sleeping."

Thornton turned casually to a bookcase.

"It sure is," he agreed. "I did half wake up once this morning, early—must have been when you first phoned; I've only a vague recollection of it. Wouldn't swear I wasn't dreaming. But it was nine fifteen by the clock when I stepped out of bed—thanks to you."

The doctor nodded silently, and he eyed Thornton's back as he bent over the books in the case, scanning the titles.

"Well, I'm going to work." Thornton straightened and turned toward the door. "Drop in before you leave, and we'll have lunch together; that is, if you don't leave too early. I've got some work to do." He turned to the door: "You saw the morning papers, I suppose?"

Doctor Lester nodded.

"They sure waded into our detective friend," he said slowly.

"Dog-gone it, Lester," Thornton stopped with one hand on the door; "it's damned queer, this whole business. I know too infernally much about these different vaults; maybe that's it. But I'd be willing to take an oath that there's not a man in the country who can get into them—any quicker than I can."

The doctor shrugged and turned toward his desk.

"Quit thinking about it," he grumbled, "and for Pete's sake, quit shooting off your mouth to everybody about your vault-entering abilities."

Thornton opened the door, laughing at the doctor's vehemence.

"Just the same, it's true," he flung back, closing the door behind him.

The doctor looked up at the closed door, a puzzled light in his eyes.

"That's the hell of it," he whispered to himself. "It is true!"

XIII. THORNTON HAS AN INSPIRATION

THORNTON stopped a moment in the outer office, and smilingly watched the office girl who was busily sewing. "Trousseau?" he teased.

The girl blushed and nodded while Thornton shook his head in mock sadness. "Seems as though everybody in the world finds some one," he complained, "except the old grouch in there—and me."

"Sure it isn't your fault, Mr. Thornton?" The girl looked sidewise at the young man.

"Oh, I don't know." Thornton turned to the doorway. "Maybe it is, and then, perhaps, I just haven't found any wonderful lady—any who would have me, that is."

"You don't sound as though you meant it, Mr. Thornton." The girl looked up, but almost immediately dropped her eyes to her work. "And, perhaps, you're mistaken about the—the lady."

Thornton seemed to know to whom she referred, for he turned red, and hastened to change the direction of the conversation.

"Well, how about Lester, then; think he will find some one—some lady one of these days?"

The girl nodded positively.

"If he wants to—yes. Every one does— invariably."

Thornton chuckled.

"That's a comforting philosophy for bachelors, Mae; wish I could believe it. But—lordy," he laughed silently, "can't you just see Lester married to—oh, anybody!"

And he turned into the hall, still laughing at the idea of the obese grumbling doctor in the role of husband.

In the hallway he collided with Franklin, the detective, who seemed to have but just arrived.

"Good morning, sir!" the detective nodded to Thornton.

Thornton smiled.

"Bright and early, eh? Even on Sunday. The early bird and the worm, is that it?"

The officer flushed and grinned.

"Yep," he nodded, "that's it. Busy in there?"

He jerked his head to indicate the doctor's office, and Thornton replied good-naturedly:

"No, I think you'll find the lady disengaged." He extended his hand. "I suppose congratulations are in order—"

The detective shook hands embarrassedly, grinning like a small boy, as Thornton laughed:

"She's a dandy, Franklin—you're to be envied."

"Sure, I know it." The detective's voice dropped to a confidential tone. "What beats me is how she fell for a rough-neck like I am."

Thornton laughed heartily.

"You never can tell, can you, Franklin? Good luck to you!" And he turned into his own office.

Franklin stood in the hall a moment after Thornton disappeared and shook his head.

"Damned foolishness," he muttered to himself, "this business o' watchin' a man like that."

The office girl looked up as Franklin entered.

"Somebody from the office—the chief, I think—wants you to call."

She nodded to the telephone on the desk, and Franklin, with a scowl and a muttered "Thanks," turned to the instrument.

In a moment he was speaking softly into the transmitter.

"Hello—yep. Franklin talkin'. Yep, talkin' from Doctor Lester's office. Uhuh; he's in his own office. Nope, just picked him up—just came in, yeh—all right."

He hung up the receiver and turned to the girl.

"Well, the chief's beginning to show sense," he commented. "I'm off the gum-shoe detail."

Franklin didn't seem any too pleased over his release, however, for he frowned heavily as he spoke.

"Just why were you watching him?" The girl's eyes met the detective's squarely.

Franklin fidgeted.

"Aw, there ain't no call to rub it in on me, Mae. I ain't responsible for details, you know. They shove a man around on the most foolish kind of detail, just to see him work, I reckon," he ran on heavily, then caught the girl's eye and stopped. The detective did not seem any too expert at avoiding answers to her questions.

"Aw, the chief thinks he knows too much about vaults," he finally explained; "and it—"

Mae laughed.

"If I couldn't make a better guess than that, I'd go and—"

"Shucks!" Franklin's ejaculation was scornful. "Of course the chief ain't nut enough to think he's mixed up in it—just watchin' him on general principles." He turned in the doorway. "I'll be back a little after twelve; you're going down the river with me this afternoon, you know."

The girl frowned, as though undecided.

"Well—you might come by—" she suggested teasingly; then, as Franklin started to reenter the office, she quickly put the table between them. "You'd better go on," she laughed, "before the chief sets somebody to watching you." And the detective turned into the corridor.

The girl sewed industriously, smiling to herself. Occasionally she raised her eyes to the door of the doctor's private office, from which emanated intermittent sounds which indicated that the doctor was at work in his laboratory.

A little later she noticed the passing and repassing of a man in the hall, a man who cast a casual glance into the doctor's office as he walked by. Without appearing to notice him, the girl watched until he came by again, and recognized the bullet-headed, heavy-faced detective. She knew Jackson. He had been pointed out to her on several occasions by Franklin.

After noting, though apparently engaged with her sewing, that Jackson had taken up a position where he could watch Thornton's door, the girl reasoned correctly that, for some reason, the man had been sent to take Franklin's place.

Impulsively she arose and tapped on the door of the doctor's consultation-room.

When the doctor's heavy "Come in" sounded, she entered, leaving the door open behind her. The doctor was reading and, for a moment, did not look up as the girl stood silently by his desk. When he raised his head he blinked his little eyes, as though he had expected to see an ailing patient.

"Well, Mae?"

The girl seemed embarrassed, playing with the tassels on her dress. She looked at the doctor quickly and away again, half turned to leave the office, and finally asked:

"Anything wrong with—with Mr. Thornton, Doctor?"

The doctor eyed her quizzically, squinting his shrewd little eyes until crinkly little crow's-feet appeared about their corners, giving him more than ever the appearance of an exalted Billiken.

"So you noticed it, too, eh?" he grunted finally.

The girl seemed surprised and shook her head. She had made the remark merely as a prelude to what she wanted to say.

"I don't know whether there is or not," the doctor rumbled on thoughtfully. "Sometimes I think he's just in the same fix that you are."

The doctor grunted scornfully at the expression of surprise that showed on the girl's face.

"Why, what is that, Doctor?"

The doctor looked at her over the lighted match he held to his cigarette.

"Ho! ho!" he rumbled finally. "Innocent this morning, ain't you?"

And the girl blushed as the doctor explained ponderously:

"What *I* think is the matter," he offered confidentially, "what really ails him, is that the little fool god—you know, the one with wings and a quiver of arrows"—the fat man in the chair gestured ridiculously—"has simply taken a pot-shot at him, and scored a bull's-eye."

"Oh!" The girl gasped. "Do you really?"

Then, "Miss Brannon?" she queried eagerly. "Is it? I was hoping that—-"

The doctor bobbed his big head in agreement.

"Yep," he advised heavily, "that's it—I *think*."

The girl smiled.

"That's—that's great! He's a dandy, isn't he, and she seems mighty sweet—"

"All o' that," the doctor interrupted. "Every bit of it and then some. And, by the way"—he raised his little eyes as though the thought had but just occurred to him—"when do you and Gum-Shoe Bill come to time?"

The girl laughed, then frowned as she remembered her errand.

"That's—that's—" she began nervously. "It's about him that I wanted to see you, Doctor."

The doctor screwed his face into an expression of astonishment.

"So-o-o," he murmured thoughtfully. Then: "Aren't you beginning a little early, Mae?"

"It isn't about *us*," she explained hastily, turning red, "but Ben—Mr. Franklin, that is—he's—been watching Mr. Thornton," she blurted.

The doctor sat up, suddenly interested. His heavy careless manner dropped immediately.

"So that's it, eh?" He reached out and patted the girl's arm with a huge hand. "You needn't bother about it, Mae—Hal's been talking too much with his mouth, that's all. Of course your man doesn't seriously think—" The doctor didn't finish the sentence, and the girl shook her head quickly.

"No," she answered, "but—but Ben has gone back to headquarters, and there's another man out in the hall. I—I just thought you would want to know it."

The doctor pondered the information, grumbling unintelligible things to himself the while, and the girl stood watching him.

Finally he turned to her again, and his heavy voice was as near soft as it could become.

"Thanks, Mae." He smiled slowly. "Thanks for telling me."

The girl nodded and closed the door behind her, and the huge fat man, left alone in his office, slumped far down in his chair, eying bale fully the lighted end of a cigarette.

When he roused himself from his contemplation of the smoldering cigarette he turned to the telephone. He leaned close to the instrument as the operator answered.

"Main—four, four, two, three," he ordered, and nodded his head as the operator repeated the number.

In another moment he smiled.

"Hello—Izzy?" The smile broadened until his huge face was creased with wrinkles. "Of course it is; who else would call you Izzy?" He chuckled heavily as he listened. "Isn't a feminine name, eh? Like to know why not? Isabel—Izzy. Natural contraction— don't contradict me." He laughed aloud into the transmitter; then, "I'm coming out your way on a call, Isabel," he explained. "May I drop in a minute? That's fine—thanks. W-e-e-1-1, yes. You might have Aunt Julie fix up one—just one, mind you! And— and—please don't put in too much sugar."

He chuckled as he lifted himself to his feet and reached for a misshaped hat.

In the outer office he nodded to the girl.

"Going out on a call," he grumbled. "If you want

me, phone Miss Brannon." He turned in the doorway. "Guess you're going off with that sleuth of yours, aren't you?" he asked with heavy jocularity.

The girl nodded, and the doctor rumbled on. "Well, wait till I get back, anyhow," he asked. "I'm coming back up this afternoon."

In the hallway he looked about keenly, but saw no sign of the detective. As he passed Thornton's door he stopped and looked in. He saw Thornton busily engaged in his laboratory and called loudly: "Hey, runt!"

Thornton turned, a test-tube held gingerly in a holder. "Well, pill-roller!" he challenged, coming to the doorway.

The doctor produced a cigarette.

"Going out Ortega way," he puffed. "Want to come along?" He eyed Thornton shrewdly.

"No—thanks—busy. I'll wait till you get back." Thornton twisted the tube in his hand, and appeared to be considering. "Say, Lester—" he finally began; "do you really think I've— Oh, I've been thinking," he hurried on, now that a beginning had been made, "and do you really believe—I—that there's a chance for me?"

The doctor eyed the young man in a friendly way.

"I'd say," he began in a heavy, consultation-voice manner, "I'd say that—if you aren't an infernal ass, you'll start something—*pronto!*"

And, because he knew his psychology and his subject, the doctor turned and without another word waddled gravely down the long hall.

Thornton stood in the doorway watching him, playing mechanically with the test-tube, a half-smile on his face and an unusual light in his eyes.

He turned slowly into his office again, but did not continue his work. Instead he turned to a small cabinet and drew out a photograph.

The smiling eyes of Isabel Brannon gazed into his own. The test-tube in his hand was forgotten, and he drew near a window, staring long and earnestly at the photograph in his hand.

"I wonder," he mused aloud—"I wonder if she really could be—"

He shook his head abruptly and turned to his work after carefully propping the picture against a rack. He began to whistle cheerfully as he shook up the contents of the test-tube and held the glass over the flame of a Bunsen burner.

Again his thoughts drifted and his eyes turned to the picture beside him. The crack of an overheated test-tube warned him to give attention to the work in hand, and, with a laugh, he threw the useless tube aside and turned to replace the photograph in the cabinet.

A roll of blue-prints caught his eye, and he drew them out thoughtfully, spreading them on the table before him. He nodded slowly as he removed a small print from the lot and studied it carefully, his eyes following each little minute line of the drawing. He refolded the drawing and replaced it with the others, placing the roll in the cabinet drawer labeled "Vault Plans—Defy Safe and Lock Company."

There was plain indecision in his steps as he paced across his office, smoking thoughtfully and frowning at nothing. Then he laughed quietly, glanced at his watch, shrugged, and dropped to a chair in front of his desk.

"I'm a fool," he whispered to himself

confidentially. "The only way to find out is to ask."

He caught his breath at the thought, and envisaged the figure of Isabel Brannon, in the manner that he imagined she might look when he put his question to her.

Then, unreasonably, there flooded over him a strangely clairvoyant feeling; a feeling of positive certainty, of encouraging assurance.

"By George!" he whispered. "I'll do it—tonight!"

XIV: Light or Dark Clothes

BEN FRANKLIN entered the chief of detective's offices in anything but a pleasant frame of mind. He didn't relish the idea of being relieved from the assignment of watching Thornton, however much he scouted the idea that Thornton could have been in any way connected with the robberies on which the department was working.

But he didn't especially care to be put back on the monotonous job of loafing around Bridge Street; watching drunken sailors and Tenderloin bums, when the time might have been spent comfortably in Doctor Lester's office, and, incidentally, with Mae.

Franklin stopped a moment to converse with the man on duty outside of the chief's offices.

"What brings the old man down here on Sunday morning?" he questioned.

The sour-faced officer shrugged heavily.

"Had some little runt in there with him up to a minute ago. 'S got a grouch on that you can feel a mile."

"Huh," Franklin nodded, "that ain't a thing new. The compliments in the papers this morning caused it, probably."

"Some compliments, all right, all right," grinned the long-faced officer. "I don't remember 'em ever wading in quite that bad on the old man before. Anything new on the bank job?"

Franklin shook his head.

"Naw; nor there ain't likely to be, the way the old

man's handling it," he criticized. "I advised him right off to get a line on some of the old-timers around Bridge Street, but he says nix. Talks about this being some gentleman's job. Gentleman, the devil! Just one of these slick crooks from up North down for a holiday. Now, if *I* was running this department, first of all I'd sort of give a peep at the private accounts of them two ginks at the Second National, and—"

The officer chuckled.

"Some head," he grinned sarcastically. "Some head."

Franklin reddened.

"What's the matter with that idea?" he demanded truculently.

"Nothing—not a thing," chuckled the other, "except you're sort of running away from the fact that not one but *three* banks has had a visit."

"What's the matter with the others just bluffing along the same way?" demanded Franklin. "Huh, what's the matter with 'em learnin' about the Second National's bull about the big vault being just walked into—and considerin' that it ain't such a bad idea to clean up a little on the side themselves? Hey, what's the matter with that?"

Franklin stopped a moment, speculating over the possibility, which really had occurred to him while he was speaking.

"Not a bad theory to work on, that ain't," he nodded; "as good as any the chief's got, anyway, and—"

"Just a little worse than none," agreed the officer sourly. "What's the matter with you, Frank," he volunteered, "is that you've just got crooks on the brain."

He grinned at the detective, then chuckled audibly as he digested Franklin's theory.

"Wholesale," he grunted scornfully—"mighty funny it would be if every bank in town suddenly went crooked. Lord, what an idea!" and he went off into another paroxysm of chortling laughter.

Franklin turned on his heel abruptly and entered the chief's office with a belligerent swagger which spoke eloquently of his humor.

The chief was sitting at his desk, chewing on the ever-present cigar and drumming the side of the desk with his stumpy fingers. He nodded when Franklin entered, and with a jerk of his head indicated a chair.

After a moment's silence he spoke without looking at the detective.

"When'd you pick up Thornton?" he asked.

Franklin crossed his legs and rocked backward in his chair. "When he came to his office," he advised. "I was down in the drug-store waiting for him to show up. Came in about ten-thirty."

"Anybody with him?" the chief questioned aimlessly.

Franklin shook his head.

"Naw. Came in by himself. Looked like he'd just got up."

"Huh?" The chief turned his eyes on Franklin. "Whaddaya mean—looked like he just got up?"

Franklin shrugged.

"All spick an' span," he explained. "Dressed up."

"Yeh?" The chief shifted his cigar about in his mouth. "Notice what he had on?"

Franklin's mouth twisted into a half sneer. It

struck him that the chief was getting more childish every day; as though it mattered what Thornton had on.

"Well," the chief snapped the word.

"White," grunted Franklin disgustedly; "serge or flannel, I don't know which. Didn't notice his shirt. White shoes; straw hat—Panama. Soft collar; black bow tie." Franklin was surprised at his own memory, and the chief nodded, satisfied.

"All right," he grunted; "and now—"

"I didn't notice how his hair was parted," volunteered Franklin cuttingly.

The chief turned red.

"Cut it, Frank," he waved a huge hand. "There ain't any call for the heavy sarcasm. I don't like the idea of being down here to-day any more'n you do, but I ain't taking it out on everybody in sight."

Franklin relapsed into shamed silence.

The chief scowled silently, contemplating his hands on the desk while Franklin fidgeted in his chair.

"Jackson picked up Thornton," he grunted finally. Then he leaned forward over his desk, eying the detective. "And, what's more, he saw Thornton this morning just before or just after the Farmer's National got theirs."

"The Farmer's National?" The legs of Franklin's chair crashed to the floor.

"Yep." The chief nodded. "Didn't hear that, eh? Somebody done 'em between nine and ten this morning; leastwise, we know it wasn't before then, for—"

Franklin whistled softly between his teeth.

"And Jackson *saw* Thornton?"

"Well," the chief modified, "he saw him near the post-office, an' what, in God's name, would the man be doin' there at that time o' day, and on Sunday? A man like Thornton?"

"What'd he get?" Franklin put the question plainly to gain time to think about this newest development.

"Little enough," grunted the chief in answer; "it ain't that, but lord, when that Carney man"—the chief scowled heavily at the thought of the cashier of the Farmer's National Bank—"gets to the newspapers with it!"

"An' you're still figuring on this Thornton chap knowing something about it?"

The chief tapped a stumpy finger on the desk to outline his argument.

"Now you get this, Frank, an' get it straight. I'm gambling that he's the one best bet we've got. First, that Second National affair—with him blowin' about his ability to open vaults right after tellin' me the thing was burglar-proof—positively!"

"But he didn't get in, did he?" Franklin reminded the chief.

"Oh, no; he didn't get in. Of course he didn't." The chief turned scornful eyes on the questioner. "If you was in his shoes and had to make good on a bluff— would you ha' gotten in? Of course not."

The chief bit fiercely on his cigar, and Franklin remained silent.

"All right, then. Then he shows that he might — mind you, might have been able to pull this— that's plain." The chief checked off the item on his finger.

"Then, there comes the St. John's business; must have happened around midnight—after midnight.

Where was Thornton?"

Franklin listened impatiently, and interrupted:

"At the dance," he answered, "we know that. Ain't the prosecuting attorney's word good enough for that?"

"Maybe he was, and maybe he wasn't," growled the chief. "At least Mr. Railey didn't see him all the time. He was there at nine o'clock—and he was there after midnight—yeh? But was he there in the *meantime?*"

Franklin's face lit up.

"Huh," he chortled, "and you think he could have come in from Ortega in about two or two and a half hours and pulled this—this and the Bay Street Bank entry—and then hop back five miles?"

The chief nodded.

"It ain't impossible—not by a long shot, it ain't. He could have come up the river?"

"Swim up?" commented Franklin sarcastically, but the chief paid no attention.

"Then finally here's this Farmer's National stunt; with Thornton seen—seen, mind you—two blocks away from the place just about when it must have happened."

Franklin's face showed his entire disbelief of the chief's argument.

"What's the matter with him being on the way, or coming from the Springfield tennis-courts? They usually play out there early Sunday morning?"

"Walking?" the chief cut in. "It's a considerable walk from the Riverside Apartments to Springfield Park—considerable walk."

Franklin tapped the floor nervously with his foot.

"Who was at the apartments this morning?"

The chief began to smile slowly. It pleased him that his subordinate should show signs of ability, and it pleased him much more to hammer home his own arguments and watch their effect on those about him.

"Hanson," he answered Franklin. "Hanson was there. I put him on Ralby's trail, that was the man he was after, and if your friend Mr. Thornton left that apartment-house Hanson'll know it."

The chief nodded to himself, pleased with the thought that his sagacity had made it possible to be definitely informed of the time of Thornton's departure from the house.

"Well, all I got to say," Franklin began defensively, when the door opened and the detective in question—Hanson—entered briskly. He was a youngish man, with a preternaturally long, earnest face which, as he entered, gave the impression that the man might be a divinity student. The thing he looked least like was a detective.

"Well, Hanson?" The chief's voice had an eager quality in it.

Hanson nodded to Franklin and turned to the chief.

"Got your message," the detective began, "and came immediately. This man, Ralby, however, seems to be making a day of it indoors. I haven't seen a sign of him this morning."

"Never mind Ralby," the chief snapped, and the detective raised his eyebrows in surprise. "It's Thornton I'm trying to get a line on," the chief explained.

Hanson shrugged.

"I didn't pay much attention to him," he said.

"You told me Ralby was the man to keep up with, and that's what I—"

"All right," the chief cut him off, "but you saw Thornton leave the house, didn't you?"

"Sure," the detective smiled. "More than once. He seems to be an early bird."

"Left more than once, did he?" The chief jerked the cigar from the corner of his mouth. "Just when did he leave the *first* time?"

"Oh, 'bout eight o'clock, I think."

"Eight, eh?"

The chief's fingers drummed a tattoo on the desk, and he nodded to Franklin.

"Yes, about eight," Hanson continued; "not exactly sure; might have been a few minutes either way. He went down to the Riverside Garage—you can see it from the house—and went off in his flivver."

"Sure he went off in a car?"

The detective grinned broadly.

"A flivver," he corrected. "Yep, sure," he nodded.

"What was he wearing? Notice?" The chief drew up on the edge of his chair, and Franklin leaned forward.

Hanson nodded; he rather prided himself on his faculty of observation.

"Black hat; blue suit," he answered promptly. "Couldn't make out anything else."

"Blue suit?" Franklin queried hurriedly.

Hanson turned.

"Well, it might ,have been black; either one, black or blue."

"Changed clothes," the chief muttered aloud. Hanson faced him again. "Yeh—how'd you know he did?"

"Go on," the chief ordered. "When?"

"He came back about an hour and a half later," the detective continued; "stayed inside about a half-hour, and came out dressed in white serge, white shoes, straw hat. That's about all I know about him."

"'S'nough," snapped the chief. "Plenty. Good work, Hanson. Mighty good work." And the detective addressed swelled visibly, although at a loss to account for the unusual praise.

Franklin seemed thoughtful.

"This fellow Thornton, Hanson—carrying anything when he left? Tennis rackets?"

The chief looked up.

"Hell, Franklin!" he exploded. "A man don't go out to play tennis in a blue suit around here, does he? And when he passed Jackson at the post-office he was *walking*—not in his flivver, remember."

Hanson looked his surprise.

"What's up?" he questioned.

"As to time," the chief went on slowly, "everything seems to fit pretty well." He looked up suddenly. "Say, Hanson, was Thornton carrying anything *when he came back?*"

"Didn't see it," the detective advised. "It wasn't anything large, or I'd have spotted it."

The chief nodded, then grinned.

"No, he hardly got enough to make a bundle of it." He got heavily to his feet. "You pick up Ralby again, Hanson," he instructed. "Needn't go back out to the apartment; try the New Era Club; he usually shows up there around noon. And when you find him, stick with him. I want to see just how much he's with this Thornton guy."

The detective nodded and turned to the door.

"And you, Franklin," the chief turned to Franklin, "you leave word where I can get to you when I want you, and you might explain to Hanson there just what's in the wind; always remembering," the chief wagged a minatory finger at Franklin, "that this Thornton chap looks mighty, mighty good to me."

When the two men departed the chief dropped again into his chair, produced a fresh cigar from a nearly depleted pocket, and, apparently addressing a newspaper on his desk, rumbled positively:

"I'll show you something," he growled, "something that'll make you sit up and take notice."

He chewed his cigar a moment, then thumbed through the pages of a telephone directory. His forefinger descended on a particular number, and he called into the transmitter of the instrument on his desk.

In a moment the connection was made.

"Hello—hello, Mr. Thornton;" the chief's voice was quietly interested. "Feeling all right this morning? That's good. No, no—nothing new, Mr. Thornton; not yet. Didn't happen to be in this neighborhood this morning, did you? What?" The chief leaned closer to the phone. *"Didn't get up until nine o'clock?* No—nothing at all; I'll call you if anything develops."

The chief hung up the receiver and chewed his cigar.

"Now, I wonder," he muttered to himself, "I wonder why Thornton lied?"

XV. The Doctor Threatens

DOCTOR LESTER'S car drew up before the home of Isabel Brannon, and the big man lowered himself gruntingly to the curb, where he stood for a moment, frowning at his automobile, then turned to the house.

In a minute he sat spraddled comfortably in a wide wicker armchair on the porch, his hat carelessly tossed to one side, and mopping his broad face with a handkerchief but one degree removed, in size, from a table-cloth.

The screened door leading into the house opened, and Isabel Brannon came lightly across the porch to the doctor. Dressed in white, with the filmiest of Georgette crepe waists, her hair tucked with seeming carelessness beneath a wide-brimmed, flopping Panama, she appeared to be the spirit of the St. Johns River breezes incarnate.

The doctor heaved a huge sigh.

"Gosh, Izzy," he grunted, "you look—well, north poleish." He grinned heavily at the expression. "Not the Slav kind," he explained, as the girl approached. He did not rise, but took her slim hand in his own huge paw. "If I get up," he apologized, "I'll flop over; I know it."

The girl smiled her acknowledgment and drew a chair next to the doctor's.

"No need," she offered. "You *do* look comfortable."

"Me? Comfortable?" The doctor's figure shook jellylike with his tremendous laugh. "Behold! Jumbo in repose!" He gestured with one short arm. "Thank the Lord, there's plenty of me to be comfortable."

The girl laughed.

"Oh—you aren't so tremendous as all that!" Her eyes twinkled as she looked at the man.

"Don't try any of that," he warned; "that's no way to lie to me. Don't I know I'm fat? Don't I?" Then: "Didn't you murmur something about—" He raised his eyebrows ludicrously.

"If you'll just wait another minute, Mr. Fat Man, the life-saver, in the shape of Aunt Julie, will arrive,"

The doctor nodded.

"There's always something worth living for, isn't there? Here I come a running to see a sick man with a tummy-ache and fill the poor devil full of Jamaica ginger, working like a slave and swearing like an Argentine cochero, and then—"

As he spoke the door burst open and a tremendous negro woman appeared, bearing carefully aloft a tray on which glistened a tall glass, carefully decorated with lemon peel, cherries, mint-leaves and two straws. The liquor it contained was amber-colored—a vague, greenish amber, and the ice tinkled musically as Aunt Julie carefully set the tray on a small table and extended the glass to the doctor.

"Ambrosial nectar!" The doctor sipped experimentally. "Aunt Julie," he growled, "why can't I ever fix'em like that?"

Aunt Julie's Amazonian figure, which rivaled the doctor's in its proportions, shook heavily.

"Ah reckon, Mr. Lester, you-all just naturally cyan't learn to make 'em nohow!"

The doctor glanced sidewise at the negress.

"Been taking exercise, Aunt Julie? Looks like you're getting thin."

A look of concern appeared on the negress' face.

"'Deed Ah ain't, Mr. Lester," she denied, arms akimbo. "Ah weighs two hun'red an' twenty pounds, Ah does, an' Ah ain't losin' a bit. Took me ten years t' git dat high, 'deed it did, an' Ah ain't goin' round tryin' to rejuce it none—nossuh!"

The doctor sucked earnestly on his straws, fumbling with his free hand in his wrinkled vest. A coin spun in the air as he flipped it to Aunt Julie, who, despite her bulk, caught it deftly.

"When you quit here," the doctor ordered, "whenever you do, just remember my address, Aunt Julie."

"Lordy, Mr. Lester," the old darky chuckled, "you-all know Ah ain't goin' to quit here no time. Who'd tek keer o' Miss Is'bel, you reckon?" And she chortled mightily.

The doctor sighed. "So it, is," he grumbled morosely. "A poor sucker of a sawbones can't even find anybody to mix his juleps."

Isabel laughed.

"Why don't you tell him how you do it, Aunt Julie?"

The big negress turned in the doorway.

"Ah'll be glad t' come by an' fix 'em up f'r you any time, Mr. Lester," she volunteered seriously, "but tellin' you how Ah fixes 'em?" She scratched a kinky head. "Ah just naturally fixes 'em, dat's all. But Ah ain't goin' to quit here no time—no time, nossuh; nor Ah ain't goin' to rejuce none either." And she waddled heavily into the house.

The doctor set his glass on the table with a sigh

that spoke volumes, while the girl shook a playful finger at him.

"Intoxicants in the daytime," she mocked.

The doctor reached for his cigarettes.

"Intoxicants? That?" He indicated the empty julep-glass. "That's no more an intoxicant than you're an old maid." His shrewd little eyes watched the girl over the lighted match.

The girl gestured lightly, dismissing the doctor's remark.

"What's new in the St. James Building?" she asked.

"Meaning with me or—" The doctor left the question unfinished; then began again: "There's nothing new in the world; there never is. There's only sick people and well people—that's all."

The girl shook her head.

"Of course that's all wrong," she smiled, "and there's a lot new—every day. The trouble is, you see too many ailers, not enough of the well kind. You're getting pessimistic in your old age," she laughed into the doctor's heavy face. "I believe you *like* to see people sick."

"Huh. A fat lot you know about it," grunted the doctor sarcastically. "There isn't a doctor in town who likes to see sick people. As for me—there's nothing I wish this burg"—he gestured with his hand—"nothing I wish this burg more than an epidemic of health."

The girl seemed but half listening, although she smiled at the doctor's expression as he fished clumsily for another cigarette.

Lester smiled ponderously to himself as he blew a cloud of smoke reflectively into the air and watched it dissipate in the sunshine. Then he turned his eyes to the empty glass at his side, puckered his lips thoughtfully, and stared musingly across the lawn. Finally, with another shrewd glance at the girl, he placed both hands on the arms of his chair as though to hoist himself to his feet, and the girl turned to face him.

"Will you be honest with me, Doctor, if I ask you something?"

The doctor noticed the seriousness in the girl's eyes, but he spoke jestingly.

"Didn't I fetch you into this world of woe?" he demanded. "And you a squalling, red-faced little brat trying to howl your lungs out." He chuckled heavily at the recollection. "And didn't I yank you through everything from croup and colic to typhoid —eh?"

The girl's hand fell on his arm.

"Of course you did, you big, fat, dear disciple of Hippocrates, and—"

"And ain't I going to see you safely married and finished off and done for?"

The girl blushed.

"Ain't I?" he demanded again. "Say?"

The girl shook her head slightly.

"I don't know," she mused. "But—but what I want to ask," she hurried on, averting her eyes, "isn't there something—don't you think—oh, you know— isn't Hal—"

The doctor laughed boisterously.

"So, that's it!" He eyed the girl with such ridiculous solemnity that she laughed aloud.

Then he spoke quietly:

"No, Isabel, there's nothing the matter with Mr. Halvey Thornton—nothing except—that is—"

"Well?" The girl's hand tightened on his arm.

"Nothing except," the doctor continued in a mock judicial fashion, "er—a—well, a bad affection, I'd say, in the—er—cardiac region." He reached over and covered the girl's hand with one of his own huge paws. "Why don't you cheer that youngster up a bit, Izzy?"

The girl's eyes were not smiling as they met the doctor's.

"He doesn't give me a chance," she whispered. "I don't think Hal likes to come here any more. Do you really think"—her eyes drifted from his and fixed intently on the top button in the doctor's pink-striped shirt—"that he—that Halvey—that—"

The doctor's laugh threatened to choke him.

"Oof!" he grunted. "You unspeakably blind little brat! And they talk of the discernment and the intuitive knowledge of the sex feminine. Ye golden gods!" And he went off into a fit of gurgling laughter.

The crimson stain on the girl's face spoke for her feelings.

"You—you needn't be so—" she began, but the doctor's bellow interrupted:

"Lord," he chuckled, "and I've been knowing it for the last ten years—every bit of it."

The girl arose and turned her back to the chuckling man in the chair, gazing fixedly out across the lawn to where the broad expanse of the St. Johns River cut a sparkling path across the sunshine, while the doctor reached surreptitiously for his glass, and swallowed the remains of the mint-julep.

When the girl turned again to the man there was a hint of tears in her eyes, and the fat doctor shook his head wisely and sagely.

"If you don't announce it in twenty-four hours," he threatened, "I wash my hands of you."

The girl laughed happily, and her fingers ran lightly through the doctor's graying hair.

"You're a dear!" she gasped, and ran into the house.

A moment the doctor sat in silence, then the smile vanished from his lips and he began his eternal muttering. A minute later his mind was far from Halvey Thornton and Isabel Brannon.

"All right," he muttered, "and if she doesn't respond to that treatment—" He visualized the tense frightened face of the little Haines girl, and frowned heavily.

"Now, I wonder," he grumbled, "I wonder what's Freud's theory—" He lifted himself slowly to his feet and waddled gravely across the porch. Still muttering, he started down the steps, to bring up abruptly at a hail from the door of the house:

"Silly! Here's your hat!"

The doctor stopped and turned, passing one hand over his bare head.

"What do you know about that?" he chuckled. "I was so busy playing Cupid I forgot." He deftly caught the hat the girl threw to him.

"I've got another julep here!" she tempted, but the doctor shook his head resolutely.

"I'm a slave," he groaned—"a hard-working slave." Then: "I want to stop by Ralby's place," he explained, "and get a book he's got. And remember," he called back, once more reverting to the main point, "if I don't hear some rumblings of that announcement in the morning, why, demme, if I don't marry you myself!"

And he heaved himself down the gravel walk
chuckling hugely at his joke.

XVI. Ralby Lends a Hand

THE automobile slid, with a series of jerks, to rest before the ornate front of the Riverside Apartments, and the doctor descended to the sidewalk. He lifted the hood of his car and peered intently into the grimy interior, muttering objurgatory comments on gasoline engines in general and those that chronically missed on one cylinder in particular.

He did not venture, however, to pry into the reasons, but satisfied himself with grumbling and eying the mechanism bale fully, after which he replaced the hood and turned to trundle across the intervening sidewalk into the apartment.

The elevator-boy brought his hand up smartly to his little red uniform cap in salute, and showed double rows of tombstonelike teeth:

"Mornin', Doctor—powerful fine mornin'."

The doctor entered the elevator nodding his acknowledgment of the greeting.

"What does the salute mean?" he grunted heavily; and the boy grinned broadly.

"Jes' a s'lute; thass all—yassuh! Jes' a 'spectful s'lute!"

"All you niggers," rumbled the doctor as the ascent began, "think that I'm a gold-mine." Even as he spoke he fished into his vest-pocket for a coin. "Some of these days I'm going to plumb surprise you. Stop at the third, you black limb of the devil!"

"And three she am. Thanks, Doctor—I's beholden

to you, suh!"

The negro pocketed the dime and the car slid from sight while the doctor turned to the door nearest the elevator. The door was slightly ajar, but he pressed heavily on the door-button and heard the answering clangor inside the apartment. After a moment's waiting he rang again.

The elevator at his side paused in its ascent and the negro boy's grinning face appeared at the grille.

"Mist'r Ralby done gone out," he advised, "done been gone out 'bout an hour."

The doctor hesitated a minute, shrugged and pushed into the apartment. He walked familiarly through the first and into the second room, a room lined with bookcases. Green rugs covered the floor, and in the center stood a heavy, square library-table. Several books were scattered on it, together with a few magazines.

The doctor lumbered to the table, seeing the book he wanted, and dropped heavily into one of the leather chairs, drawing the volume to him.

Soon he seemed as much at home as in his office, slouched far down in the chair and puffing thoughtfully on a cigarette as he read page after page, stopping now and then to pause and scratch his head and wrinkle his forehead when he did not quite agree with the words on the pages before him.

Once he rose to his feet and his hand reached out before him. When, however, his hand did not come into contact with a desk-top, the doctor looked about him in a surprised fashion. It seemed that he had forgotten his whereabouts, and he grinned to himself, muttering heavily.

He had reached to the top of the desk, which

wasn't there, to check up a reference in the book before him, and now he trundled across Ralby's library, peering intently into bookcases. He found the book he sought, returned to the table and in a few minutes was again engrossed in a huge volume.

"Sounds all right," he muttered to himself, "sounds fine, but does it work out?" He turned to a case reference and studied a history sheet duplicated in the book. "Huh," he chuckled, "I knew it wasn't that easy; took four treatments, eh?" He carefully read over the history sheet a second time and closed the book.

He looked up, rubbed his eyes, and stared about him. Ralby had not returned, and with a shrug the big doctor arose, placing the volume under his arm. As he turned another book on the table caught his eye, and he picked it up, glancing interestedly at the title on the cover. *On the Psychic Phenomena*, he read, and paged idly through the book, grunting his scientific disgust as he read an occasional line.

"Prep school stuff!" he grunted sarcastically. "Kindergarten junk!"

He replaced the book and turned to one of the wall cases.

"Whew!" he whistled softly as he ran his eyes over a set of red bindings. "Didn't know he went in for it so seriously."

He drew out one of the volumes and opened it at random. In a very short time he was keenly interested and read on carefully.

"That man ain't a fool," he commented praisingly. "Oh, no wonder—"

He had turned to the title-page to note the author's name and found him to be the professor of experimental psychology in a large eastern university.

"Dog-gone it." The doctor glanced at his watch. "Mae's waiting for me, too," he grumbled and turned. In the doorway he collided with Ralby, who was entering. Ralby's eyes leaped from the doctor's around the room and back again, and, noting the volume under the doctor's arm, he nodded. "Oh, hello—come in; don't leave yet. I wonder who left my door open."

The doctor seemed to forget his haste of a moment before and returned into the room, placing the book on the table.

"I don't know," he grumbled. "Your infernal door was wide open and in I sailed. Wanted this Jung book for a day or two—don't mind, do you?"

"Surely not." Ralby pushed a humidor of cigarettes across the table to the doctor. "You're welcome to anything in the place," and he laughed pleasantly.

"I was just wondering," continued the doctor, sinking back into the chair he had vacated a moment before, "if it mightn't be worth while to try this psychoanalysis on that little Haines kid."

Ralby was changing into a smoking-jacket, and he shrugged his silk-clad shoulders.

"You ought to know, Lester. I don't imagine you'd get much results from a kid, though. She'd probably be—well—impossible."

The doctor reached mechanically into Ralby's humidor and lighted a cigarette. He puffed it twice, then dropped it hurriedly into an ash-tray, reaching into his own pocket.

"Phew!" he snorted. "Infernal Turkish things!

Now here—" he displayed a battered package of a notoriously cheap domestic cigarette, "here's a white man's smoke," and he lit a cigarette with visible signs of satisfaction.

"Matter of taste," Ralby commented lightly. "I couldn't smoke one of those things of yours in a century."

"Psychic," the doctor grumbled, "psychic, and you know it."

"Well, why don't you smoke the Turkish ones then, if it's all the same?" challenged Ralby, and his deep black eyes twinkled amusedly at the man across the table.

The doctor straightened a little in his chair.

"Could," he grumbled, "just don't like the odor."

"Psychic," mocked Ralby, "purely psychic."

The doctor's smile creased his heavy face.

"*Touche!*" he admitted. Then, indicating the bookcase he had so interestedly examined: "I didn't know you went in all that seriously for this sort of stuff, Ralby."

Ralby shrugged deprecatingly.

"I'm only a beginner," he demurred.

"All that new thought and hypnosis dope," the doctor waved his hand again—"been over all of it?"

Ralby's eyes flashed a moment, but the doctor's heavy face was impassive and free from any sign of guile or sarcasm. Then he nodded.

"Yes, pretty thoroughly. By the way, when are you going to give that mania patient another treatment?"

Doctor Lester hunched his fat shoulders.

"Can't say," he admitted. "I don't know whether to repeat it or not. But if she doesn't show any response to the treatment, I'll have to. I've tried everything else in the catalog."

Ralby nodded and tapped his cigarette on an ashtray.

"Rather peculiar, wasn't it," he ventured speculatively, "Thornton's attack yesterday." He eyed the doctor with elaborate casualness as he put the question. The doctor nodded.

"Yes, rather," he admitted, then chuckled throatily: "Won't happen again, I don't think."

Ralby appeared mildly interested.

"Too high-strung, that's Thornton's trouble. I've been watching him lately. One of these days he's simply going all to pieces all at once."

The doctor nodded.

"Can't make the ass see reason," he grumbled. "Works harder than any man in town, and that's a fact. And now this infernal bank-robbery business piled on top of it—" The doctor muttered his disrespect for any man who would worry over something that really did not concern him.

"Still, I can understand that, all right," Ralby nodded. "Thornton feels somehow responsible; I can appreciate that, but that he should bother himself about it—" Ralby's airy gesture indicated that he, for one, gave no great thought to the troubles of the Jacksonville detective department.

"Find myself thinking about it in spite of myself," grumbled the doctor. "It *is* a mighty interesting problem."

"It is that," Ralby agreed, "but after all, we'll find an absurdly simple answer to it when they finally get the man."

The doctor looked up.

"Changed your mind?" he grinned; "think they'll get him now, do you? Five hundred dollars' worth?"

"Oh, no," Ralby denied quickly, "I'm going to win that bet. Make it more if you like." Then, as the doctor shook his head: "But, of course, they'll get him—not here maybe—but when he tries it somewhere else."

"What's the rule this time?" questioned the doctor interestedly. Ralby's theories were usually worth hearing.

"Same old thing," laughed Ralby. "There is always a man somewhere just a little bit better than the other. Here these people make a vault, and along comes a man with just a little more imagination and ability—and the first one might not have made the vault at all, for all the good it does him. Then Mr. Burglar will feel a little too much above the average run and—bing! Along comes some one just a little bit more intelligent—and up goes Mr. Burglar." Ralby's face shone interestedly with his subject. "Think! That's the keynote. Why, man, there are men in this country—a half dozen of 'em—in the universities— who could work this seemingly impossible problem by sheer ability to *think*."

The doctor nodded.

"Sounds fine, Ralby, but where are your intellectual giants?"

"Oh, they exist," Ralby stated positively. "Of course, though," he smiled, "the chief of detectives is hardly one of them—nor am I; but there are two or three detectives in the world—not fiction detectives, either—who would make short work of the question."

"Well, I wish one'd turn up," chuckled the doctor, "I need the five hundred, and, what's really more important, I want Thornton to forget this whole bally business and get his mind down to more definite things. Overworked, that's all he is;" the doctor blew a cloud of smoke thoughtfully ceilingward; "and— maybe—a little emotional disturbance to help things along, like, well—" The doctor gestured widely.

"Like what?" questioned Ralby.

The doctor turned his little sunken eyes on the questioner.

"Aw, don't play innocent," he grunted; "I know you're hit, too."

Ralby stiffened in his chair, and his voice was a bit too quiet:

"I assure you, Lester—I—that I haven't the remotest idea what—"

The doctor's laugh cut off his explanation.

"No," he mocked. "Oh, no, you haven't." The doctor produced a fresh cigarette and his eyes drifted to the picture of Isabel Brannon which stood in a frame on one of the bookcases.

The younger man's eyes followed the doctor's gaze and a tiny frown appeared in his forehead. Very suddenly Ralby understood what the doctor was driving at and his respect for the big man's almost uncanny intuition was too great to dismiss lightly anything he might have to say on a subject that was very near to Ralby.

"And you think—what?" he ventured.

"I think," replied the doctor brutally, "I think, young man, that we'll be offering congratulations— mighty soon!" He turned his head to note the effect of his words on Ralby, and, for the moment, the doctor appeared to be puzzled.

Ralby was not caught napping. He smiled openly

and frankly.

"By George!" he ejaculated, "that *is* news; she's a girl in a million, and Thornton—well, he deserves her, I guess."

"You're mighty right he does," the doctor rumbled heavily, still eying Ralby in a puzzled fashion. "There's not a cleaner cut fellow in the city than Hal, and not a man I'd rather see Isabel tie up with." The doctor hesitated a moment, then added: "You see I've just about been everything but a father to Izzy since she was born," he apologized. "That's why I'm so interested."

Ralby nodded and studied the photograph of the girl on the bookcase.

"I wonder," the doctor smiled twistedly, "I wonder just how hard you're hit."

Ralby laughed clearly.

"How hard *I'm* hit? Not at all—not a little bit, except to be rather glad for Isabel. And I'll be among the first to offer congratulations."

The doctor got slowly to his feet, and Ralby followed suit.

"Then drag out the silver," offered the medical man, "for something is sure goin' to bust loose, as my nigger says."

The two men walked together to the door.

"Thanks for this." The doctor nodded to the book under his arm. "Fetch it back to you in a day or two."

Ralby nodded.

"And I'll call you," the doctor finished as he pushed the elevator signal-button, "when I give the kid another treatment."

"Thanks," Ralby called as the doctor entered the car. "I'll be glad to see what results you get." And he turned to reenter his apartment while the doctor grumbled to the uncomprehending but grinning elevator-boy: "Yeh, so will I; mighty glad!"

XVII. THE IRREFUTABLE FACT

THE doctor, grouchily anathematizing the second cylinder of the engine of his automobile, waddled down the long corridor of the third floor of the St. James Building leading to his offices.

He walked, as he did everything else, in a fashion peculiar to him; lurching from side to side ponderously like a squat tramp steamer wallowing through a heavy sea and making progress ahead where he seemed, crablike, to be making progress abeam. His huge head was sunk on his chest, as though making a study of the tile of the flooring, and his continual muttering seemed to originate deep down in his barrel-chest.

When he neared his door he brought up sharply and lifted his head. From his office came the sound of voices, and he recognized immediately Mae's voice, unmistakable, irritable and impatient.

"How many times have I got to tell you," the girl was demanding, "that I don't know when he'll be back? Now you can either sit there or hang around, as you've been doing all day, out in the corridor. Why didn't you see him when he was here?"

And the answer came in a heavy voice that seemed trying hard to mollify the angry girl:

"Can't a bloke ask a respectable question? Aw, say, I ain't done you nothin', have I? I wouldn't—"

The doctor's huge form filled the doorway, and his little eyes caught the sudden stare of the startled detective; the bullet-headed Jackson.

The doctor's voice rumbled heavily.

"Mae, what does this—er—*gentleman* want?" He emphasized the word prominently.

The girl, standing by the magazine-littered table, eyed Jackson threateningly.

"Oh, he's been asking for you, Doctor."

"Well?" The doctor's monosyllable was threatening as he turned to Jackson, and the bullet-headed one shuffled nervously and twisted a derby in his hands. "Well—I'm the doctor!" A little ominous gleam came into the big doctor's eyes, and his frown was thunderous.

"I—I—I," Jackson began stuttering. "I'm from headquarters!" he blurted out, with an air of great bravado.

The doctor's frown lightened not one bit.

"Headquarters?" he bellowed. "Headquarters of what?"

The bullet-headed detective was taken aback, and Mae turned to giggle silently into the palm of her hand. The doctor's face was a ludicrous study of anger, and held an expression that was almost too funny in its incongruity with his round jovial face. Nor could the girl decide whether the doctor was angry in earnest.

As for the detective, he never for a moment indulged in any other thought than that he had suddenly loosed on himself, for some unknown reason, the anger of this colossus who stood threateningly blocking the only means of egress.

"Well, headquarters of what?" repeated the big man, scowling at the detective.

Jackson gazed anxiously toward the girl, whose back was turned, fidgeted a moment, glanced toward the telephone as though seeking means of escape in that direction, and, finally, evidently relinquishing the idea of making a hasty exit, answered sullenly:

"Detective headquarters."

The hint of a smile began to dawn in the doctor's eyes, as though the news was amusing. He looked at Jackson a moment, then grunted:

"Well, I'm here. What's the big idea? What's been done, and who did it?"

The detective drew closer to the doctor, and dropped his voice to a confidential undertone, after the manner of a true detective of fiction, for Mr. Jackson—when he donned his badge of office—brought with him some juvenile ideas of what constituted the proper behavior of a sleuth.

"I'd like to see you—private!"

The doctor's eyebrows shot up quizzically.

"Yeh?" He eyed Jackson until that gentleman fidgeted again. Then: "In there, then," the doctor ordered, indicating his private consultation-room, and Jackson, with a look of triumph in the direction of Mae and a look of extreme secretiveness in his eyes, entered the office.

The doctor turned to the girl.

"Been bothering you, Mae?"

She shook her head.

"No—not that—but he's been hanging around ever since you left, and I saw him even before that." She dropped her voice: "He's the man who is watching Mr. Thornton."

The doctor chuckled.

"Oh, is he? I thought maybe," and his eyes twinkled, "that our gum-shoe friend, Franklin, had a rival!" And he waddled across into his office, slamming the door behind him.

"Take a seat." The doctor nodded to the leather chair close beside his desk. "Talk to you in a minute."

He shrugged out of his wrinkled coat, rolled up his shirt-sleeves and put on a white office-coat, the sleeves of which were cut off at the elbows, leaving exposed the doctor's huge brawny forearms. Then he turned into his laboratory, talking as he rummaged about in an instrument case:

"Be with you in a minute, Mr.—er—from headquarters."

He returned bearing a huge wicked-looking instrument and a stiletto-like operating knife. These he placed on the desk before him, seated himself heavily, and slowly began to unwind the protective wrappings on the blade of the knife.

"Now, Mr.—er—er—what was it?"

"Jackson," grunted the detective, ill at ease and watching the doctor's hand fascinatedly.

"All right, Mr. Jackson," the doctor gestured easily with his knife, "I'm Lester, Edward Lester, B. Sc., from the University of Georgia, and M. D. from Tulane; any further information?"

The detective was plainly puzzled and covertly shot a glance at the doctor's heavy face.

"Well, just what can I do for you?" The doctor thoughtfully tested the knife on the end of his thumb and slowly began to polish the blade, breathing on the steel and polishing off the resultant cloud on the metal with meticulous care.

The detective twisted in his chair.

"I don't want nothin' particular," he began.

"No?" The doctor frowned heavily. "Then why are you disturbing my office girl at her—ahem—labors, heh?" Again the wide gesture with the wicked-looking scalpel.

The detective shrank visibly before the shining steel, tentatively trying to push the heavy chair farther away with his feet, while his eyes followed each move of the knife.

"I—that is—I'm watchin' a guy on this floor," he admitted.

The doctor nodded nonchalantly.

"Sure, I know it. My friend, Mr. Thornton, isn't it? Shall I call him in?"

The detective stared wide-eyed a moment, while the doctor resumed his polishing of the knife. Suddenly the detective got to his feet. It had but that moment occurred to him that all this talk and byplay was meant to serve but one fell purpose: that of allowing Thornton to leave the building while he — the valiant officer of the law—was in the doctor's office, unable to take note of Thornton's movements.

Doctor Lester seemed in no way surprised by the detective's sudden desire to leave, and he smiled engagingly as he addressed the detective.

"Oh, no, he isn't leaving," he assured him, and once more Jackson's eyes popped wide. "Sit down," invited the doctor cordially, "sit down!" The big man's voice grew crisp, and with one startled glance at the doctor's hand the detective sank into the chair while the big man rumbled aloud: "Oh, Mae!"

When the girl appeared he turned to her smilingly.

"Call Mr. Thornton, will you? I want him to meet this—er—gentleman from headquarters."

The detective sat stupidly gazing for a moment, then made as though to rise again.

"Oh, but just a minute now—" The doctor's voice

boomed, and his hand shot out gesticulating.

The detective drew back, for the instrument in the doctor's hand had come perilously close to the uppermost button of his coat.

"Aw, say, Doctor—" he began, but stopped short as Thornton entered.

Thornton nodded to the doctor and glanced unconcernedly at Jackson.

"Hal, here's a gentleman from headquarters— from detective headquarters I believe you said, didn't you?" The doctor turned questioningly and Jackson nodded sullenly. "You want to meet him," the doctor continued to Thornton. "Mr. Jackson—Mr. Thornton." The doctor smiled and nodded, then explained: "Mr. Jackson has been detailed, so I gather, to keep a sort of eye on you, Hal."

Thornton started, but the doctor only nodded heavily.

"Yep—so I thought," he smiled ingenuously, "that you two ought to know each other."

The detective turned a brick-red and resolved to brave the doctor's scalpel. He got hurriedly to his feet and turned to the door.

"Ah, what's your hurry?" The doctor's tone was elaborately ironical. "You must go? Just help yourself to my reception-room, then," he invited, "it's nicer than waiting in the corridor." And as the bullet-headed Jackson, utterly bewildered, shuffled out, the doctor turned laughingly to Thornton:

"Well, young hopeful?"

Thornton found words.

"Is that idiot actually watching *me?*" he demanded. "What in heaven's name is the idea?"

The doctor laughed.

"What for?" He smiled at Thornton as he offered his cigarettes. "Oh, I reckon he wants to see what you've been doing with all the money you've been lifting from these vaults."

There seemed the faintest suggestion of a gleam in the doctor's shrewd eyes, which contrasted strangely with the laughing wrinkles of his face, as he rumbled the words, a gleam that seemed intensified for a puzzled moment as Thornton's face mantled with a flush of anger and Thornton turned impulsively to the door.

The doctor's heavy hand fell on the younger man's arm.

"Easy, Hal," he counseled, and watched Thornton closely as he stopped short, with a laugh, and dropped into the chair vacated by the detective.

"Can't the department have a right to its own opinions?" grumbled the doctor. "And you did blow almost too almighty loud about the impregnability of that vault and your own miraculous powers as an expert."

Thornton laughed aloud.

"That's good," he chuckled, "and I'm the only clue the blithering asses have unearthed. I'm afraid it looks bad for your five hundred dollars, Lester."

The doctor shrugged resignedly.

"If I lose, I lose," he grunted, "and Ralby will be five hundred in, that's all. But they think you'll bear watching, anyhow, and that beetle-browed friend of ours is unquestionably on your trail."

Thornton tapped a cigarette on the arm of his chair.

"H-m," he mused aloud, "that was why the chief called then—to try to locate me exactly."

The doctor's face expressed his sudden interest.

"Did the chief call you?" he questioned. "When, and what for?"

Thornton lighted his cigarette.

"Some time after you left," he said. "I thought it was funny that he should suddenly take an interest in my health. Asked how I felt and whether I was completely recovered from yesterday's attack."

The doctor pondered this, and the little wrinkles began to creep slowly into his face as he raised his eyes to Thornton's face, took in that smiling young man's eyes, and traveled to the sign above his desk, the sign with the one word. "Think!"

"Didn't have anything else to say?" queried the doctor mildly after a moment. "Nothing about developments in the case?"

Thornton shook his head.

"No, just talked a minute with him; inconsequentials—asked what I'd been doing, I think—whether I was out this morning—"

"What?" the word jerked from the doctor suddenly.

Thornton started.

"What?" he repeated, and laughed: "What—what?" And grinned at the doctor's heavy face.

Doctor Lester shook his head.

"Getting batty," he grumbled; "what were you saying—something about the chief, wasn't it?"

Thornton nodded.

"Nothing," he laughed; "you'd better quit worrying about cases and come to earth. You're a nice one to preach the ill effects of too much work," he laughed.

The doctor growled, and picked up a history sheet

from the desk before him.

"*Vamose*," he grunted. "I just wanted you to become acquainted with the embryonic Sherlock Holmes, that's all. And I've got to get to work."

Thornon rose to his feet.

"Thanks, old man, for telling me. I'd rather know it if I'm to be shadowed about," and, as the doctor nodded absently, he queried: "But how did you know it?"

"Mae's friend was on the job first," the doctor explained, and smiled; "she thought you ought to know." He raised his voice slightly. "Damned good sort, Mae," he grunted, "and don't forget she's going to be a party of the first part to a wedding ceremony soon."

Thornton nodded.

"It *was* nice of her." He looked at the doctor a moment. "Why did she tell you, do you think?"

The doctor laughed his rumbling laugh.

"Well, sonny, maybe she wants to see you safely through," he advised finally, with which cryptic utterance he turned to rewrap his operating instruments carefully.

Thornton stood silent a moment, gazing down on the big man in the chair.

"I think I know what you mean," he smiled. "And—and—Lester!"

The doctor looked up.

"Shoot it," he advised, "what's up all of a sudden?"

Thornton grinned as though embarrassed. "I'm—I'm going to do it, too—to-night!"

The doctor's heavy laugh and bellowed "Go to it!" followed Thornton as he left the room.

After the door was closed, however, the doctor sat gazing absently at his one word motto, puffing thoughtfully on a cigarette which he had not even lighted.

"But, dammit all," he growled, "I saw him myself!"

XVIII. Jackson Observes a Phenomenon

THORNTON did not lunch with Doctor Lester, despite that gentleman's reiterated grumbling comment that any man who worked on Sundays — except, of course, doctors—was a fit subject for an alienist's attentions.

Instead, Thornton pottered about in his laboratory, although he knew himself that he accomplished but little. He looked forward tremblingly to the coming of night and rehearsed many speeches in his laboratory, speeches which were to be delivered to Isabel Brannon—the gods willing.

In the late afternoon he left his office and made for the street, recognizing in the doorway the dour-eyed Jackson.

On the sidewalk Thornton stopped before his machine and motioned to the detective. There was no way for Jackson to ignore the gesture, so he shuffled forward, mentally casting about for some accredited line of action under the unusual circumstances.

"You might as well come with me," Thornton laughed. "I'm going home to dress, and then to call on a lady."

"Say, you tryin' to kid me?" The detective's eyes met Thornton's laughing ones.

"Heavens, no!" Thornton smiled politely. "I am merely telling you. There's room in my car. You see,

I'm going all the way to Riverside," he explained, "and you'd never be able to keep up with me, you know. And if you just must watch me, why —come along. I live in the Riverside Apartments, as you perhaps know, and I'm going there. Hop in."

"By cripes, I will!" Jackson swaggered around the car and let himself into the rumble seat behind the roadster. And, as Thornton dropped into the driver's seat and pressed the starter with his foot, the detective muttered: "But don't you try to start nothin' funny, young feller, or—"

The car shot forward and the detective grabbed the seat in front of him. He felt extremely foolish, perched behind Thornton in the automobile, and hoped that he would not be seen by any of his acquaintances from headquarters.

It was bad enough to be detailed to follow a man who explained carefully his destination and the reasons for it, but to accompany him was worse still, and not in accordance—as Jackson well knew—with the best precedents.

Something was awry, that he knew definitely, but what it was he had no more idea than the unconcerned pedestrians on the streets. He puzzled the thing over as he sat perched in his seat and concluded that, while this method of procedure on the part of a detective might not be in accord with the recognized and professional technique, at least it had its advantages.

The automobile turned down Forsythe Street and continued into Bay. Thornton, busy with his driving, paid no attention to the man behind him. He twisted the car expertly in the traffic of Bay Street and guided it carefully through the congestion at Broad then turned, with a sudden burst of speed, up the sharply inclined viaduct.

In a few moments he was rolling easily down Riverside Avenue, to bring up, a moment later, before the much decorated front of the Riverside Apartments.

Here Thornton climbed out, locked the car, nodded to the detective and remarked casually: "I'm going in for a while," he explained, "to change clothes. Then I'm going out to Ortega to have dinner with a—er—young lady. You can come in or wait here, just as you please."

Jackson muttered something inarticulate and climbed down on the opposite side of the car. It had begun to sink through his thick skull that his position was hardly dignified, but he didn't know what to do about it.

Thornton swung into his apartment, let himself in and commenced to dress.

The detective followed half-heartedly a moment later, and stood before Thornton's door. Here he heard snatches of song rising above the splashing of water, and then the cheerful whistling of a man very much pleased with himself, or whistling to keep his courage up.

The detective lounged uneasily in the hallway and wondered what course would be the best to pursue. It had grown almost dark when the brilliant idea occurred to him to get in touch with the chief of detectives, report, and demand instructions. That would relieve him of the necessity of acting on his own initiative, and if Thornton were indeed going, as he said, to Ortega, several miles beyond, Jackson could scarcely see the necessity for shadowing him, especially if the shadowing was to be done from the back seat of Thornton's roadster.

With a glance at Thornton's closed door the detective emerged into the street, cast suspicious glances about him, eyed Thornton's windows for one speculative moment, then turned to swagger a short distance down the street to a garage.

The chief was not in his office, he was informed, and he tried the chief's residence.

He had not, however, returned, and Jackson walked slowly into the street before the garage, hurried to make sure that the lights in Thornton's apartment had not been darkened while he was telephoning, his beetle-brow deeply corrugated with the effort of thinking.

The garage manager became immediately suave and polite at the sight of Jackson's badge. The latter demanded an automobile, determined to follow Thornton wherever he went. But he decided also that it did not become an officer of the law to associate too closely with a potential criminal which Thornton was, so Jackson concluded.

He did not, for an instant, doubt that Thornton's open-handed invitation to accompany him was anything save a deep laid plot of dire import, and he started suddenly with a furtive look about as though half-expecting ah ambush in the quiet garage.

The garage manager offered two cars, already mentally figuring the items of the bill he would present to the detective department on the following day, and Jackson picked the smaller of the two, one that he was certain he could drive without mishap.

With a great show of secrecy, he demanded that the tank be filled to the top, signed the receipt tendered him by the manager, rolled the car in front of the garage, felt carefully and ostentatiously of his hip-pocket, started the engine and leaned back in his seat, ready for anything; regretting only that there was not some official superior to behold the sagacious manner in which he had made ready for the pursuit of Thornton.

Some time later Thornton emerged from the apartment, immaculate in evening clothes. The detective, who in the meantime had taken up a position across the street, with the automobile carefully parked around a near-by corner, watched closely as Thornton donned a large, loose automobile-duster, and gazed about for the detective.

Thornton seemed in no hurry to enter his car, for he stood some time on the sidewalk leisurely smoking. Then he turned to his automobile.

The ride to Ortega was uneventful and the detective thanked his stars that the road was smooth and the engine in the hood of his car running well. There was no question but that Officer Jackson, of the Jacksonville detective department, was obeying orders literally and exactly.

Thornton, a short distance ahead of Jackson, had no thoughts for anything save his destination. The detective had not entered his thoughts, nor did he make any effort to ascertain whether he was followed.

But when his auto turned into the broad drive leading to the Brannon home, he might have seen, had he turned, a figure dodging furtively through the trees, and might have heard, had he been near enough, a puzzled muttering from the detective, muttering which took the form of:

"Well, he didn't lie about it, anyhow."

But Thornton's thoughts were far removed from the detective—and even from steel vaults. And his eyes were only for the girl who stood on the dimly lighted veranda and the welcoming hand she extended to him.

Perhaps five hundred times in his life Thornton had so seen her, yet never before had there been—so it seemed to him—the same quickly returned pressure of her slender fingers, nor had she ever, in his eyes, appeared quite so desirably wonderful.

"You look well, Mr. Chemist." The girl's compliment sent an unaccustomed flush to his cheek.

"I feel well, lady," he smiled, "and why shouldn't I?"

The girl disclaimed any knowledge, and together they entered the house, while the detective, gazing in true sleuth fashion from behind a tree, scratched his head in perplexity.

He wandered once around the long low house; then returned to his place. Here he stood for some minutes, wondering whether it would be advisable to go any nearer the lighted windows which gleamed so brightly before him, and which were but a few feet from the ground. He debated the question seriously and decided definitely against the idea.

After a while he made his way to his automobile, drove it carefully into the trees that encroached on the driveway, smoked a preliminary cigarette, and leaned back in his seat, contemplating with no small amount of grumbling the possibility of a several-hour wait and speculating on whether the chief would send a relief for him when he returned to the apartment.

An hour later found him pacing restlessly about, cursing his luck and trying to recall some reason why he should not at least return to the city for dinner and then again take up his watch. Against this idea he also decided, remembering that his orders had come direct from the chief, and doubting not that in good time the chief would discover his predicament and send him aid.

After another century of waiting, and just as he had decided to look into the lighted windows and ascertain whether Thornton was visible, the detective drew up abruptly as two figures descended from the porch and came toward him across the lawn. He recognized immediately, in the now bright moonlight, Thornton and the girl. Thornton was bareheaded and the bosom of his dress-shirt gleamed plainly in the light, while the girl's dress seemed wraithlike and elusive.

The detective rubbed his eyes and stared and the couple, oblivious of his presence, turned to one side and continued along the walk which led around the house. In another moment the house itself hid them from the detective's sight.

Jackson sighed his relief as he carefully followed. This was a job he could understand, and his orders were to keep an eye on Thornton.

When he passed the out jutting veranda in the rear he once more saw Thornton and the girl making their way to the river. Jackson followed, taking advantage of the shadows thrown by the long lines of evergreen bushes of the lawn.

He drew closer to the moving couple as they drifted into the darkness of the river-bank, where the overhanging branches of the weeping willows shut out and dimmed the moonlight.

Jackson harbored no illusory romantic ideas, and he mumbled his disapproval of any man foolish enough to wander along a darkened river-bank when he might sit in comfort in a house as pleasant as the Brannon home seemed to be. But he followed tenaciously and with considerable skill the meandering couple, never for an instant losing sight of them, although it seemed to him that they were making unnecessarily slow progress.

It was almost a relief when he saw the man and girl seat themselves on a bench that faced the river, and Jackson carefully took up a position behind an accommodating sycamore some fifteen yards removed from the river-bank.

He took up again his train of wondering how long this ridiculous assignment was going to last. Mr. Jackson of headquarters had just begun to realize that his watching of Thornton was ridiculous; it had never before been his experience to shadow a man who seemed quite willing to be followed, and who cared so little about the fact that he invited the shadower to accompany him, after giving him a careful and complete itinerary of his contemplated movements.

For a long time there was a silence between Thornton and the girl as they sat together. Then, in a neighboring marsh, the frogs struck up their nightly discord, and their hoarse croaking broke the stillness: "Co-ax, co-ax, co-ax." The detective crouched against his tree, grumbling against the disconcerting and continued croaking.

The girl smiled slightly to herself.

"I love to hear them," she ventured softly, apropos of nothing. "And they never fail. They remind me always of Aristophanes' play."

Thornton nodded absently and Mr. Jackson of headquarters leaned stiffly against his tree.

"Do you really think," the girl continued quietly, "that they are saying anything?"

Thornton lifted his head.

"What was it, Isabel? Oh—the frogs, you mean," and they listened in silence to the continued croaking which arose from the marsh.

The girl thoughtfully studied the man beside her, and Thornton was entirely oblivious to her scrutiny. He had relapsed again into an absent study of the river at their feet,'gazing moodily across the swiftly hurrying water. The girl sighed a little, but he paid no heed, and finally she spoke again:

"Still worrying, Hal?"

He shook his head.

"Why, no, Isabel—not any more than usual." Thornton turned to her, but turned as quickly away again. "Well, yes, then, I am worried."

The girl nodded slightly, seeming aware of what he spoke.

"And don't you think they will catch him? Surely he can't just go on and on without somebody—" she glanced quickly into Thornton's eyes as he turned to her again, and a puzzled expression came into her face as Thornton laughed shortly.

"Oh, yes, they'll get him, I suppose. Why, they are even watching me."

"No?" The girl was incredulous and Thornton, seeming to shake his lassitude from him with an effort, spoke again.

"Oh, yes, there's some evil-faced individual trailing me about; at least, there was this morning. It seems that the detective department thinks I might have had a hand in it."

"But why?" The girl turned again to look directly into Thornton's face. "Why, Hal? What makes them think so?"

Thornton shrugged.

"How should I know, Isabel? The ways of detectives are past finding out, you know—like the ways of a woman."

The girl glanced covertly at the man, but Thornton was again looking out over the river, where the frogs, having silenced their croaking for a while, had once again resumed their eternal: "Co-ax, co-ax, co-ax."

Jackson shifted his position awkwardly behind his tree, wondering if it was Thornton's intention to remain on the bench for the balance of the night.

Thornton did not seem disposed to speak, and finally the girl began again:

"What else is it, Hal? Something is the matter, I know." There was genuine concern in her low voice.

He shook his head.

"Nothing, Isabel; nothing—"

The girl drew imperceptibly closer to him, and a white hand gleamed on the black of his coat-sleeve.

"There is, Hal; I know;" the girl's voice was very low. "Aren't we pals any more, Hal? A year ago you would have told me."

Thornton's hand closed spasmodically.

"I—I know I would have, little lady;" and the girl smiled at the familiar address; "just as I—as I —as I will tell you now."

"Yes?" The little hand on the man's arm closed slightly, closed encouragingly on the hard forearm beneath it.

Suddenly the man turned, and his own hand covered the girl's.

"Good God, Isabel! Don't you see—can't you see? Look at me!" he cried fiercely. "Look at me! Now—do you see—do you understand—sweetheart?"

A little gasp from the girl was his answer and for a moment he was frightened at his own vehemence.

Then her voice came to him, infinitely sweet:

"It—it—it took you a long time, boy! Oh, why did you wait?" Her face was hidden on his shoulder, and all the pent-up feeling of his heart went into the little oft-repeated endearments he whispered into her hair.

When finally she raised her eyes to the man, a great light burned far in their depths, and the bullet-headed Jackson of headquarters beheld a phenomenon—for the moon cast only one bulky shadow on the ground before the bench.

XIX. Ralby Elucidates

NOT once in all the long drive back to his apartment, a drive which led along the boulevard skirting the river, did Thornton know that behind him lurched the automobile of the bullet-headed detective; not even when—on occasions—the momentary brilliant flash of a search-light crossed his path as the pursuing auto wound about the numberless curves, making it imperative for the detective to switch on his headlights to prevent catapulting into the river beneath him.

A misty, hazy fog obscured the moon, and the stars twinkled uncertainly through the gossamer drift, the river reflecting their radiance in a dimmed, ghostly fashion.

For Thornton it was a night of wonder, and he reveled in the breeze that swept in from the river, heavy with the odor of pines. The stars to him had never seemed so brightly numerous—this despite the unnoticed fog—nor had the moon ever held the same inexplicable brilliance. Even the branches of the palm trees seemed to sway toward him as he drove by, and the dust that arose from the avenue beneath his turning wheels went, for the time being, unnoticed.

Thornton drove mechanically, with no conscious thought or effort, and the wind, whistling across his lowered wind-shield, caught and flung back to the pursuing detective strange snatches of song, hilarious and uncalled for, so the detective thought as he bent low over the wheel of his machine striving to keep well in sight of the lights of Thornton's car ahead of him.

Thornton turned into Riverside Avenue, passed the Riverside Apartments, and, at the garage beyond, left his car, shouting a cheery good night to the yawning negro boy who came out, as the detective's car shot past him unheeded.

Jackson brought his machine to a grinding stop a half block beyond, carefully backed and turned, and parked the borrowed automobile near by. Then he made his way along the opposite side of the street from the apartment, until he came abreast of Thornton's lighted windows.

Here he took up his position, mentally determining that he would remain until it appeared beyond doubt that Thornton was in for the night, after which he would endeavor to get into communication with the chief to discover whether he was expected to remain on his post until morning.

So the bullet-headed detective loitered complainingly in the shadows, giving vent to his uncomplimentary thoughts of a chief of detectives who would leave a subordinate for hours without orders, and who sent no relief to that subordinate when he had been steadily on his job for an interminable string of hours.

Jackson began to have faint glimmerings of the reason that moved Thornton to invite him to accompany him, reasons that took the shape, eventually, of a feeling of certainty that—whatever Thornton might be—he contemplated nothing nefarious on this night; hence, argued the detective, his willingness not only to be watched, but to be constantly accompanied by the watcher.

What had taken place on the Brannon lawn the detective did not know. Romance was not in his make-up, and to him the girl and man who had sat so utterly oblivious to their surroundings for such an unholily long time, a time so long that the detective had shivered in the cool night wind, and had become cramped and cold from his vigil, were only "two blasted fools," not to be either understood or counted in the detective's scheme of things.

He noted, with small curiosity, Ralby's arrival at the house a moment later, saw him glance sharply at Thornton's lighted windows, and, in a moment, saw another light appear several stories up in the apartment-house, a light which, the detective reasoned, came from Ralby's apartment.

Then he became aware of another furtive figure drawing closer to the apartment-house across the street, and he watched interestedly as the man sidled up to the house, stood as if hesitating a moment, and then continued up the street.

Jackson's eyes followed the man until he was lost in the darkness, and just as the detective with a shrug was giving up the puzzle of who it might have been, a whistle behind him brought him to startled attention; then followed the whispered call:

"Hey, Jacks."

A grin overspread the detective's face. It seemed that the chief had not forgotten him after all, and he sent back a tentative:

"Yeh—where are you?"

A figure detached itself from the side of the house, a figure which Jackson immediately recognized as that of the man he had seen passing the apartment but a moment since, and Hanson, the officer of the preternaturally long face and earnest demeanor, approached Jackson.

"Well," Jackson greeted surlily. "Do I get a relief or don't I?" He had small love for the other detective, whom he had often classified as "too damn highbrow," and he turned for the man's answer.

The recently arrived detective only smiled quietly.

"I don't know, I'm sure," he answered politely. "I'm watching the man who just went in there, a Mr. Ralby."

Jackson snorted his disgust at the other's tone.

"An' 'r' you goin' to hang around here all night?" he demanded.

Hanson smiled again. His smile was chronic.

"Well, perhaps," he admitted. He held a watch up to catch a light reflection on the crystal. "I was told to report to the chief at one o'clock," he advised. "It is only a few minutes past midnight."

"We both report then," Jackson grunted, and turned to survey the silent street.

Ralby's light snapped out, and, had the detectives' point of observation been the inside of the apartment-house, they might have seen Ralby coming down the darkened stairway, pause a moment at Thornton's door and knock.

Thornton, struggling with his collar, called, "Come in," and, as Ralby entered, closing the door behind him carefully, Thornton turned a radiantly smiling face to the man.

"Well, old man," Thornton chuckled, "congratulate me."

It seemed that Ralby misunderstood for a

moment, for he frowned slightly as he put the question:

"Congratulate? Have you worked out your steel problem?"

Thornton laughed happily.

"Steel? Good lord, no!" He turned his eyes to a photograph on the table, a duplicate of the picture which decorated Ralby's bookcase. "That's the reason."

Ralby jerked erect.

"When?" There was unquestioned eagerness in his voice now.

"To-night; a little while ago." And Thornton grasped Ralby's outstretched hand.

"By George, I do congratulate you. It's—it's great. Maybe that isn't some news to tickle the doctor with, eh?" He eyed Thornton quizzically. Thornton, still smiling, sank into a chair by the table.

"Have a seat," he invited. "Man, but I'm glad you dropped in; couldn't go to sleep to save my life." He smiled fatuously. "Just get in?"

Ralby nodded as he took a chair directly opposite Thornton. "Just this minute. Feeling rather wide awake myself."

Thornton lighted a cigarette and impatiently threw it aside, and almost immediately lighted another.

Ralby watched the man opposite in silence for a minute, then continued:

"Saw Bernice and Max to-night; Max inquired about you. I had told him you were somewhat under the weather."

Thornton nodded and stretched both arms in an all-embracing gesture.

"Feel great, Ralby—absolutely never felt better in my life." He laughed aloud at Ralby's expression. "Why don't you try it?" Thornton chuckled. "Greatest little panacea for human ills that ever was, Ralby," he rambled on, not noting the gleam in Ralby's eyes, nor the slight frown which corrugated his forehead.

Finally Ralby looked at the man opposite.

"I'm not a kill-joy, Hal, but, remember, 'there's many a slip.'" There was a nuance of prophecy and bitterness in Ralby's light tone, but Thornton took no heed.

"And how about your steel proposition?" Ralby questioned, blowing rings of smoke toward the ceiling.

Thornton seemed not to hear, or at least seemed uninterested.

"Isn't she the most adorable—" His eyes were on the picture before him, and Ralby smiled leniently in a superior, tolerant fashion.

"Oh, well then—if you just must talk of the lady. When is the big event to be?"

"Haven't decided." Thornton dropped his half-smoked cigarette into an ash-tray and arose to pace the room restlessly. "But soon—yes, man—soon. Think of it! I've known her nearly all my life, and it took this long to—"

Ralby's laugh cut into his monologue.

"Going to announce it, aren't you?"

"Sure; in the morning. Say, don't mention it to Lester if you see him before I do. I want to spring this on him myself," and Thornton chuckled with anticipatory pleasure.

Ralby nodded.

"Afraid it won't be news to him, though," he

commented, and Thornton only laughed.

"Lord, I've been blind," he smiled, "blind as a bat; but whoever would have thought—"

"Oh, come to earth," Ralby bantered with a show of good nature, and, as Thornton resumed his seat, Ralby reached for a fresh cigarette and continued: "Any new developments to-day in the matter of the robbery?" he questioned casually. "Or the robberies, rather, since our friend seems to have gone in for it on the wholesale plan."

"None that I know of, except that there's an ass from police headquarters that has been following me around."

"Following you?" Ralby seemed interested.

"Started this morning, I think. Lester introduced me to the gentleman," and with much gusto he related the manner in which the doctor had accomplished the introduction of Mr. Jackson from headquarters.

Ralby pondered the readily volunteered information.

"It is a bit funny," he remarked at length, "that they should have picked you out. Now if it had been me, there might have been some reason. I don't think I personally stand exactly ace high with the chief."

"What's the difference?" laughed Thornton. "He no doubt felt that he had to make a bluff of doing something, and perhaps Lester's explanation is the right one."

Ralby's face expressed a query.

"Lester says," Thornton explained, "that I talked too much, and the chief got suspicious."

Ralby nodded.

"He had a right to, I think. You did boast pretty loudly, you remember." And as Thornton did not reply, Ralby rose slowly to his feet: "Well, it looks as though I'm in five hundred from our medico friend," he smiled.

"I hope you're not," Thornton commented. "I'm afraid, however, that you stand a pretty good chance to win."

Ralby picked up a richly bound book from the table, riffled the pages, and played with it absently. "This the sort of stuff you read?" He glanced at the title and turned to Thornton.

Thornton leaned over, looking at the book.

"What is it?" he asked, and took the book from Ralby. On the cover he read: *Memoirs of a Physician*; and below, the author, Alexandre Dumas. "No," he shook his head, placing the book on the table. "That's one of Lester's. He's amusing himself with Dumas lately; swears he's going to wade through an entire twenty-eight-volume edition."

Ralby dismissed the subject with a shrug. He lingered, however, by the table, as though he wanted to speak of something else, and seemed uncertain what to say first.

At last he began:

"Don't think I'm an infernal meddler, Thornton," he apologized embarrassedly, gesturing with a cigarette. "But this news of you and Isabel—well, it's interesting," he finished lamely.

Thornton nodded. He could see that there was something else Ralby had to say of the matter, and he was only too glad of any occasion to talk of that which was, at that moment, nearest to his heart and to his mind.

"I know you both pretty well," Ralby continued uneasily, "and I'd like to see you two—oh, dammit, Thornton," he grinned ruefully, "can't I ever talk any more?"

Thornton laughed.

"What are you driving at? I haven't the least idea. If I knew I'd help."

"Well," Ralby continued slowly, methodically opening and closing a book on the table, "about this marriage business, Thornton. It's a whole lot—well —it's more, a bigger thing, something larger than most of you young people think it is."

Thornton raised serious eyes to the man opposite him.

"I know, Ralby, and I don't think you're butting in where you've no business. Fact is, I'm glad you spoke of it, not that"—Thornton grinned—"your great age makes you any more capable." He chuckled aloud as Ralby smiled. Ralby's three years' seniority hardly seemed much to Thornton. "But you know a lot more than I ever will, Ralby, about—well—about sex psychology, and all that sort of thing. Don't think I'm just a darned fool, Ralby. I'm simply a little light-headed to-night—happiness, I suppose, but I know that there's more—as you say—to it than just marrying, settling down, and living happily ever after."

Ralby, still standing, nodded with averted face.

"You're right, there is, Thornton, and, if you'll let me, I'd like to lend you a book or two which you ought to see."

Thornton looked his appreciation.

"Sit down, won't you?" he invited. "You're not tired, I know."

Ralby took the indicated chair.

"Lester can tell you about all these things—oh, all sorts of reactions—" he gestured with his cigarette, "and he doubtless will. But, remember, Hal, Lester's a medical man, and bound more or less by the often stupid contentions of the materialistic school to which he belongs."

Thornton was gazing thoughtfully at the table, listening interestedly, and Ralby continued quietly and earnestly:

"There is more than just what is material," he said slowly, his voice dropping to a colorless drawl, "and it was Havelock Ellis, I think, in one of his volumes of the *Studies*, who took up the question of marriage, and handled it infinitely better than—"

XX. With the Goods

MR. JACKSON of headquarters kicked viciously against a telegraph post and snapped a finished cigarette into the street.

"Say, ain't it time yet?"

His colleague, Hanson, raised studious eyes from the ground which he had been contemplating for fifteen minutes.

"Time? Oh, to report, you mean. You're rather impatient, Jackson."

"Impatient!" snorted Jackson disgustedly. "If you'd been on this silly watch as long as I have you'd be worse than impatient; you'd be mighty damned sore, that's what. Here I chase a guy all over the state of Florida for a day—a guy, mind you, who *knows* I'm chasing him and don't give a whoop—and then stand out here in this blankety-blank street for another half year, with no relief in sight! You're mighty right I'm impatient! I'm impatient to eat." Jackson thought hungrily of the down-town restaurants.

Hanson yawned slightly, and held his watch up to catch the moonlight.

"Five minutes of one," he advised. "What is it you desire me to say to the chief for you?"

"I don't desire nothin'," Jackson snapped in answer. "You tell him I want relief from this job out here *pronto*, or he might as well send an undertaker for me in the mornin'. I'll be starved."

Hanson permitted himself the luxury of an amused smile at the bullet-headed detective's rare

humor. Hanson could afford to smile; he had dined
well, previous to following Ralby to the apartment,
and Jackson seemed to divine the fact.

"That's right, grin!" he growled. "You ain't got no
better sense nohow—grin, dammit!" And he stormed
off up the street, careful, however, not to get too far
from the apartment-house.

Hanson leisurely watched the irate Jackson turn
about and prepare again to take up his tirade,
whereupon he yawned impolitely, and walked in the
direction of the garage near by, from there to get in
communication with the chief of detectives and
report; also to request relief for his wrathful
colleague.

"Huh," Jackson snorted, as the darkness engulfed
Hanson, "now maybe somebody else can come out
and rubber at the front of that house for a while."

And Jackson produced a cigar—his last—and
clamped his tobacco-stained teeth down hard on the
end.

It was no part of Jackson's program to remain
there all night and he impatiently waited the return
of the slow Hanson, the while he wondered casually,
and finally interestedly, why Thornton's light—
which had been burning the better part of an hour—
should not yet have been extinguished.

For just an instant it crossed his twenty-two-
caliber mind that it might be a good thing to
endeavor to take a peep into the windows. This
thought however was soon dismissed. Initiative was
no outstanding part of the detective's character, and
he chewed his cigar impatiently, envisioning sundry
delectable viands with which he would regale
himself when a substitute arrived.

He scowled in the direction of the garage, into which Hanson had disappeared, and mumbled his intense disapproval of "any man with a face like a horse and the brain of a peanut, who didn't have no better sense than—"

The mutter stuck in his bull-neck, and his eyes popped open as he stared across the street.

Thornton had come out of the apartment—the light in his room remaining burning—and stood in the doorway for a moment, as though undecided what to do. Then he turned north, walking leisurely up Riverside Avenue.

Jackson found voice:

"Now what in the name of the devil—" he groaned aloud, watching the disappearing figure of Thornton.

Then he turned to look toward the garage, but there was yet no sign of a returning Hanson. For an instant Jackson was tempted to let Thornton go where he pleased without surveillance, but the habit of obedience was strong, and, cursing his luck in no uncertain terms, the detective hurried across the street and began to follow the man ahead.

"An" he's gonna walk," the detective growled, chewing his cigar, as Thornton made no effort to turn in the direction of the garage, but, instead, continued slowly and leisurely up the avenue in the general direction of the city.

Twice beneath faintly sputtering arc-lights Jackson dived hurriedly behind a near-by tree, fearful lest the man ahead of him should grow suspicious and turn suddenly, and, though his steps made no sound, Jackson rose frequently to tiptoe forward with painful silence that he might make sure it was indeed Thornton he was following, and not some other resident of the apartment-house.

On lower Riverside Avenue the long lines of electric sidewalk lights brightly illuminated the deserted street, and, when Thornton hesitated for an instant at the approach to the viaduct which led to Broad Street, Jackson flattened himself painfully against a wall, peering intently forward.

The man before him, however, seemed to resolve on a definite course, and began again to walk slowly on, while Jackson crept behind him, squeezing himself against the walls and windows of the stores he passed to reduce his visibility to a minimum should Thornton suddenly stop and wheel about.

Beneath the viaduct a passenger-train shot with a loud screeching from its engine. The suddenly shattered silence echoed with the sound, and Jackson swore violently under his breath. The man who walked in front of him, however, seemed in nowise startled by the sudden ear-splitting noise, and, when they crossed Broad Street, near the center of the city, the detective was close enough to notice that Thornton had changed from his evening clothes, and that he was now wearing a dark sack suit.

Jackson drew breathlessly closer to his quarry as he continued along Broad Street to Forsythe, and ran silently forward as the figure turned sharply down Forsythe Street, fearful of losing his man.

On peering around the corner, however, he breathed a sigh of relief to see Thornton still continuing his leisurely stroll, and Jackson now crossed boldly to the opposite side of the street, from where he kept almost abreast of the walking man.

Only occasionally did any one pass, and then Thornton seemed to pay them no attention whatever, but continued nonchalantly on, as though certain of his destination and of arriving there in due time to accomplish whatever purpose he had in mind.

At one corner, Jackson wigwagged a greeting to a drowsy policeman, and nodded his head in the direction of Thornton, to explain his haste.

And still making apparently not the slightest effort to hide his movements, Thornton crossed the street at a sharp angle, while the detective, grown tense now, drew closer and closer to the unsuspecting figure.

And when Thornton stopped abruptly before the ornate building of the Second National Bank, the detective was but a few feet behind, literally holding his breath with excitement.

Thornton turned to go around the building, and the detective's eyes blazed eagerly as he stopped at the entrance to the areaway on which the Second National Bank building backed.

Here it was darker, but the detective's ears, grown suddenly keen, heard the unmistakable jingle of keys, and the shadow which had indicated Thornton to his eyes disappeared suddenly, followed immediately by a slight creaking noise, as that of a door carefully closed.

The detective hurried forward into the darkness and reached the alleyway. He turned quickly to the small door which led into the rear of the bank building, and, with a strained, eager expression on his face, he twisted the knob slowly, pushing easily against the door.

It resisted his efforts, and he muttered a soft curse. For a second he hesitated, then dashed out and around the building to the front doors. Edging gently around a pillar, the detective pressed his face close to the glass panels of a door, but could make out nothing within. The building stood silent and empty, and no sound came to the bullet-headed detective as he slipped quietly down the steps.

He dived across the street into an all-night lunchroom and snatched at a telephone. While he waited, moving about impatiently, he kept one keen eye on the door of the bank across the street. Irritably he jangled at the receiver, and barked commandingly at the operator: "Keep ringing—it's important!"

In a moment the connection was made, and a drowsy voice came across the wire.

"Yes—yes," panted Jackson into the instrument, keenly alive with the excitement of it, "went into the bank—saw him myself—the back way—I'm talking from Demos's place—yeh—all right—all right."

An interested waiter inquired what was up, and Jackson, as though the sight of the white-coated man had suddenly reminded him of something, growled an order from the doorway, and stood there impatiently while it was filled. Then he recrossed the street, taking huge bites from sandwiches in his hand, and literally choking with the impatience of his wait.

An automobile slowed up from the direction of Main Street and jerked to a halt, and the half-dressed chief of detectives jumped out.

"No, he ain't come out—went in the back I tell you—yes, sir, with a key. 'Course I'm sure it's him—ain't I been on his trail all day?"

"All right; you keep an eye out," was the chief's

superlative advice to his subordinate, and the chief in turn took his position at the telephone in the café. The waiter, now knowing that something was undoubtedly going on, appeared in the doorway, volubly offering aid.

In a very few minutes a second automobile drew up before the café, and the bank president arrived, followed almost immediately by a half dozen plain-clothes men from headquarters, among whom was Franklin.

Jackson, swollen visibly from the effects of the sudden spotlight in which he found himself, gave the details of the trip from Riverside, a trip which Jackson made—according to himself—with a revolver in one hand and a flashlight in the other, ready for any and all contingencies.

"And he's *in* there?" gasped the banker.

"He is," nodded Jackson dramatically.

The chief turned to Franklin and another of the men.

"You two take the areaway; watch that doorway, and stop any one who comes out. If he don't stop on order—shoot!"

Franklin turned to obey, followed by the other man detailed, to whom Franklin confided in no uncertain terms that Jackson had been the victim of a sudden nightmare, and that, furthermore, Jackson was a complete and utter ass, and that—still further —Thornton was no doubt safely asleep in his own apartment; and the furtive figure which Jackson shadowed from Riverside so stealthily and belligerently was none other than some harmless citizen returning from a late game of draw poker.

The chief, meanwhile, placed men at each of the

bank's doors, and, taking the keys extended by the banker, he motioned to Jackson and the bank president to follow him. Very carefully he made his way up the wide steps, and unlocked one of the large front doors; he swung it open but the smallest space and squeezed into the bank, followed by the financier and Jackson, who crouched in the most approved fashion and carried a tremendous forty-five in one hand.

With infinite care the chief closed the door behind him, and the three men drew breath sharply as a slight squeak met the chief's efforts silently to close the door.

They stood huddled together in the interior of the bank building breathing softly. Not a sound broke the silence, and Jackson covered his heart with a huge paw, wondering why the sound of it was not disturbing the other two men.

"I wonder," the banker whispered, "I wonder where Jensen is. He ought to be right—"

A rough hand on his mouth, the chief's hand, was his answer, and he bit his lips silently.

The chief leading the way, the three crept carefully around toward the left, and past the long row of tellers' cages. Once they heard a sharp click, metallic and penetrating, and held their breaths anxiously, and once Jackson gave voice to a whispered "damn" as he all but collided with a writing stand on the bank floor.

The chief stopped dead in his tracks in the deep gloom as a circle of light appeared outlined on the enormous closed door of the vault and traveled slowly to the clock above.

The banker gasped.

"Look at the clock." His whisper seemed to Jackson considerably louder than a shout, and again that warning hand descended on the banker's mouth, as they strained their eyes to see the manipulator of the flashlight.

Jackson gazed pop-eyed at the brightly illuminated clock. The hands stood at eight-thirty, the hour at which the vault could be opened by the combinations, and the detective felt a vague panic of something being entirely wrong as he gazed fascinated until the light disappeared as suddenly as it had come, leaving the darkness more thickly intense.

The chief drew a revolver from his pocket and held it grimly before him, leaning forward with a sudden tenseness as there came a tiny squeak—as that of a man endeavoring to walk silently and stepping on a bit of bad flooring. The floor on which the men stood was tiled, but behind the tellers' cages it was of wood, so the watchers remained motionless for a long minute listening strainedly for a repetition of the sound.

A few steps farther on, and a crouching figure could be made out bending over the dials of the combinations of the vault, endeavoring to see them without the aid of a light. From the ventilating space above there filtered the tiniest ray of soft gray. The chief of detectives' hand trembled with eagerness.

Again that tiny circle of light flashed on the glistening vault surface. The man worked silently and steadily, and, while the watchers gazed with amazement, there came a soft sound as of the sliding of heavy bolts.

The banker's own hand covered his mouth—

covered it to prevent a startled outcry. There was something familiar in that almost silent slide as the huge bolts of the immense vault dropped from their grooves in answer to the manipulated combinations.

The man before the vault backed slowly away a few paces and stood quiet an instant, while the three breathless watchers having reached the end of the tiled flooring dared make no farther step in his direction.

A spasm of apprehension twisted Jackson's face as the figure at the vault straightened slowly from his stooped position, but the man did not turn, only stood gazing at the door for the smallest fraction of an instant.

Then he stepped forward—a bundle of shadows merely—and only the banker recognized the metallic clang that echoed through the bank, a clang that bespoke the fact that the steel floor plate directly in front of the circular door had dropped to a lower level to permit the swinging open of the door itself.

The watchers gasped in amazement as the inert thing of steel suddenly seemed to acquire life, and the eight-ply steel door of the Second National Bank vault began to sway open slowly on its tremendous hinges.

The chief raised his revolver at the precise instant that the electric globes in the domed ceiling of the bank leaped to life, stabbing the dark with a blinding flood of brilliance—

"Hands up!"

It was the voice of Jensen, the night watchman, from the other side of the bank vault. A quick flash of the watchman's eyes revealed the three unconsciously crouching men on the opposite side, headed by the detective chief with his revolver extended menacingly.

The tableau lasted but an instant.

The man at the vault-door seemed to cringe, sway forward and suddenly jerk upright, blinking in the glaring electric light.

"Got 'im!" exulted the chief, leaping forward.

"Got 'im with the goods!"

XXI. To the Rescue

THE early gray dawn filtered through the branches of the sycamore trees that grew about the windows of Doctor Lester's bedroom, and threw a ghastly light into the room, vaguely outlining its furnishings.

Breathing in a stentorian fashion, a checkered quilt drawn high over his huge shoulders, Doctor Lester slept heavily. On his face was an expression of cherubic peace and contentment, and the quilt rose and fell regularly over his barrel-like chest.

The telephone on a small stand by the doctor's bed rang sharply and insistently, and the doctor turned grumblingly in the bed which creaked beneath him as he slid farther under the cover in an effort to shut out the sound of the telephone.

For a moment there was silence; then the jangling began again, and, half awake, the doctor reached out one short arm for the instrument. Laboriously he hoisted himself upright, and grunted sleepily:

"H'lo—yes—Doctor Lester—uhuh!"

Then his drowsiness dropped from him magic-like and he jerked tense in the creaking bed. "What's that—what's that? Man, you're crazy! Who's talking? Chief? What's that again? *You got Thornton!* The devil you did; yes, I'm coming—all right, coming now."

The doctor's heavy face was expressionless as he stupidly surveyed the room in the dim light of the early morning, his eyes coming to rest finally on the telephone he had mechanically replaced on its stand.

Then, as though but just realizing the import of the words that had come to him, the doctor slid from his bed. As he threw on his clothes, with even less regard for them than usual, he muttered aloud a stream of invectives against the detective department.

The doctor knew that Thornton was to have called on Isabel Brannon the evening previous, and for an instant the thought crossed his mind that, perhaps, things had not gone so well as expected in Ortega.

As he stooped groaningly over his shoes he raised his eyes to a clock on his dresser, and saw that it was three A. M. This startled him for a moment, for, in his sudden awakening, he had taken no note of the gray dawn.

Mechanically he felt in his pockets for his hypodermic case, stethoscope and the small blood-pressure apparatus he carried about with him habitually. The doctor's thoughts had not yet finally adjusted themselves to the fact that Thornton had, in some manner and for some reason, been apprehended by the detective department.

When eventually he rolled out to the garage in back of his house, the light had grown stronger over the deep bend in the river east of the doctor's home, and that individual, with lines of worry beginning to appear in his face, steered a reckless course to the city.

Fortunately the streets were deserted at that early hour, or the doctor might never have reached his destination, and for once as the car drew up before the building which housed the detective offices the doctor was not muttering wrathfully against the second cylinder of his automobile.

The chief was momentarily alone when the doctor puffed into his office. He seemed more than satisfied, did the chief of detectives, and chewed his very black cigar with evident relish as he contemplated, in his own imagination, the profuse apologies that were to be extended him by the newspaper boys when the story was given to them.

He raised his eyes smilingly as the doctor entered, and indicated a chair near his own by the desk; and the doctor, glancing heavily about him as though expecting to see Thornton, perhaps, took the indicated chair.

"Well," the detective greeted jocosely, "I got 'im!" The words seemed to have a delectable flavor, for the chief detective hung on them smilingly and repeated, after a moment: "Yes, I've got him—all right."

The doctor controlled himself with visible effort, and only slumped in his chair grumbling a "good morning." It was the doctor's professional manner to begin always at the beginning.

"Will you tell me about it?" he questioned the chief slowly. And it spoke eloquently for the state of the doctor's mind that, up to the moment he spoke, his hand had not gone into his coat-pocket for his cigarettes.

The mere mechanical act of lighting the cigarette and drawing a long puff seemed to steady him. The frown which had gathered on his face was dissipated, and the heavy man was once again the phlegmatic, unimaginative doctor, face immobile, heavy and entirely expressionless.

"Sure, I'll tell you," chuckled the chief pridefully.

"It was pretty good work—if I do say it."

He drew his cigar from his mouth and leaned toward the doctor.

"Now, first," he began dramatically, "first let me tell you that I suspected him all along; he didn't exactly ever have me buffaloed."

The chief glanced at the doctor's heavy face, but the remark elicited no response from the man beyond a grunt to signify that he was listening.

"And when he began to talk so big—" the chief continued amiably—"and then flivvered at the bank after stalling around for half an hour—well, right there I began to smell a rat. He seemed entirely too anxious to prove that he couldn't get in, rather than he could—that's how I doped it out."

The doctor still sat silent, and in silence the chief resumed his cigar. After a puff, he continued:

"And what cinched it—cinched it for me—was Thornton's wandering around Sunday morning—oh, I know he was out all right, all right—I had the goods on him there—and when I asked him, what did he say? Eh?"

The chief paused dramatically.

"Said he hadn't been out of the place, when I knew blamed well he had—and a man don't lie like that 'less he's got some mighty good reasons." The chief puffed again meditatively. "It took time," he admitted; "it took time to dope it all out, but we'd had the goods even if we hadn't caught him dead to rights. There wasn't much need to hunt for motive — easy money was enough, and Thornton never did have much; there's a note of his down at the bank right now—"

The doctor had slid down in his chair while the

chief continued his narrative, telling of the shadowing of Thornton, of his trip to Ortega, his return, and then the final walk from the Riverside Apartments to the city and to the bank; nor did the chief neglect to dwell with much gusto on the tense scene on the floor of the bank itself, and of the sudden dramatic capture of Thornton at just the moment the vault door swung ponderously open.

The doctor's mind, even as he listened, was already busy with the problem. It seemed to him so wildly, improbably incongruous. He passed a huge hand over an elephantine chin, and started inwardly with the memory of the night of Isabel Brannon's ball when he had turned to the river and had seen, for the first time, the yacht which had been tied there —the bow of the yacht had pointed up the river! There was not the slightest question of it; and when he saw it again, the bow was pointed down, as though some one had returned in it from the city.

And Thornton had been out on Sunday morning; the chief was right, of course, although he did not know that the doctor knew it. That was the first thing to explain satisfactorily.

The chief concluded his narrative, and the doctor's little eyes turned on him coldly.

"What'd he say?" grunted the doctor, sparring for time to fit in the various parts of his suddenly disconcerting thoughts.

The chief chuckled.

"Lord, there never was a more surprised hombre in this town—and no wonder—he'd done the thing so often that he never had the least thought of any one being in the neighborhood." The chief's smile grew to a wide chuckle of satisfaction.

"He just stood there," continued the detective. "Just stood there rubbering straight ahead; then one hand—a hand holding a flashlight—wandered across his eyes as though he was trying to shut out the light. An' say, Doc, he's some great little actor, that guy. When he turned his face to me I never saw a better expression of surprise in all my life. Plumb astonished he looked, and I reckon he was. He just stared and stared, and then, when I starts to him he makes a step back and slumps like he's going to fall. We had the goods on him—oh, we had 'em, and, what's *more—he knew it!*"

The doctor pondered, scowling at the pattern of the chief's carpet—one of a particularly atrocious design. The woven figures seemed to interest the big man keenly, while the chief watched him closely.

The chief did not for a moment doubt—he knew the big doctor too well for that—that Doctor Lester was going to advance some theory to account for Thornton's presence in the bank, and, while he did not know what it was, the chief waited with a mild degree of anticipatory pleasure, for his evidence was too Gibraltar-like, too unshakable to be affected by anything the doctor might say or do.

After a while Lester pursed his lips slowly, and the chief leaned forward to catch the one word that the doctor muttered hopefully:

"Somnambulism."

"Hell!" exploded the chief. "That's what he'll try to get away with, is it? A fat chance he's got. A man don't walk in his sleep from Riverside to town and then sneak in behind a bank and let himself in—no, nor he don't open vaults in his sleep either—not much he don't!"

The chief knocked the ashes from his cigar with a careless gesture.

"You'll have to dope out something better than that, Doctor," he chuckled. "Funny he'd look, wouldn't he, tryin' to convince a judge that a vault he couldn't open when he was wide awake was pie from mama for him when he was asleep? Oh, my!"

And the chief shook with his laughter, amused at the prospect. Then he turned again to the doctor, who had made no reply to the outburst.

"Oh, we've got 'im all right," the chief exulted, "and none of this somnambulism stuff is going to get him anywhere at all."

The doctor continued to study the floor with great attention. His dead cigarette dropped from his fingers, and mechanically he lighted a second.

"How'd he get into the bank?" he asked finally.

The chief pulled open a drawer in the desk and jangled a little bunch of keys.

"Here you are"—he extended the keys to the doctor—" a key for every bank door in the damned town! Oh, he was going in wholesale, all right."

The doctor took the keys in a big hand and eyed them listlessly. There were four ordinary paracentric keys, tied together with a bit of silvered string, such as might have originally been used to tie up a package of chocolates.

The doctor threaded the string carelessly across his spatulate thumb, seeming interested in the silvered bit. There was something in the manner in which the doctor played with the keys that caused the chief of detectives to lean near to him to ascertain whether there was anything peculiar in the keys themselves; something, perhaps, that he had, himself, not noticed. But he saw only the harmless appearing keys strung on their bit of cord, a cord which the doctor was twisting absently.

Silently the doctor handed the keys back to the detective, and that individual dropped them again into the drawer of his desk.

"Of course"—the doctor straightened slowly in his chair—"of course there is something wrong."

The chief laughed boisterously.

"Oh, yes!" he agreed heartily. "There sure is; there's something mighty wrong with your friend Mr. Thornton."

The doctor ignored the sarcasm.

"And somnambulism," the doctor continued heavily, tentatively, as he might have diagnosed the case of a patient in consultation with other physicians, "and somnambulism offers a certain possibility. The symptoms seem—"

The chief reddened under the monologue.

"You know darned well, Doctor," he broke out, "that the man's a crook—and that's all there is to it. A crook and a good one. Believe me, I'll see that scientific dope don't affect a jury none—not much."

The doctor seemed not to have heard, and the fingers of one hand beat a slow monotonous tattoo on the arm of his chair as he sucked in his thick lips softly and mused aloud, grumblingly:

"—Went home first—h-m—changed clothes and waited an hour—" The doctor nodded his big head, continuing his drumming, and the chief scowled at him thunderously, chewing his cigar.

"I'm telling you, Doctor," the chief began again, "that I never saw a more certain open-and-shut case in this town, and I'll take my oath—"

The doctor raised one hand.

"Just a minute," he growled heavily. "Use your head—why do you suppose he never attempted anything like this before, if it is all that easy?"

The chief studied this a minute, then laughed shortly.

"Aw, g'wan, that ain't an argument. Never was a man who didn't have to begin somewhere, was there?" The chief chuckled at the crushing logic of his retort.

The doctor made as though to speak, when the door opened and Franklin stepped in.

"Well?" The chief turned quickly to the detective, leaning forward eagerly.

"He says," Franklin began shamefacedly, turning to the chief but really eying the doctor in his chair; "he says that he don't know a thing and can't make any explanation. Says he went home—went to sleep, and the next thing he remembers is you standing there with your gun in his face. That's all."

The detective twisted his hat nervously. On the face of it, even the skeptical Franklin had to come to the one inevitable conclusion.

"And what about the other?" asked the chief. "Did you put it up to him that it might go easier if he came across with the money he stole first?"

Franklin reddened.

"Yeh," he nodded, "an' he looked at me like I was dippy. Didn't know what I was talkin' about, and if ever a man looked clean, Chief—"

The chief snorted.

"By God, I'll make him—"

"He says," Franklin broke in, "that he'd like for you to phone for the doctor here; he wants to see him."

The chief turned to the doctor, whose little eyes brightened on hearing the detective's advice. He was afraid that perhaps Thornton's mind was deranged, but his request to see the doctor evidenced the fact that at least he thought lucidly. The doctor drew himself up heavily in his chair.

"All right, Doc," the chief grumbled, "but you ain't going to try to frame up nothin' on me, are you?"

The doctor did not answer, and the chief's fist crashed on his desk.

"Damn!" he ejaculated. "Go ahead—talk to him — do what you please—talk all the scientific dope you like—it's an open-and-shut case, I tell you." The chief's face reddened under the mild little eyes Doctor Lester turned on him, and he curbed his vehemence: "We've got him," grunted the chief, "and we're going to keep him, and all your claiming he was walkin' in his sleep ain't going—" he broke off angrily and turned to Franklin.

"Let the doctor see him, and you stay with 'em," he ordered. "Take Jackson in with you, too. Then, take *Mister* Thornton," he underlined the mister sneeringly, "down to headquarters and see that he's given a nice warm place to stay until we want him."

The doctor turned with the detective to the door, and waddled heavily into the corridor, the chief's eyes flashing balefully as the door closed behind them. It was no part of the chief's intentions to be done out of his just deserts by any scientific dope, as he called it, and he set his shrewd mind to work to counteract and refute the doctor's suggestions.

His eyes fell upon the keys on his desk, and suddenly the chief of detectives leaned back in his chair, chuckling hugely.

"I reckon he made these keys in his sleep, too—" and he went off into a fit of laughter at the thought of what a squashing blow to the doctor's theory lay in the keys before him, strung harmlessly on the little bit of silver cord.

The detective in the corridor leaned toward the doctor hesitatingly.

"You—you know, Doc," he pleaded, "I ain't had nothing to do with this—this—honest. But—but—" the detective hesitated again, and the doctor rumbled a heavy:

"All right, but what?"

"It does look mighty bad for him," the detective finished. "I ain't sayin'," he added hastily, "that he did 'em all, y' understand—maybe he just thought he could get away with this."

The doctor did not answer as they turned into a corridor leading in the opposite direction and brought up before a door guarded by the bullet-headed Jackson.

The men entered the room, a sub-office belonging to the detective department. In one corner, his head buried in his hands, sat Thornton. He did not look up when the men entered, and it was only when the doctor's heavy hand fell on his shoulder, and he shrank instinctively, that he raised his eyes.

For an instant Thornton's gaze was expressionless, then he grasped the doctor's outstretched hamlike hand in a crushing grip.

XXII. THE DOCTOR MAKES A PROMISE

A LITTLE before eight o'clock A.M. found Franklin, the detective, standing before a house on a side street, whistling with what he believed was a certain cheerfulness, but which, in reality, sounded more like a funeral dirge.

The detective glanced at his watch, kicked the ground thoughtfully, then turned to the front door of the house, as though impatient.

Ben Franklin's impatience, in itself, spoke volumes, for the innumerable times he had stood in exactly this place—every morning, as a matter of fact—awaiting the appearance of the lady of his heart, had taught him that promptness was not exactly the most prominent of Mae's virtues.

It was the detective's custom to walk with the girl each morning from her house to the doctor's office, and leave her there, discussing on the way such topics of absorbing interest as the doctor's latest witticisms, Mae's favorite moving-picture hero, the latest song hit, and—of late—the atrociously high rental rates of certain apartments on which Mr. Ben Franklin had long cast an expectant eye.

Mae finally came from the house, a mere matter of fifteen minutes late, and waved a greeting from the porch, whereupon Ben Franklin's face screwed itself into a smile of greeting, and the impatience of waiting was forgotten utterly.

During the short walk that followed Franklin seemed most unaccountably embarrassed, and the girl, with the keen intuition of the woman, talked lightly of this and that, knowing that, in good time, the man at her side would interrupt her inconsequentialities.

Twice it seemed that her intuition was correct, for Franklin stuttered the beginning of a sentence, only to relapse into a sullen silence, his face flaming red as the girl paid no attention to his efforts to speak.

There is small question that, if the walk had been longer, Franklin would have relieved his feelings by speech of his own accord. The time was short, however, and the girl stopped suddenly:

"Ben Franklin, you might just as well tell me now —whatever it is—as later."

Franklin looked at her stupidly.

"Aw, Mae—" he began expostulating weakly. "You know I ain't—"

The girl shrugged and moved on, the man falling into step beside her, and they walked nearly a block.

Then Franklin seemed to screw his courage up, for he began again, fumblingly:

"Say, Mae, you know about—about—aw, about my watching that feller—about—"

The girl tossed her head impatiently and quickened her steps.

"They got him this morning!" Franklin suddenly exclaimed, and his great relief at having got the words out appeared on his face.

If he had hoped to startle the girl into a display of interest he succeeded admirably. She stopped suddenly when she realized what the detective meant, and her face paled.

"What? What—did—you—say?"

Then, seeing that they were attracting attention,

she clutched his arm and literally dragged him along with her.

Franklin explained hurriedly, his words fairly toppling over one another in his anxiety to make her understand how it had come about, and to show her that he really had had no hand in the capture, for to Franklin the idea that he might have offended the girl was of considerably more importance than the capture of a half dozen bank robbers. So he explained volubly and continuously, reiterating his own belief in Thornton's innocence of having perpetrated the robberies on which the department had been at work.

When finally they stepped from the elevator of the St. James Building and started down the comparatively deserted corridor, the girl spoke:

"It isn't right!" she cried vehemently. "It isn't, I tell you. He didn't do it. I know he didn't. I—" She choked suddenly and Franklin patted her arm clumsily.

Then as they neared the door of the doctor's offices she turned fiercely on the man at her side.

"And don't you ever dare speak to me again— you—you—" She dashed into the office, leaving the detective staring ruefully at his hat, and shaking his head sadly.

"Ain't that just like a woman?" mused Franklin aloud. "Ain't it?" he inquired again of the empty corridor, and turned slowly to retrace his steps, sighing hugely.

In her excitement the girl gave no heed to the unusual fact that the door of the office was open. She hurried through the reception-room blindly, and pushed open the door leading to the doctor's consultation room.

On the threshold she started back, one hand going to her mouth in a sudden gesture.

The doctor raised his head from his arms outstretched on the desk before him. Books were scattered haphazard about the desk and on the floor beside the chair in which he sat. His collar was open and his great throat seemed to bulge from his shoulders. The face he turned to the girl was streaked with deep lines; blue pouches showed beneath his dull bloodshot eyes, and a great weariness seemed to depress his hunched shoulders.

The smile he tried to call forth in greeting was slightly twisted, and absently he brushed at splotches of cigarette ashes on his clothes.

"Mae—you'll—you'll not let any one interrupt me."

The heavy voice did not boom with its accustomed joyousness, and the doctor rubbed his face with a soiled hand.

"I want to be—"

The girl came forward impulsively.

"I just heard about it," she began. "It isn't so—I know it isn't so."

The big doctor shook his head slowly.

"Don't get excited, Mae—bad for your heart;" a bit of his usual bantering lightness crept into his voice. "Of—of course, it isn't so," he went on more seriously. "We'll simply have to work it out, that's all. Now—"

"Can't I do something?" the girl pleaded, "Can't I help you in—"

The doctor's eyes softened.

"Yes, Mae—you can go down the hall to Doctor

Hale's and get me—tell him I'll return it immediately—a volume of Coriat he has. It's on *Abnormal Psychology.* Thanks."

He sat quietly after the girl had left, his hands hanging listlessly on each side of his chair, and when in a few moments the girl returned with a red-bound volume he took it from her mechanically and dropped it on the littered desk before which he sat.

"And—and—Miss Isabel—" the girl began slowly but the doctor's voice interrupted softly:

"She promised, last night, to marry Halvey."

"I'm glad—oh, I'm glad!" The girl's hands went to her breast. "Now—" A weary gesture from the doctor stopped her, and she turned from the room, closing the door softly behind her.

In the outer office she dropped into a chair, and sat, staring wide-eyed before her, making no movement to clear the magazine-covered table, or rearrange—as was her invariable custom—the chairs about the large reception-room.

She seemed fascinated by the telephone which stood on a little side table, and she wondered whether she dared use it to call Isabel Brannon. She did not know whether the girl knew of Thornton's arrest; the doctor had not said, and she did not even consider again disturbing the huge man in the inner office.

The picture of his lined tired face was still in her eyes, and she knew him too well to fail to appreciate his feelings.

For the doctor, his few friendships were a passion, although he conducted himself, usually, in a grumbling, grouchy fashion which successfully concealed his feelings. But she had heard him, on one rare occasion, explain to the young prosecuting attorney, who had taunted him with being possessed of an impractical idealism, just what his friendships meant to him, and in the girl's ears thundered again the man's booming, earnest voice.

Slowly she arose and turned to the telephone on the table, her eyes watching the door behind which ihe doctor sat stupidly at his desk, his eyes fixed on his two pudgy hands. He lifted his eyes wearily and turned again to his book.

It was an hour later that there came to the doctor, deeply buried though he was in the volume before him, the sound of an altercation from the outer office.

He raised his head, listened a moment, then called out:

"All right, Ralby—come in, come in!"

Ralby appeared in the doorway, fresh and immaculate.

"What's wrong, Lester?" he queried. "You look like the wrath of seven gods." He eyed the confusion in the doctor's office with evident surprise, then, chuckling whimsically, he bantered:

"Well, I lose my five hundred—more's the pity." The doctor's little eyes glared, and Ralby hurried on: "Why, what's wrong? Haven't you heard? They caught him last night."

The doctor gasped, running a finger around his disarrayed collar. His big chest heaved strangely; then he seemed to sense the reason for the other man's joking tone.

"Don't you know who it is?" The doctor's voice was incredulous.

Ralby started at the ominous question.

"Why, no. I haven't heard. I only heard that some one was caught in the Second National Bank—there's nothing in the papers—fancy a man trying it twice—who was it?"

The doctor slumped farther in his chair. "Thornton."

"No!" Ralby stiffened visibly. "Good lord, man, what are you talking about?"

The doctor waved Ralby to a chair, and in a heavy monotone outlined the events of the early morning as he had learned them.

Ralby listened with intense eagerness while the doctor was speaking, watching the big man keenly as he rumbled on, telling the story—a story which seemed to damn Thornton utterly. The doctor made no effort to gloss over the grim evidence against his friend.

When he finished, Ralby leaned back with a sigh. He produced a cigarette-case and tapped a cigarette absently against the arm of his chair, while a tiny frown appeared between his eyes.

"Somnambulism?"

The doctor groaned.

"That's what I'm trying to determine. It's not—man, it's inexplicable. There's no similar case on record, and yet—what else?" The doctor's hand made a gesture of helplessness. "It is—it was somnambulism, or something close akin to it—an obsession—that's it!—he worried day and night about his ability to enter that vault. His subconscious mind held the idea—held it always—then, in his sleep—well?"

The doctor's jerky sentence ended abruptly, ended as the huge unwieldy man recognized the futility of his own arguments.

Ralby, however, who knew only what the doctor had but just told him, nodded his head.

"Um. It *might* have been possible. He acted in his sleep on the suggestion of his subconscious mind—on the subconscious certainty that he could get into the place—but—" Ralby shot a quick glance at the doctor as he shrugged. "It's far-fetched, Lester; damnably far-fetched, and as for trying to prove it to a lay jury—"

The doctor leaned forward.

"You don't believe—be candid, Ralby—you don't believe he did it consciously?"

Ralby frowned.

"I don't know, Lester," he apologized. "He's just engaged—oh, yes, he told me—and he needed money —he's not rich, you know—" Ralby broke off at the light which leaped into the little eyes of the man opposite.

"You don't believe that, Ralby." The doctor's voice was ominously quiet. "You know damned well you don't. Money? Great God, I've got plenty—he could have had it for the asking, and he knew it, and Isabel—" The doctor slumped forward in his chair again.

"Help me out, Ralby," he said slowly. "I'll need all the help you can give me—there *is* a way out, as certainly as I'm here before you there *is* a way!" He passed a hand over his forehead. "And there's nothing I wouldn't do—and Max will help; I know he will—dammit, I'll make him help!"

Ralby sat silent for a long moment while the doctor wearily pushed his books aside. He knew how useless his theories were—how hopeless it was to

arrive at any satisfactory conclusion as long as a tiny
bit of string blocked his every thought—the tiny bit
of string that held together the keys with which
Thornton had gained entrance to the bank.

Ralby blew a cloud of smoke thoughtfully as he
arose.

"How did he get into the bank itself, Lester?" The
question—an obvious one in itself—seemed to startle
the doctor violently. It seemed as though Ralby had
uncannily read his thoughts.

He did not answer immediately, and Ralby
waited a moment, then:

"I'll do what I can, Lester," he assured the doctor.
"I'll, of course—" He stopped short as the door
crashed open and Isabel Brannon appeared on the
threshold.

The doctor came swiftly to his feet, both hands
extended.

"Come in, Isabel, I—"

Ralby nodded and passed into the outer office,
closing the door noiselessly behind him.

The girl sank into the chair Ralby had just
vacated. She stared at the figure of the doctor—
stared vacantly.

"Mae called me up," she explained in a dead
voice.

The doctor patted her shoulder encouragingly.

"Of course—of course we'll work it out," he
assured her heavily. "It's some blunder—some
ridiculous—"

"Tell me about it. Tell me everything—everything
you know. I—I—promised last night—"

The doctor nodded hurriedly.

"I know, Izzy; Hal told me of it—told me this

morning—"

"Then you've seen him?" The girl's hands went out eagerly. "Oh, tell me—"

After a little while the girl rose slowly to her feet and turned to face the doctor.

"I'm going to give the announcements of our engagement to the papers now," she said quietly.

The stodgy doctor coughed to hide his feelings, and his eyes blazed earnestly.

"He deserves—" he began chokingly, but the reserve which the girl had held so long gave way completely and she dropped to the couch sobbing.

The big man stood over her helplessly. He was glad she was crying. Tears would do no harm.

When the girl raised her face the doctor's little eyes were none too clear.

"You promise you won't give up—you'll—"

Her voice broke and the doctor dropped to the couch beside her. One short fat arm fell over the girl's shoulders, and she buried her face in the doctor's ill-fitting wrinkled coat.

"I promise, Isabel." The doctor's voice was low and deep. "He'll be free in twenty-four hours— I give you my word!"

The girl drew herself up.

"Oh, if you can—" she gasped.

She did not know the effort it cost the big man to force the tiny smile which tugged at the corners of his mouth.

"Say," he grumbled heavily, "didn't I fetch you into this world, eh?" The words sounded but a little less jokingly than they usually did. "And did I ever fall down on any job you know of?" He pushed the girl gently to her feet. "Stand up—be a man!"

But when the door had closed behind her and he heard the voice of Mae earnestly assuring the girl that of course there was no question of it, and that everything would come out all right—the doctor dropped heavily into his chair. He heard Ralby urging the girl to come with him; that he would see her home; that everything possible was being done—

Footsteps outside indicated that they had left together, and the doctor sat before his littered desk, a dead cigarette between his fingers, his eyes staring ahead—seeing nothing.

XXIII. The String to It

IT WAS past noon when the doctor again stirred heavily in his chair, leaning back for a moment to rest his eyes from reading. Mechanically he lighted still another cigarette, and puffed slowly and deeply, burning the rolled tobacco rapidly, unconscious of the bite of the smoke against his tongue.

He closed his little eyes tightly to relieve the stinging burning pain beneath the lids, and when he opened them he focused them far out through the windows which overlooked the park.

A timid knock on the door, followed by a louder one, finally drew his attention, and he called hoarsely "Come in."

Mae entered the office and approached the man in the chair. He rose to his feet to stretch his cramped muscles, and nodded to the girl.

"What is it, Mae?"

The girl stooped to replace two books from the floor to the top of the desk, and without turning directly to the doctor questioned in a low tone:

"Aren't you going to eat lunch?"

The doctor started.

"Lunch?" He repeated the word inanely, as though it was devoid of meaning. Then: "Oh, yes — yes—of course—later."

The girl hesitated.

"Please—" she began again, but the doctor interrupted with a gesture, and with a sigh the girl turned to the door, leaving the huge man standing in the middle of the small office, his whole immense body sagging with weariness, his eyes dull and bloodshot, and the heavy wrinkles of his face accentuated by a strange pallor.

From above the doctor's desk a small framed motto stared at him, level with his eyes. The letters of the word burned into his brain, and seemed, through some trick of his senses, to contain the whole universe:

"Think!"

His eyes protruded weirdly from their fleshy sockets, and his mouth hung half open as he stared as though hypnotized by the five black, block letters of the motto.

He moved toward his chair with an automatonlike gait, his eyes still fixed on the motto, and dropped into the seat, nodding his head slightly and muttering aloud:

"Think! Think!"

One hand lay inert on his desk; with the other he toyed nervously with the penholder, then dropped it and twisted a small paper-weight in his fingers. This, too, he discarded, and continued, all unconsciously, playing with first one article and then another on his littered desk.

"Think!"

The motto seemed to glare at him from the wall, and finally he tore his eyes from it with an effort, and resolutely stared at the books on his desk.

As he gazed a look of amazement came into his eyes; a look of incredulity, and he held his breath for an instant, with wide-open mouth, staring at the fingers of his hand.

His stained, soiled fingers were carelessly twisting something between them, twisting it and untwisting it in a haphazard fashion, winding it first into a tiny ball, then unrolling it again.

He opened his hand slowly and easily, as though fearful that the thing would vanish from under his eyes. Carefully he withdrew his hand and dropped it to his side.

"Now where—where in God's name did I get that?" he whispered hoarsely.

Lying twisted on his desk was a bit of silvered string; just such a piece as represented the impassable barrier over which his thoughts could not travel; the same kind of string—it might have been from the same piece that he had seen in the chief of detective's office, and which tied together the several keys—keys which the chief of detectives had said were to the banks of the city.

The doctor picked up the string and straightened it slowly.

"Think!" Commanded the framed motto, and the man's face grew set and tense with the tremendous effort that he made—an effort of pure will —an effort calling on his mind, commanding it to bring to his consciousness a remembrance of the first time he had seen this bit of string—and where?

Before him lay an open volume, and his eyes dropped to the page and read mechanically:

. . . and the subconscious will retain tenaciously any suggestion given it, no matter . . .

Again his eyes traveled to the piece of string in his hand, and his hand closed tightly over it, closed until the knuckles shone white under the puffed skin. The doctor had remembered.

The bit of sentence that he read from the page before him stuck in his mind: "will *retain* any suggestion *given* it—"

Hardly aware now of the process of thinking, his mind sharply underlined the two words.

Nervously he crushed a cigarette between his fingers, dropped it and lighted another, his eyes growing large as he began to grasp the idea.

His thoughts leaped over the events of the preceding several days—a kaleidoscopic picture of them flashed before his eyes—Thornton in his laboratory—the news of the first robbery of the Second National Bank—Thornton's astonishment and assertion that he himself, perhaps, but no other, could open the bank's vault—the dance at Isabel Brannon's house, and Thornton's queer behavior— the matter of the launch turned inexplicably about— his own visit to the little patient in the Riverside Apartment, and his call on Thornton—

The cigarette burned his fingers and fell to the floor unheeded. A weirdly triumphant light shone in the doctor's eyes as the leaping brain behind them accepted this and rejected that, until a complete and entire structure of logic was reared behind the man's lined forehead.

The heavy face remained immobile, even for a moment after the unquestionable conclusion smote him with the crash of a trip-hammer.

He raised his eyes once more to the motto on his wall, and there blazed in them a burning fire of accomplishment.

"Think!"

The doctor laughed aloud harshly, almost hysterically. It was too absurd—too unbelievable that he should not instantly have known it all—

With surprising agility he leaped to his feet, jerked open the door, and literally dashed across the reception-room, followed by the startled eyes of the girl in the outer office.

"To Max's—to Mr. Railey's" he flung over his shoulder as he ran, bareheaded, into the corridor, and scorning the elevators, leaped down the stairs three at a time, his huge body jolting and shaking.

The office of the prosecuting attorney was not far removed from the St. James Building, and unheeding the stares of the people on the crowded street, the doctor scrambled into his automobile, fumbled with the gears, and shot recklessly into the traffic.

A policeman on the corner, recognizing the doctor's face and beholding his condition, held the cross traffic to give the doctor's auto the right of way. The car lurched by the policeman, barely escaped disaster from a heavy truck and careened down the street.

The doctor burst into the office of the attorney breathless and shaking, and that young man looked up from his desk with a startled gasp.

"Lester—what in the name of—"

"Sit down, Max—sit down!" bellowed the doctor as he dropped, panting, in a chair. He waved an irritable arm to indicate the two subordinates who crowded in the doorway, and Railey nodded to them. They departed, closing the door behind them. Doctor Lester was not unknown there.

"Now what in God's name has hit you?" The young man seemed genuinely concerned.

The doctor's laugh held much the quality of

hysteria, save that it thundered boomingly in the
little office.

"Hit me?" he roared, "hit me?" He repeated the
words between gasps.

The young attorney tried to smile carelessly, as
though the doctor's whirlwind entrance had not
really been surprising, and that it was the huge
man's regular custom to rush into the office, hatless,
collar open and eyes blazing like a madman's.

"I say, Lester," he began, "what's the idea? You
dash in here like—like—" he cast about to find a
word.

The doctor, regaining his breath with difficulty,
pulled his chair against the desk.

"Now don't say a word," he urged; "not one word
until I finish. *I* know who really did this bank
robbing!"

The young man raised his eyebrows slightly, and
a sudden expression of keen interest came into his
face. The piled-up work on his desk—unfinished
work—told its own story of an idle morning spent by
the young attorney, a morning full of puzzled
speculation and wonder.

He had expected to hear from the doctor before—
since the news of Thornton's arrest had reached him.
So he did not speak, but only nodded eagerly to
signify his attention.

The doctor gazed about him, then launched into
his story, emphasizing his remarks, and hammering
home each phrase with a clenched fist which beat on
the table.

The story bristled with scientific terms, bits of
Latin phraseology, medical jargon, and constant
mention of the names of Claparede, Charcot, Jung,

Munsterberg—

The telling seemed to sap even the huge man's vitality, for, when he finished, he leaned back weakly in his chair and fished for a cigarette in his sagging coat-pocket. His hand trembled as he held a match to it, trembled violently, and his eyes bored into the face of the young attorney at his side.

"Well, Max?"

The attorney jerked suddenly erect, as though startled by the question.

"If anybody on earth but you, Lester," he began slowly, "had come to me with such an idea—" he stopped speaking an instant, then his fist crashed on to the desk: "By the Lord, it sounds right!"

A great laugh of relief boomed from the doctor's throat. Now he had no doubt. His hand shot out for the telephone.

"Main—four, four, two, three." He smiled slightly while waiting for the connection.

"Hello—Miss Isabel, please. Oh—hello, Izzy? Yes. Yes." The doctor's voice trembled. "Ralby with you? All right. No—nothing, Isabel; nothing definite that is—I'm in Max's office—yes, I'm there now—I want you to come down, yes. Let Ralby bring you—come right away, please. Now Isabel, please don't get excited—please—all right."

He hung up the receiver and turned to the younger man.

"Now get the chief and tell him." The doctor smiled grimly as he recalled the chief's warnings of the little good that "scientific dope" was to do Thornton.

In a few minutes the necessary instructions were given to a very irritable chief of detectives, and he was on his way to the prosecuting attorney's office, together with another plain-clothes man and Halvey Thornton.

The three men were the first to arrive, and, when Thornton's eyes met the doctor's he stepped forward with a tense eagerness, and the chief of detective's face was a study in conflicting emotions as the young attorney came from behind his desk and approached Thornton, hand extended.

"Damned tough luck, Hal," he said quietly.

The doctor shook hands with Thornton violently, growling to hide his feelings.

"Just a little longer," he grunted. "You go in there with Franklin;" the doctor nodded a short greeting to the plain-clothes man who had accompanied the chief. "And you stay there, whatever happens—you hear?—you stay there!"

The chief removed his cigar to expostulate against this high-handed dealing with his prisoner, but Max Railey cut in before the detective could speak.

"This whole thing will be handled on my responsibility, Chief; we'll be here; there's no other exit."

Thornton moved to the indicated door, the doctor at his side clutching one arm and whispering jerky sentences into his ear.

The chief, watching the ungainly figure of the doctor, took a seat at the broad table which served the young prosecuting attorney for a desk. Skepticism shone plainly in his glance, skepticism which was easily translated into an expression of the fact that he was not to be done out of his deserts at this stage of the game.

Once more the doctor, transformed suddenly into a colossal human dynamo, talked rapidly into the telephone:

"Mae? Listen, now—careful. Bring me that book of Coriat's—yes, the one you borrowed, and the little black box on the top of my desk. Yes, to Mr. Railey's office, and hurry, please. Besides, there's some one here you might want to see," and the doctor chuckled with his old naturalness as he hung up the receiver.

He drummed his fingers impatiently on the desk while he awaited the girl's arrival, and drew from his pocket a moment later a tiny bit of silvered string. This he eyed smilingly, and wound carefully around his finger, then unwound it again, as though loath to replace it, but finally put it into his pocket.

Mae came breathlessly into the office. The doctor dropped the box she extended into his pocket.

"If you'll wait a few minutes over there, Mae,"— he indicated a chair in one corner—"there'll be some one in here you want to see, I reckon." The doctor grinned, and even the chief of detectives, watching hawk-like everything that happened, smiled sourly.

The doctor turned to Railey, opening the book.

"See, Max," he said heavily, "this chapter here." He pushed the book across the table.

Isabel Brannon and Ralby entered, the former plainly on the verge of hysteria, and Ralby coolly nonchalant. He nodded to the attorney and shook hands.

"What's up?" he questioned.

Railey shrugged his shoulders and greeted the girl.

"Some idea of Lester's—I don't know myself—"

The doctor turned to Isabel, taking both her

hands. He led her to the door opening into the adjoining office.

"You're to stay in here a moment, girly—now—not a word—just leave it to me—and—" He opened the door slightly, and the chief started belligerently to his feet.

"Here now—" he began, but again the prosecuting attorney cut in coldly.

"I told you, Chief, that this was on my responsibility," he repeated, and the chief subsided into his chair.

"Sit over here, Ralby"—the doctor indicated a chair on one side of the table—"and you'd better draw up closer, Chief," he grunted, dropping into a chair opposite Ralby and the young attorney. To the girl in the corner the doctor only smiled. "You stay put, Mae," he chortled. "Your time's coming."

The doctor spread his hands on the table before him. He seemed to be very calm and cool under the battery of eyes: the young attorney's eager, the chief's scornful, and Ralby's mildly inquiring.

"Let's begin at the beginning," the doctor smiled leisurely, "begin with a study of the phenomenon of somnambulism."

The chief of detectives sighed with relief and smiled inwardly, resolving to allow the doctor to say what he pleased and then squash him utterly by simply producing a little bit of string on which there were threaded several keys.

XXIV. PROVING THE PUDDING

"SOMNAMBULISM," Doctor Lester began slowly and heavily, "as the best modern school of psychology has recognized and defined it, is not always to be considered—"

And the doctor drifted into an exposition of the theories of the psychologists concerning the phenomenon of sleep-walking. He dwelt at length on the various ideas advanced at different times, seeming really to have but little interest in the subject, for his voice dropped to a slow, drawling monotone —drowsy and soothing.

The chief of detectives fidgeted now and then in his chair, waiting only until the doctor should begin to apply his theories to the case in hand, while Ralby, to whom this was nothing new, lounged comfortably in his chair. Only the young attorney, elbows on table, listened interestedly.

The doctor's lecture became deathly tiresome; so deadly monotonous was his unending flow of words that the girl, sitting in the corner of the office, clutched tightly the arms of her chair and clenched her teeth resolutely to prevent an involuntary outcry; anything to break the interminable roll of the doctor's voice.

The doctor, still talking, dropped his hand casually into the gaping side-pocket of his coat where he kept his cigarettes, but when he drew it forth, he held lightly between his fingers a shimmering, glistening crystal, which seemed to hold a spot of fire far down in its center. This he spun about in his fingers, now and then gesticulating slightly with the hand that held it.

The chief of detectives, gazing unconcernedly at the ceiling, was smoking silently and had not noticed the doctor's hands; the young attorney resolutely kept his eyes on the doctor's heavy, expressionless face, following each movement of the man's lips as he continued his dull exposition.

Ralby's eyes dropped and fixed themselves on the crystal, and as the doctor's voice droned on his eyes followed fascinatedly each movement of the sphere. Once he made a violent effort—a visible effort—to remove his gaze from the shimmering globe.

Suddenly the doctor ceased speaking and whirled in his chair. His eyes, blazing strangely, were fixed on the protruding eyes of Ralby which stared at the crystal before him. Small beads of perspiration broke on the doctor's forehead, and his face took on a strange unwonted pallor.

Ralby's cheek muscles tensed; the veins of his forehead stood out visibly; his body seemed taut. Then he relaxed easily and naturally into his chair.

Very calmly then, but with a hand that shook, the doctor lighted a cigarette.

The detective, who had been staring with open mouth, seemed brought to sudden life by the doctor's natural gesture, and he straightened in his chair.

The doctor turned to the young attorney.

"Entire hypnosis, Max—absolute—" he said slowly.

The young man peered intently into the vacant staring eyes of the man in the chair.

"Look," the doctor offered.

He stepped to Ralby's side and touched the end of

a stumpy forefinger to the staring eyeball. The girl, watching his movements, closed her eyes tightly, and the chief leaned forward, expecting to hear a cry of pain.

For all the reaction noted, the doctor might as well have touched the eyeball of the small marble bust of Gladstone which decorated the attorney's table!

"Now, get Thornton," demanded the doctor, and the chief rose without speaking to obey.

Together with Isabel, Thornton stepped into the room, behind them the detective Franklin. For a moment both the man and the girl looked from one face to another, seeing nothing peculiar or startling in the room.

Franklin caught sight of Mae and immediately made his way toward her. She rose to her feet as he neared, and held out her hands to him. Very gently then the detective, with a side glance at his chief, drew the girl into the room from which he had just come, and closed the door.

The eyes of Isabel and Thornton, following the glances of the others, fell on Ralby, and Thornton started at the sight of the figure in the chair, staring intently. The girl gasped frightenedly.

The doctor raised his hand. "Just one more minute now," he muttered, "and I'll—I'll be through."

He seemed suddenly very tired.

From his pocket he drew a bit of string—a bit of silvered string, that looked as though it might have originally bound up a box of chocolates.

"This is what started me." He played with the bit of string in his hand. "You'll remember, Chief, that a little piece of string held together the keys you took from Thornton—a little piece of string that looked like this. I found this piece on my desk."

Utter bewilderment was written large on the face of the chief of detectives, and the big doctor rumbled on heavily.

"It took me a long time—much too long," he grumbled, "to remember how it got there, but finally I did. I borrowed a book from him the other day," — he jerked his head to indicate the unconscious Ralby—"and this was in it; been using it for a

book-mark evidently."

The doctor smiled reminiscently as he recalled the feeling which had overcome him when first the remembrance came to him.

"Now"—once more the doctor raised a short arm —"now, you listen—"

Thornton's arm went about Isabel and drew her closer to him. The chief stared wide-eyed, and the young attorney lighted a cigarette nervously.

"Ralby—you hear me, don't you?"

The figure in the chair remained immobile.

"Yes."

"Now tell me," the doctor went on commandingly, "tell me just how you made Thornton get into the vault of that bank."

The statue-like figure of Ralby in the chair opened its mouth. "I hypnotized him—I told him to go there—I told him he would awaken when the door of the vault swung open—"

There was no expression in the voice, not a shade of tone; the words fell flat.

"How did you get the combinations?" The doctor's voice rumbled the question, and the chief of detective's cigar dropped from his mouth in amazement as he listened.

"I got them through Thornton. When the two bank men were opening the vault one morning, Thornton was there."

Thornton started violently.

"I—" he began, but the doctor waved an impatient hand.

"You mean you *sent* him there."

"Yes."

"How?"

"I hypnotized him and sent him there. I made him see, and I had him read the combinations to me as they were turned."

Plain incredulity showed on the chief of detective's face, and the young attorney bit his lips in a puzzled fashion. Thornton turned inquiring eyes to the doctor, who turned and explained:

"Here's how it is—ever read Dumas? Hey? *Joseph Balsamo* for one, or *Memoirs of a Physician*, or *The Queen's Necklace*?"

A light began to dawn in the young attorney's eyes, and he caught his breath sharply. The chief of detectives, however, scowled darkly.

"What was this *Doo-maah* guy?" he queried; "what's he got to do—"

The doctor gave no heed.

"Remember the figure of Balsamo, eh, Max? *Cagliostro* he was called; and recall the Italian girl whom he experimented with and who was such an extraordinary subject for hypnosis? That's what Ralby used; the same method; he hypnotized Hal there and impressed upon him the fact that he— Hal—was at that moment standing before the door of the Second National Bank vault and he made him read those combinations just as though he were there. Understand?"

The chief's face showed very plainly that he did not understand, and the doctor smiled wearily.

"All right, I'll try to show you."

He approached Ralby, gazing intently into his face, and placed both hands on his temples, speaking to him softly, soothingly. The staring eyes closed, and Ralby lay in his chair as though asleep.

The doctor turned briefly to the chief.

"Where do you live?"

"Huh? Where do I—"

"Your house—what street?" The doctor was growing impatient.

"Thirteen-o-five Laura," answered the bewildered head of the detective department.

The doctor turned to Ralby.

"Listen," he ordered softly. "You're standing on the corner of Laura and Adams Streets—the corner of Laura and Adams Streets."

For an instant the doctor was silent, then:

"Where are you, Ralby?"

"On the corner of Laura and Adams Streets."

"All right, come—we're walking up the street— now we're passing Hemming Park and the St. James Building—now the power-house at First Street—now we stop—we are standing before number thirteen-o-five on Laura Street—we are going in—you are inside, Ralby—inside of the house—*what do you see?*"

Ralby spoke slowly:

"A large room."

The doctor frowned.

"Describe it; describe what you see in it—"

"There are four windows—and two doors—a large table in the center. There are pictures on the walls— I only see two walls—picture of a ship in a storm, and a picture of a man—he's a big heavy man—he looks like—like—"

"Like whom?" the doctor's voice commanded.

"Like—the chief of the detective department, but younger; and the man in the picture has on a navy uniform—and I see—"

The chief of detectives gasped. He was convinced. Certainly Ralby had never seen the interior of his own home, and the picture of the sailor—the chief was proud of that picture—was his own, taken years ago.

The doctor nodded, and talked again, low and soothingly, to the man in the chair.

Isabel lay against Thornton, trembling; the scene was beginning to tell on her; the young attorney was twisting his hands nervously, and the chief licked his dry lips in a frightened fashion, staring at the doctor as though he considered the fat man but one degree removed from the devil.

But the doctor had not finished, and his merciless questioning began again.

"You got all your combinations in the same way?"

"Yes."

"Why did you want Thornton caught?" The doctor's voice grew hard on the question.

"He told me he was engaged to Isabel, and I wanted—"

"Stop!" the doctor cried sharply, and the voice trailed off on the unfinished sentence.

Isabel hid her face on Thornton's shoulder with a choking sob, and his arms held her protectively.

The doctor turned at the sound.

"Ask him," stammered the chief, "ask him what he did with the money he got."

The doctor nodded and turned again.

"Where is the money you stole?"

The voice, still deadly monotonous, answered: "I stole no money."

A queer expression flitted across the doctor's face, and he chuckled softly, remembering a contention of Charcot, that a subject answered directly—and literally.

"Where is the money Thornton brought to you?" he questioned.

"In my room. In my trunk."

The doctor leaned back in his chair, his hands toying with the crystal.

"Well?" he turned to the young attorney.

Railey drew a deep breath.

"God, man, it is marvelous! I'm satisfied—are you?" he asked the chief.

The chief had not recovered sufficiently to speak his thoughts, but he nodded in unquestionable acquiescence.

The doctor turned his heavy head toward Thornton and Isabel, and fumbled clumsily at his wide-open collar.

"My car's down-stairs," he grumbled; "take it—go on—" He turned as Thornton would have spoken; then boomed in a thunder of irritability; "What! Not gone yet? Get out! Get out!"

Together Thornton and the girl passed through the doorway.

"Now *awaken!*" The doctor snapped the command at the man in the chair.

Ralby moved tentatively, passed a hand dazedly over his eyes, and then, suddenly realizing what had transpired, he leaped to his feet.

"My God, I—"

The heavy hand of the chief of detectives fell on his shoulder.

"Sa-a-ay,"—the chief turned an apologetic face to the big doctor, but averted his eyes in an embarrassed fashion—"maybe there is something in this scientific dope, after all."

The doctor's laugh boomed out.

"Yeh," he grunted, "just a little, I reckon." Then his eyes fixed on Ralby's: "And there is always, somewhere," he said slowly, "a man who can undo what another man has done; somewhere there is always a man who can think."

The door closed behind the detective and his prisoner.

For a moment the doctor sat silent, then lighted the inevitable cigarette. He eyed the young attorney across from him.

"A bit of string—a book of Dumas—and just plain *think!*" he grunted.

He puffed deeply and exhaled the smoke with much sign of pleasure; then a lugubriously comical expression came into his heavy face; he scratched his head thoughtfully, and remarked ruefully, much to the bewilderment of the young man:

"But—who the devil is going to pay me that five hundred?"

THE END

Resurrected Press Books in *The Chief Inspector Pointer Mystery* Series

RESURRECTED PRESS BOOKS FROM *THE ETHEL THOMAS DETECTIVE STORY* SERIES BY CORTLAND FITZSIMMON'S

The Whispering Window

The Moving Finger

Mystery at Hidden Harbor

The Evil Men Do

AVAILABLE FROM RESURRECTED PRESS!

THE EDWARDIAN DETECTIVES
LITERARY SLEUTHS OF THE EDWARDIAN ERA

The exploits of the great Victorian Detectives, Poe's C. Auguste Dupin, Gaboriau's Lecoq, and most famously, Arthur Conan Doyle's Sherlock Holmes, are well known. But what of those fictional detectives that came after, those of the Edwardian Age? The period between the death of Queen Victoria and the First World War had been called the Golden Age of the detective short story, but how familiar is the modern reader with the sleuths of this era? And such an extraordinary group they were, including in their numbers an unassuming English priest, a blind man, a master of disguises, a lecturer in medical jurisprudence, a noble woman working for Scotland Yard, and a savant so brilliant he was known as "The Thinking Machine."

To introduce readers to these detectives, Resurrected Press has assembled a collection of stories featuring these and other remarkable sleuths in The Edwardian Detectives.

- The Case of Laker, Absconded by Arthur Morrison
- The Fenchurch Street Mystery by Baroness Orczy
- The Crime of the French Café by Nick Carter
- The Man with Nailed Shoes by R Austin Freeman
- The Blue Cross by G. K. Chesterton
- The Case of the Pocket Diary Found in the Snow by Augusta Groner
- The Ninescore Mystery by Baroness Orczy
- The Riddle of the Ninth Finger by Thomas W. Hanshew
- The Knight's Cross Signal Problem by Ernest Bramah

- The Problem of Cell 13 by Jacques Futrelle
- The Conundrum of the Golf Links by Percy James Brebner
- The Silkworms of Florence by Clifford Ashdown
- The Gateway of the Monster by William Hope Hodgson
- The Affair at the Semiramis Hotel by A. E. W. Mason
- The Affair of the Avalanche Bicycle & Tyre Co., LTD by Arthur Morrison

RESURRECTED PRESS CLASSIC MYSTERY CATALOGUE

The Middle of Things
Ravensdene Court
Scarhaven Keep
The Orange-Yellow Diamond
The Middle Temple Murder
The Tallyrand Maxim
The Borough Treasurer
In the Mayor's Parlour
The Saftey Pin

R. Austin Freeman
*The Mystery of 31 New Inn from the Dr. Thorndyke
Series*
*John Thorndyke's Cases from the Dr. Thorndyke
Series*
The Red Thumb Mark from The Dr. Thorndyke Series
The Eye of Osiris from The Dr. Thorndyke Series
A Silent Witness from the Dr. John Thorndyke Series
The Cat's Eye from the Dr. John Thorndyke Series
*Helen Vardon's Confession: A Dr. John Thorndyke
Story*
As a Thief in the Night: A Dr. John Thorndyke Story
*Mr. Pottermack's Oversight: A Dr. John Thorndyke
Story*
*Dr. Thorndyke Intervenes: A Dr. John Thorndyke
Story*
The Singing Bone: The Adventures of Dr. Thorndyke
The Stoneware Monkey: A Dr. John Thorndyke Story
*The Great Portrait Mystery, and Other Stories: A
Collection of Dr. John Thorndyke and Other Stories*
The Penrose Mystery: A Dr. John Thorndyke Story
The Uttermost Farthing: A Savant's Vendetta

Arthur Griffiths
The Passenger From Calais
The Rome Express

Fergus Hume
The Mystery of a Hansom Cab
The Green Mummy
The Silent House
The Secret Passage

Edgar Jepson
The Loudwater Mystery

A. E. W. Mason
At the Villa Rose

A. A. Milne
The Red House Mystery
Baroness Emma Orczy
The Old Man in the Corner

Edgar Allan Poe
The Detective Stories of Edgar Allan Poe

Arthur J. Rees
The Hampstead Mystery
The Shrieking Pit
The Hand In The Dark
The Moon Rock
The Mystery of the Downs

Mary Roberts Rinehart
Sight Unseen and The Confession

Dorothy L. Sayers
Whose Body?

Sir William Magnay
The Hunt Ball Mystery

Mabel and Paul Thorne
The Sheridan Road Mystery

Raoul Whitfield
Death in a Bowl

And much more!
Visit ResurrectedPress.com
for our complete catalogue

About Resurrected Press

A division of Intrepid Ink, LLC, Resurrected Press is dedicated to bringing high quality, vintage books back into publication. See our entire catalogue and find out more at www.ResurrectedPress.com.

About Intrepid Ink, LLC

Intrepid Ink, LLC provides full publishing services to authors of fiction and non-fiction books, eBooks and websites. From editing to formatting, from publishing to marketing, Intrepid Ink gets your creative works into the hands of the people who want to read them. Find out more at www.IntrepidInk.com.

www.ingramcontent.com/pod-product-compliance
Lightning Source LLC
Chambersburg PA
CBHW070835250626
47159CB00003B/789